THE EMPTIEST QUARTER

THE EMPTIEST QUARTER

NOVELLAS

RAYMOND BEAUCHEMIN

EDITIONS

Cover design by Doowah Design.
Photo of Raymond Beauchemin by Ariel Tarr.

This book was printed on Ancient Forest Friendly paper.
Printed and bound in Canada by Hignell Book Printing Inc.

We acknowledge the support of the Canada Council for the Arts and the Manitoba Arts Council for our publishing program.

Library and Archives Canada Cataloguing in Publication

Title: The emptiest quarter : novellas / Raymond Beauchemin.
Names: Beauchemin, Raymond, 1962- author. | Container of (work): Beauchemin, Raymond, 1962- Tent. | Container of (work): Beauchemin, Raymond, 1962- Oil. | Container of (work): Beauchemin, Raymond, 1962- Identity.
Description: A collection of three novellas.
Identifiers: Canadiana (print) 20230585876 |
Canadiana (ebook) 20230585884 |
ISBN 9781773241401 (softcover) |
ISBN 9781773241418 (EPUB)
Subjects: LCGFT: Novellas.
Classification: LCC PS8603.E36318 E47 2023 | DDC C813/.6—dc23

Signature Editions
P.O. Box 206, RPO Corydon, Winnipeg, Manitoba, R3M 3S7
www.signature-editions.com

For Denise and Georgia,
my desert roses

THE EMPTIEST QUARTER

The trees die, the flowers wither, the walls crumble into unheeded decay, and in a few years the tiny paradise has been swept forgotten from the face of the earth, and the conquering desert spreads its dust and ashes once more over it all.

— Gertrude Bell

We did what we set out to do, and have satisfaction of that knowledge.

— T.E. Lawrence

TENT

To the foreigner, the wind in the dunes outside Liwa conveys nothing on its back. To the foreigner, the edge of the Rub al Khali is so dead the air transmits no sound and one's voice carries no farther than inside the empty quarter of one's own skull. But for us, these million square miles of emptiness we call the Sands, or al Rimal, are not empty. Here, our fathers worshipped The One God who created the expansive sand and sky and sea to remind us of our insignificance; from whom The Prophet, peace be upon him, received blessing and grace and His Holy Word, and to whom are turned the face and breath of those who have lived and will live here. The sand is dense with their stories; their memories reverberate in the wind, echo in the waves. This is what we hear.

The wind blew my people here many years ago. In search of water, they smelled moisture in the air and followed the scent to Liwa. The village rose around wells of water and groves of date palms on the edge of al Rimal. The settlers were from old, once-upon-a-time tribes. The clans stood shoulder to shoulder with one another, like siblings: sometimes given to quarrel, sometimes to defence of the blood. They peopled the desert in the summer and the coast in the winter. Their names are legend. They were the Manasir and the Al Bu Mahair. The Rumaithat, the Qubaisat, the Mazari and Sudan. And although the stitching of their rugs was different one from the other, though some spoke with an accent as flat as the roof of their *arysh* homes, they shared the common element of their faith; every one of them Maliki Sunnis. They were not Wahhabi Sunnis. These people were from the west, from the lands of the Saud, and their fighting with the Bani Yas in the 1800s and 1900s, when my grandfather and father lived, led to the creation of the frontier between Saudi Arabia and what would become this country.

When the wind blows, I can feel dust from the ruin of their long-ago encampments coat my skin, my lips. Those are the times I think this is what it was like at the beginning, when a people rose up out of the sand, gathered at the sea, and looked to the skies.

Kan ya ma kan. Maybe it was, maybe it wasn't. At the very beginning was my grandfather, the father of my father, who was born before Hayla Tower was built. My father was elderly when I was born. His own father was already on in years as well when my father had come along. They counted their years by the winter rains that pelted the desert sands with infrequency. When I was born, my father had already counted seventy such storms, but there were years when the rains did not come and the sand absorbed nothing but sun and heat and the bones of animals and men too fragile to survive. It is likely he was many years older than he thought.

It is always the hope of one generation that the one to follow will have a better life. For a people who have submitted to an unforgiving sun for a thousand years, who have bent to the will of the wind, it was often enough to hope a child would live. The woman who gave birth to my grandfather was one of those. All she had was hope, because she never saw her son, my grandfather, grow up, to mature into a desert fortress, a man forged by the elements to become a strong, wise and respected man.

In the desert, one can watch weather develop miles—meaning hours if not days—away. A storm of dust or a spear of rain in the desert is neither predictable nor surprising. A desert plant thirsts with such desperation that when a rain falls the plant stands in its fullness to take in as much as it can. A desert people thirst with equal desperation, so that when a rain falls, somewhere on the horizon, they pack and go to it and absorb what they can.

Striking a desert encampment involves shaking and dusting away the sand, a near-impossible feat, before giving up the endeavour and simply concentrating on not packing scorpions. The reed mat for sleeping is rolled, then the poles holding up the inside of the tent are removed and the ropes tethering it are unleashed one by one and the tent collapses like a camel folding at the knees. The folded tent and rolled mat are strapped to the family's pack animal first, whether camel or donkey. Then come the few articles of clothing, the tripod and sack used to make cheese, the bags of flour and rice and tiny sacks of spices and dried herbs, the few pots, pans, bowls and utensils. Last on, so they may be first off, are the cardamom, the coffee and the pot for coffee, the *dallah*.

Then off they go: the husband, his sons, the pack animals, the women. This is the way it always has been.

In the spot where the rain has fallen, the Bedouin leads his camel to graze on newly sprouted grasses, thin, proud and erect as camel hair. In the holes among the rocks where the rain has fallen, the Bedouin wife collects water for coffee, for rice, for bread. She fills goatskins. Water will be set aside for the ablutions before prayer.

So it happened on one such trip to collect rainwater and feed the camels that a woman, riding the last camel in the caravan, cradled a baby in her arms. The baby was rolled in a bundle no different than the rolls of sleeping mats and tents strapped to the dromedaries in front of her. The dunes undulated in soft, low waves; the wind swept at the camels' hooves; and the sun was white behind the sand clouds. The woman, tired from a night spent trying to calm her restless baby, hypnotized by the desert *djinn*, dozed and, somewhere in the vast, uninterrupted expanse, the boy-child slipped from her grasp. The caravan had gone many miles before the young woman was startled from her hypnotic sleep and realized she was childless.

What words passed between husband and wife, father and mother, at this point, or weeks and months and years later, were important to these people; but these are Bedouin and until the Bedouin had settled in one place and oil was found and trade began and an identity emerged, no one paid attention enough to the Bedouin to gather and record their stories; so these words, of pain, of acrimony, are gone. We know the couple, part of a caravan of several families, did not go back for the child. They had gone miles, and they had miles to go. The wind blew from the direction from which they'd come, but there was no cry.

The desert in those days was dotted with tribal encampments and travellers who came upon such a camp could expect warmth and welcome. Travellers with frankincense to sell, or saffron or musk, or cardamom for coffee; or people, dark-skinned and slight as reeds from lands south of here: they were welcomed no matter what they offered for trade. And so it was the caravan, which included the childless mother and her cold, angry husband, stopped at a Bedouin tent. While the leader of the group and the owner of the tent spoke, the man and the young wife had words. "What is the matter with this young couple?" the Bedouin tent-owner asked the caravan leader.

"They have lost their child to the desert sands," the caravan master replied.

What bad luck did these people carry in their hearts? the host of the camp wondered—but he was honour-bound by the customs of desert men to offer hospitality. "Dear *msaafir*, you have travelled a long way and you have some distance to your journey. I should offer you and your party some coffee," he said, keeping his eye on the arguing couple. By coffee, he meant he would provide protection to the caravan until it was out of sight of the encampment.

"*Shukran*," said the caravan leader, "but it is late in the day and we are tired. We have had a most arduous journey. We are weary and should like to stay the night."

The woman was sobbing now, a cowering figure rolled tightly on the desert floor. Her husband menaced her from above.

The Bedouin host shifted his attention back to the negotiations. Under other circumstances perhaps the host would have offered accommodation, but an overnight stay meant protection for three days; it meant having this couple in his tent. How had they lost their child to the desert sands? Was the child ill and left behind? Was it taken by wild dogs? Had they been cursed by *djinn*? It meant upsetting his own family, possibly sending his eldest son, who was only eleven, or a slave, out on a camel with this caravan and returning on his own. It was too much to ask.

The *msaafir*, the traveller, could sense the host's hesitation. He looked to the sky above, to the horizon toward which they were bound. "We have perhaps not so much farther. There is plenty of light left to this day. We shall stay for a meal perhaps."

There was dust in the smile of the Bedouin *mu'dhiif*. This, the host could live with. A meal meant his son would have to travel with the caravan only one day; they would offer protection to this caravan of people, curious yet querulous at the same time, for only one day. He swept his arm toward a tarp, his *majlis*, under which was a fire, a pot of coffee, and his slave Bashir, the one with the chipped front tooth, and two sons, Hassan and Karim, who displayed beadwork and embroidery made by their mother and sisters: camel bags, donkey packs, pouches for silver Maria Theresa coins, *annas* and rupees; jewellery of coloured stone; stamped metal bracelets. The travellers now were expected to barter, but the *msaafir*, the leader of the caravan, bought little and this further soured the host toward his guests.

The host—we may name him now, for we have become familiar—
was Abdul Qader bin Ali Al Ghurair and he was not a bitter man. He
knew his role as host was to provide comfort and protection to those
he welcomed in his tent. He told Bashir to prepare coffee and bring out
the meal Abdul Qader's wife and her servant had prepared. Alongside
the coffee, the guests ate dates. Then out came cheese from the milk
of Abdul Qader's goat; *shorbut*, a spicy soup of orange lentils; rice and
yogurt. Abdul Qader asked the men about the caravan's travels, where
they had come from, what they had seen, where they were headed, and
the travellers answered in terse clips, Bashir ladling more soup and more
rice until there were no longer any questions to answer, and only the
scraping of fingernails against the shared tin metal plates interrupted
the silence that followed. When the men had finished eating, Bashir
took the plates away, the men left the *majlis* and the women were
allowed to eat. They were no more talkative than the men and soon the
leader of the caravan said they would go.

"Should travellers who come this way find the child who was lost,
I ask that you care for him until our return," the traveller said.

"Should the child who was lost be found, *insha'allah*," Abdul
Qader replied.

"*Shukran*," the father of the baby spoke, as if it pained him.

Abdul Qader blessed them as they departed, "*masalaama*," because
this was the polite thing to say.

The guests departed with Hassan, his eldest boy, and Othman, the
slave who watched over the livestock. When Abdul Qader could no
longer see the last camel in the caravan, he told his family he would
not foster the child for the couple. "The desert grass dies without rain,"
Abdul Qader said. "A child would wither in such a family."

Should the child come to them, by a family or caravan, he would
raise it as his own, he vowed.

The slave Bashir left the family that night, sneaking, and went out
into the desert astride one of Abdul Qader's dromedaries, a small one,
but one he knew was strong; and he followed the trail the caravan's
leader had described at dinner.

When he returned early the following morning, after having ridden
many hours into the Sands, into the unknown, and back, he brought
with him a male child about three months old cocooned in a white
shift of tightly woven cotton. He laid him at the knees of his master.
He said a fat-tailed scorpion had ambled onto the bundle. Bashir had
found a stick, however, and placed it near the scorpion. When it had

climbed high enough along the stick, he'd lifted the stick gently and moved it away from the baby. Then he placed the stick on the sand and let the scorpion go. "It hadn't stung the boy," he said. Shrugging, he left the *majlis*.

It was at this point Abdul Qader understood the true worth of Bashir and the precise nature of their relationship. Yes, Bashir was a slave. In fact, he was the son of a slave, as Abdul Qader was the son of a master. Abdul Qader was near in age to Bashir; they had known each other all their lives. Abdul Qader spoke and Bashir acted. Abdul Qader sat and Bashir acted. Until Bashir had gone out into the desert, however, Abdul Qader had not realized how firm Bashir's allegiance was to him. Abdul Qader considered Bashir's actions a genuine sign of the love he held for his family and the only way to repay such affection was to grant Bashir his freedom.

"Sir," Bashir said, "I am a poor man. I have no education. I have no money. I have you. I have been yours or your father's all my life. I know nothing but service. I owe you everything I have."

"Bashir, all this is true," Abdul Qader said. "I ask you to look at this service you have done me. Look at how I had misjudged you. When I awoke this morning and I saw you were gone and one of the camels was missing, I wronged you: I believed you had absconded with that malicious traveller. But you returned, with the gift of this child, and proved to me how disloyal I was to you and the memory of your father who served *my* father so well. I must repay you. I must."

Bashir was beginning to turn red, like saffron. "Where would I go? How would I manage?"

Abdul Qader, who was not a man to act rashly, without deliberation, could see how the limitations of Bashir's education and his lack of money were shackles tighter than any servitude. He said, "Then, Bashir, you are free here, within our family, to live with us as one of the family. You shall take my name, Al Ghurair, so all will know you are a free man. Whatever we have is yours. Should, one day, you wish to marry, to settle within or outside this family, you will do so with my blessing." Then Abdul Qader took the baby into the tent where he and his wife would begin to raise him.

When a year had passed and the caravan had not returned, Abdul Qader was convinced he had made the right decision. He taught the boy to call him *Baba* and he taught the boy the words for the sand underfoot and the sky up above, for the mountains behind them, the sea they could not see and everything in between. He named him Aidam bin Abdul Qader Al Ghurair al Rimali: Aidam, because he was the first of his line; al Rimali, because he had come from the Sands.

As Aidam grew, he learned from his father and his older brothers; he was respectful of his mother and sisters. Aidam was fond of Bashir, for he knew the story of how Bashir had plucked him from the desert with only a shift on his back and a scorpion for companionship. Of the scorpion, Aidam needed no stories. On his chest, curled over his heart, was a reddish mark, a mark like a tail, to remind him daily.

It was from his mother that Aidam learned the story of his family, stories she told him as she fed him and cleaned him and put him to sleep. The Al Ghurair clan had been traders for as long as there have been goods to trade and animals to transport them. They had sold dates and cheese, handicrafts and metal goods, spices and essential oils, throughout the Arabian Peninsula, going as far west as the great pyramids of Giza, north to Damascus, south to the Horn of Africa, east overwater to the land of the Pashtu and the region of the Indus.

"Our fathers traded gold from Mali, whose traders forded the Senegal, then streamed across the Sahara, for turmeric and cumin, cinnamon and nutmeg, then we traded the gold to the Indians who took it home to make bracelets, rings and hoops which dangle from the ears," his mother said. "Like this." She leaned forward over Aidam on his mat and dangled her earrings and the baby shrieked in pleasure.

"From the south, came men. And women. Sometimes children. Darker than a moonless night. In those days, a well-crafted pair of earrings could buy you a child, and a beadwork necklace might fetch you a girl. For a pound of salt, ah, what some men wouldn't give up for salt in those days. The men who traded other men also brought with them ivory and cola nuts for which we paid the odd weapon: a knife, a *jambiya* dagger, short, curved and pointy as a snake's tooth."

Those who went to the sea could expect to find fish, which they would salt and dry to take back to their wives, picking up the flesh of goat and camel on the way. There on the beaches arrived voyagers from many distant shores whose stories were as valued as the spices and jewels they traded.

These were the stories with which Aidam filled his heart.

When he was older, Aidam often followed Bashir to fetch firewood or sometimes with Othman to watch over the goats as they grazed. One day, Bashir told Aidam he had a surprise for him and took him to the family's grove of date palms. He counted out the trees—*wahaid*, *ithnain, teletha, arba*—glancing all the while at their tops, judging the colouration of the dates to report to Abdul Qader and projecting when they would be ready for picking. When they reached the fifth tree in, he tapped the trunk and smiled with satisfaction.

"Why are we stopped at this tree?" Aidam asked, "and not that one, or that?"

"This tree is a special tree," Bashir said. "I planted this tree on my own. It was my thanks to Allah for finding you. This tree is the same age as you. We have had eight Ramadan since you were born. That makes this tree eight years old, like you."

Bashir pointed further into the grove. "You see those trees are still much bigger. This one has not reached maturity. Maybe four years, *insha'allah.*"

"But it bears fruit now," Aidam observed.

"Yes, yes," Bashir said. "And it will bear fruit for one hundred years."

Aidam laughed. "Nothing lives one hundred years!"

Bashir grew serious. He crouched down so he and Aidam were at eye level. "This tree I planted in your name will give you food when you are hungry. It will give you timber to make furniture. It will provide leaves for houses and fences and fabric to make a place for you to sleep at night or when you are ill and need comfort. You will make rope, and your wife and daughters will make baskets and crates. The stalks you will burn as fuel to warm your coffee and your rice. Your slave will make vinegar and syrups from the fruit. Then you will die and this tree will do the same it did for you but for your children and then your children's children. Little Sheikh, this tree is your life and your people will show gratitude to you for it."

Flushed, Aidam knew to say nothing, so he nodded to show he understood. Bashir stood and took Aidam's hand. They stood at the bottom of Aidam's date palm, and looked up. They saw five or six bunches of dates, all of them bright yellow. Each group might contain a thousand fruit, Bashir said, before strapping rope around his waist. Aidam watched as Bashir, all sinew and muscle, brown as roasted coffee, wrapped the rope around the spiralled trunk of the tree and climbed.

Aidam ran his hand over the rough scars at the base of the tree. They were scallop-shaped memories of the feathery leaves. The boy fingered his chest, where he had his own memory. He grunted and groaned as he tried shaking the trunk, but the tree did not budge.

Aidam heard Bashir laughing above him. "No fresh dates will fall on you from this tree," he called. "Though it is but eight years old, it is already too stubborn."

With one swipe of his knife, Bashir cut the stalk and a cluster of fruit fell heavy in his hand. He placed it in a palm-leaf basket, careful not to bruise the still-ripening fruit, and cut another stalk. When the three baskets were full, he descended.

Aidam pulled the strap of a basket over his shoulder, but he could not lift the harvested fruit.

"You are not a camel," Bashir said.

"Neither are you, yet you carried three baskets down from the tree."

"I may not have the hump of a camel," Bashir started, and then stopped. He no longer worked like a camel. It had been eight years since he'd earned his freedom by retracing the path of the caravan and going into the desert to find Aidam, eight years since he began saving rupees and Maria Theresa dollars to someday… He wasn't sure what he would do when someday came, but whatever it was, he would do it. For now, it was enough to dream someday would come.

Aidam was too small to climb the tree, had not the strength to carry a basketful of dates, yet he was not so young or unwise he did not know what Bashir kept himself from saying. Perhaps out of loyalty to Aidam's father, perhaps out of gratitude.

"Why does this tree have fruit and that one none?" Aidam asked, pointing to one several metres away.

Bashir thought about the answer, considered the age of Aidam. Then he thought about Abdul Qader, who was a wealthy and busy man, but who, still, was Aidam's father, better suited to answering such questions. "This is a female tree. That is a male. Beyond that, you'll have to ask your father."

By the time he remembered to ask about dates and palms, and males and females, Aidam had another question, one that had developed when he was watching Bashir fifteen metres up, his hair brushing the leaves, his hands cutting the stalks, his bare feet and the rope securing him to the trunk.

"Can you see the sea from the top of the palm tree?" he asked his father on another occasion.

"Our trees are tall but the distance too far to see the sea from here," Abdul Qader said.

Aidam thought about the dates. When they were young on the tree, they were green. When Bashir picked them, they were yellow. Already, spread out on palm-leaf matting in front of the family *majlis*, some were half-yellow and half-brown. Soon, they would be all brown and they would be sweet and sticky in the mouth. Each stage of the process had a name: *khalal, bassar, rotab, tamar*. The change itself, the ripening—how did it happen? was it external? was it something from within?—also had a name. This made him think of the sea again.

"Why do we name something we cannot see?" he asked his father.

"I do not see your heart," his father replied, "yet I know it is present and it has a name."

"I do not see my heart, but I feel it beat so I know it is there," Aidam said.

"The sand knows the ocean is there from the beating it takes," his father said.

"Does the sea go as a river goes?" Aidam asked another time.

"The sea is not a river, son," his father answered. "As Allah is, so is the sea. It is content to be. As should you."

When he was a bit older still, when he understood certain things but not others, Aidam approached his father. "I can touch the sand and I can see the sky. I have climbed the palm tree and collected dates, been to the mountain on my own to retrieve a lost goat. When shall I see the sea?"

"Soon, my son, *insha'allah*."

And soon it was that Abdul Qader told Othman to roll his sleeping mat and those of his youngest sons, Mahmoud and Aidam, and of Bashir, to sort through the pots and the pans and set aside those the women would need, to gather firewood, to find containers for rice and lentils, to check the goatskins for holes, to load the baskets with his collection of *rotab*-stage dates and, finally, to pack a coffee pot, for Abdul Qader bin Ali Al Ghurair and his two youngest sons would lead his trade caravan north to the sea and to the market by the sea.

Before they would reach the shores of the Arab Gulf, however, there were miles following miles in the Sands. They moved as their camels moved, slowly, kneeling high on their saddled dromedaries or, when their animals were tired, walking alongside them, the men's feet protected from the hot sands of daytime by thick, coarse-haired stockings, like the padded feet of the fox or the sand cat. The camels were tied, one to the other, muzzle to tail, so when one stopped to dawdle, to piss, to strip a mouthful of leaves and thorns from a salt bush, to graze on rare grasses, the entire caravan stopped. At their pace, little escaped the gaze and study of the would-be traders. Abdul Qader pointed out to his young sons how the sharp ridges of the dunes were formed by the wind. Aidam said the colour of one reminded him of the sun as it broke the last thin film of night and Mahmoud said another was the red of a ripening date.

"Where are all the animals?" Aidam asked. "Why do we not see signs of them even if we do not see them in the flesh?"

Abdul Qader explained, "In the desert summer, animals sleep during the day and forage or hunt for food when it is cool. Now the season is changing. But it is still cooler at night than in the day."

Aidam said he understood, but, still, where were the animals? "They must sleep somewhere."

"By and by, you shall see."

And they did. Bashir showed the boys the side-winding tracks of a horned viper, ripples in the sand that resembled a man's cane thrown in the sand at regular intervals. The curled hedgehog, the den of the red fox. The displaced sand at the root of a water-rich plant showed an oryx had been digging at it with its hooves, but leaves remained: something had caused it to flee. They saw bone-dry fecal pellets of the desert hare and the dark, elongated hair of a striped hyena that had brushed by a thorny bush.

"From this *abal* plant comes a dye to turn cloth a russet tint," Abdul Qader said. "Othman shall pack some to bring home to Umm Hassan, your mother."

The men let their hair down to protect their necks, then wrapped themselves in cotton sheets and wound cloths around their heads until only the eyes showed. They would sweat and the sweat would build up into a cool layer on their skin. At dinner, as the day deposited the sun in the west, toward Mecca, the men shed the extra clothing.

Only when it was time to make camp for the night would they couch their camels, seeking wind-protected troughs among the dunes. No one was idle. The camels were led to whatever they could feed from. Aidam greased the waterskins to keep the supple goat leather from cracking and leaking. Mahmoud twisted rope or mended a saddle.

Othman loosened the wrap of cloth he had around his loins and tore off a piece before wrapping himself again in decency. The cloth, which once had been white as teeth, was gray with dark splotches, worn thin. Abdul Qader would buy a new cloth for Othman at the market that he would wear for the next year. He used the torn piece of loincloth as tinder and, with flint and steel, created a small fire. While the fire burned and created embers, Bashir crouched beside it and baked flatbreads, which he then offered to Aidam, his brother and father, and to Othman. Their evening meals began in this way.

On the first night, Bashir made a tray of rice into which he had thrown joints of goat meat. He prepared only what could be eaten by the five of them that night. For the rest of the journey, they would eat salted, preserved meats. Each night, after they had eaten, as Othman wiped down the bowls and prepared the bedding for each, Abdul Qader removed tobacco and a stemless soft stone pipe from a small leather bag he carried under his shirt. The men talked about their trip as they shared the pipe. Then they unfurled their rugs and, on their knees, shoulder to shoulder, Abdul Qader the master, his sons Mahmoud and Aidam, the free man Bashir and Othman the slave, equal in the sight of the Almighty, praised the holy name of Allah. Afterward, each found a shallow scrape in the sand or between boulders, and slept.

When the supply of preserved meat started to run low, they adopted the hunting habits of the foxes and cats, large and small, which populated the desert. They hunted at night. This pleased Aidam, who longed to see the desert animals. For meat, they would have liked gazelle but they made do with the hare Othman caught. It twitched in the trap Othman had made and Aidam wished for Othman to release it.

"Its leg is broken," Bashir said. "It would be cruel for us to release it now."

He handed Aidam his dagger. "Under the throat, right here," Bashir pointed out.

Othman stepped aside and Aidam killed the hare. Let the blood soak into the sand. He thanked Allah for the life of the hare and the health of those who would eat its flesh and use its skin.

Later, they came across a three-week-old oryx calf, lying near a bush that in daytime provided it with shade. They carried on past it and when Aidam took aim at an adult oryx eating a plant, Bashir stayed his hand. "This would be the calf's mother," he said. "Have sympathy."

On the eighth night of overland travel, Abdul Qader and his sons Mahmoud and Aidam arrived at the sea. The caravan broke camp after the first prayer, and within two hours father and sons were cresting a dune. The air tasted of wet salt. Aidam heard it before he saw it and if one could listen with one's eyes, then Aidam heard everything he saw.

There was the timpani of tongues from Toamasina and Tehran, the babel of Baghdadis and Bengalis, the sibilance of speakers from Shiraz and Ceylon, shouting, and selling, and laughing, calling to comrades, grunting and heaving as they lifted boxes of goods and hoisted cables and sails. He heard the clang of a hammer against metal, the bray of a recalcitrant donkey and the soft cajoling of its master. He heard the grate of rope the size of a wrist rubbing against the gunwale of a trader's dhow and women haggling over the price of chickpeas.

"Is this the sea?" Aidam wondered.

Abdul Qader studied his child and tried to see what the boy saw and heard, to recall his first encounter with the sea and the men whom it called. He pointed. "Out there, son; beyond Qasr al Hosn, the fortress of our sheikh, you see the light-emerald water with the diamonds dancing on the waves. That is the sea."

When he closed his eyes, Aidam could hear beneath the cacophony of the seaside marketplace the pulse of a heart crashing against a rib cage of sand and stone, as his father had said. In time, he would feel it was his heart and his heart was the sea. He would know this as deeply as he knew the white shift that was his story.

"*This* is the *souq* of Abu Dhabi," Abdul Qader said. "Come. Let us enter." First father, then sons, tapped their camels' hind quarters with a reed switch and the animals dropped to their knees. Abdul Qader led the caravan down the dune, over a causeway, and into the *souq*, squeezing past barrels of spices, the scales and trays of the jewellers, the ropemakers and their coils, the perfumers and their oils, to an empty stall, where they stopped.

"It is six in the morning and already we are late," Abdul Qader said. "Ah, we shall make do." In front of the stall, he unstrapped the baskets of Liwa dates, then Mahmoud led the camels away. Aidam helped his father display the dates and soon they were busy, counting and weighing and negotiating.

"These aren't even ripe dates," one man said.

"This is true," Abdul Qader said. "Ramadan is one month away. These dates you buy today, even though they are fully edible now, will all be completely at the *tamar* stage by your first *iftar*. They will be at their driest, at their sweetest and most fully ripe, *insha'allah*."

"All right, all right. Your talk is all sugar," the man said. "How much for these dates? Ten pounds, I need."

"Ten pounds I can provide."

"What is your bottom price?"

A smile tugged at the corners of Abdul Qader's lips and eyes, and the haggling began. Abdul Qader was an honest man and did not set his initial price too high; and he expected to deal with honest men, and hoped not to be forced to sell too low. Aidam watched and listened while he lifted baskets of fruit and spread some of the contents along a wooden shelf.

"Eight *annas*? Hmmmm, half a rupee. What do you think, Aidam?" Abdul Qader said.

"Six, plus three of those chickens he is selling in his own stall," Aidam said.

Abdul Qader admired his son. Where did he garner such information when the boy had not left his side?

"You heard the boy. That is our final, bottom price," Abdul Qader said.

The chicken-seller brought out a tiny cloth purse and handed over six *annas*. "Have your son bring the dates. He can carry back the hens."

The man turned quickly and Abdul Qader had a moment to query his son how he knew the man sold fowl. Aidam looked down at the dirt in front of the stall. "Feathers on the soles of his sandals," he said and smiled.

Abdul Qader laughed at this boy-falcon who observed the minutest movement and detail from his aerie perch. "Good boy; now go."

Aidam rushed behind the man to another part of the *souq*, and collected the hens without incident. The chicken-seller told him how and when to retrieve eggs, what grain the birds needed for feed, how to protect them from desert predators. Aidam thanked the man, then lashed a cage to each end of a pole and lifted it to his shoulder.

On the way back to his father's stall, Aidam left the marketplace and walked to the beach. The sand was wet and he felt the grains cling between his toes and to his soles. It was so unlike the sand of the dunes, which one could dust off with one sweep of a hand. With the chickens clucking and squawking, he made his way past teams of scrawny men pulling large boats onto the beach, others repairing gouges in the wooden undersides of the vessels or sewing torn sails, still more loading and unloading baskets and crates of unknown goods, the boxes marked by black lines and waves, that yet another man, the only man among them who covered his torso and arms with a blouse, examined, marked again, then indicated where in the *souq* the box was to be delivered.

Aidam stood watching the toil, the exertion of men, all shoulders and arms, for long enough he felt water lapping at his ankles, felt it rise to him and then pull away, like his brother and sisters when they were at play. He fixed his attention on the marketplace. Though he couldn't see his father's stall, he knew where it was, could see in his mind the driftwood sides, the baskets of dates, the crisscrossed pattern on the shelf formed by the sun squeezing through the braided roof. He sensed the water at his feet and turned back toward the sea. It was real, this thing that had a name he'd known since he was a child but which he'd never seen. A wave crashed at his feet and the water splashed his knees and the thin cotton sheet wrapped around his thighs and groin. As the rivulets retreated, leaving tiny canyons in the sand beneath his feet, Aidam felt something under his toe. "What have I got here?" he wondered aloud to his passengers. It didn't feel like a pebble or stone. It was smooth and round. Fearful that the seawater would sweep it away if he moved his foot and tried to pick it up with his hand, he wrapped his toes around the stone, and brought his leg up, balancing himself all the while like a flamingo on one leg, with the chickens in their cages on the pole as a counterweight. "What is this?" he asked on examining the grayish little globe.

"Yes," a voice said. "What is this?"

Aidam stumbled and the chickens protested. "Father," he said.

"Where have you been, son? You missed the afternoon prayer."

"I…" Aidam didn't believe he'd been gone so long. Had his thoughts been so caught up in the seaside activity he had missed the call of the *muezzin*? "I am sorry, Baba. I was watching the sea."

"Yes, yes, I can see." His father tugged him at the elbow. "Come. We must pack for the night."

With the hollow echo of the waves in his ears, and the smooth sphere in his hand, Aidam returned with his father.

Mahmoud laughed at the sight of his brother returning with the chickens. Then his father cut him off. "You won't be laughing when you have to feed them and collect their eggs every morning."

"Every morning?" Mahmoud said. "Aidam bargained for them. It's his job."

The sun dipped behind a cloud and cast the *souq* in momentary shade. Abdul Qader looked at Aidam, who was untying the cages from the pole. The boy was already lost to him; in a way, perhaps, he never was truly his. In a matter of time, he knew, Aidam would leave the tent he called home and would follow the sea. Though Abdul Qader wished it were not so, it felt ordained. Mahmoud would remain with his older brothers, Hassan and Karim.

"Aidam," Abdul Qader said, "show us what you found."

Aidam brought out the stone from the folds of his cloth. He held it out in his palm. With his thumb and forefinger, he rubbed the sphere free of the beach sand to reveal a shiny blue globe. "What is it, Father?"

"Haven't you seen a pearl before?" Mahmoud said.

Abdul Qader shushed the elder son. "Until last year, I believe, you hadn't either, young man."

Mahmoud shrugged.

"What is a pearl?" the younger boy asked. "Is it a waterstone? A seastone?"

"It is not a stone at all," said Abdul Qader. "But it does come from the sea. It comes from the belly of an oyster, a mollusk, which clings to the rocks in shallow water. It has a hard shell to protect itself, and a very thin mouth through which sometimes a grain of sand might enter."

"I thought it was rainwater that entered," Mahmoud said. "This is what the divers say."

"You live in the desert, do you not?" Abdul Qader asked.

Mahmoud nodded.

"What happens to a raindrop when it reaches earth?"

"It is absorbed in the sand."

"Then what should happen to a raindrop when it meets the sea, a body of water?"

"It would be absorbed, Baba," Mahmoud said.

"Correct," their father said. "Now you have won the prize, pack up those dates."

Abdul Qader turned to Aidam. "When something you don't like enters your mouth, what do you do?"

"I spit it out," he said.

"Not the oyster. The oyster is the most forgiving, most generous, of hosts. It guards the irritant within. Months go by, perhaps years, until this most secretive of sea animals is forced to reveal its mysterious guest."

"This pearl was a grain of sand?" Aidam said.

"Yes, it was," his father said. "This one, I suspect, fell from someone's bag, or was rejected."

"Now I have found it," Aidam said. "May I keep it?"

"For now, son. Some day, you will want to give it away."

It felt much too soon. Yet perhaps it was time. "Now go; go help your brother."

Aidam took a few steps. "Baba, how long shall we stay?" His eyes met his father's, then his focus moved past him, to the sea.

"We stay until the dates are sold," Abdul Qader said. "*Insha'allah.*"

"*Shukran*, Baba."

"*Afwan*, my son; you're welcome. Now go."

Mahmoud had worked fast. He, Bashir and Othman had gathered the dates they'd put out for display and placed them in baskets. Then they'd set the baskets against a wall of their kiosk, ready for hauling and mounting on the dromedary when Abdul Qader returned.

"Father sent me to help but you left me nothing to do," Aidam said. "You worked too fast."

"You were too slow," Mahmoud said. He cracked a smile in his dusty face.

He sat down. Aidam sat next to him. They leaned against the containers of fruit. Soon the sun would descend into the sea, and the call to worship would rise and swell in waves into the hearts of everyone within hearing.

"You want to go, don't you?" Mahmoud said. "To the sea."

Aidam said no, not at all, he wished to stay with their father. The grain had entered his thoughts, however, and there it would agitate.

In the evening, after their meal and after prayers, traders sat or crouched around a fire, some with their pipes, others sucking on twigs with which they cleaned their teeth. Occasionally a man threw wood into the fire and it sizzled and hissed, and sparks flew up in response.

One by one the men around the fire participated in sharing, whether it was news, testimony, a song, a poem, a story.

"I am Khalifa. I am from the west, near the desert islands," one began.

"I am Ali. I raise goats near Al Ain," said another.

"Hamdan is my name. It is the name of my father too; may he be remembered. I come from Buraimi," said a third, then he continued. "I am here by the grace of Allah."

There were murmurings of acknowledgment, of approval. Every man believed the same.

One spoke of such a storm in the desert he and his clansmen believed they were under attack. "But the clatter was not a battle cry. It was a wailing mass of air that had come up from nowhere, the mother of all winds, paying her children a visit unannounced, gathering with it thousands of miles of desert sand, fine granules of salty rock that had succumbed to nature and time, and depositing the entirety a thousand miles away from where their journey began. Anything standing was forced to sit. Anything sitting lay down. We dared not speak for fear of death by swallowing sand. We lay by our camels, covering our faces with cloth and protecting our camels' mouths, noses, eyes and ears in like manner. For half an hour, for an hour even, this unwelcome guest howled, but it could not break our spirit, nor sever our ties to Allah, to whom we prayed and prayed. The choice was Allah's alone to make whether we should live or we should die. Then as quickly as this hell had descended on us, the invasion ended. Our oppressor had moved on. We were alive and we rose from our sandy burial grounds, one after the other, and brought our camels to standing. Man and camel, camel and man, shook off the sand. Every man in the caravan fell to his knees and gave thanks to Allah the merciful."

The men repeated the words and gave thanks to Allah, and quiet descended upon them until another, a young man, with only the beginnings of a beard, spoke with warnings regarding the Wahhabi Sunnis of Saud. "Our sheikh, Shakhbut, will require great armies with which to counter-attack the Wahhab, and it will be the duty of each family to give up a son, to raise money, that we might protect what is ours."

The end of his speech, which went on for a long time, was greeted with grumbling from some, acceptance from others. After a time, they quieted. There was one whom all respected who had not responded to these dire warnings. Bilal bin Khaled al Mansoori was an old man who owned the land upon which the marketplace stood. The land had been given his family for services rendered during previous tribal skirmishes. He had long white hair kept tied in the back, and his beard, also white, was thin and covered a long pink scar from a long-ago knife wound. "Yesterday was as Allah willed it. Tomorrow will be as Allah wills it. We have heard with our own ears tonight the story of the caravan beset by a desert dust storm. They are here. You are here, and only Allah and you know the tribulations you encountered on your road. Why concern yourself with matters of states and taxes and armies? Eat when the plate is placed in front of you. Drink when you are offered the cup. Raise your boys to be righteous men. That is all."

Al Mansoori looked at the young man who had given the warning, who was now chastened, and nodded.

There was a song then and a poem, one which many of those gathered knew by heart, and they repeated the lines that ended each passage so in the end even the youngest among them would also remember the words.

The next day, Aidam and his brother and father sold more dates than the day before. They would have enough for the following morning and, if those were sold, they would be able to leave by midday. Aidam thought a noon departure too soon. He'd returned to the shore on the second day and watched the work of the men, tall ones, short ones, brown ones like him, darker brown ones like Bashir, speaking languages he'd never heard before. One man with a white turban and great flowing robes sat with his legs crossed at the end of a wooden pier. People came to him with cloths of varying sizes and hues that they opened at his feet. Aidam drew closer to watch. The turbaned man—Aidam had never seen such elaborate clothes; surely, this was a man of wealth and stature—unknotted the cloths before him and picked up the pearls inside, letting them fall through his fingers like water. Then he sorted them—how, Aidam could not see, but he understood one pile was good and one pile was less good. For the pearlers, who stood around the turbaned man, this was judgment day.

This time Aidam was more attentive to the afternoon call to prayer, so when "*Allahu akbar*" cracked through the cacophony of the marketplace, Aidam rushed off to join his father and brother and the hundreds of other men on their mats to face Mecca.

At night the men gathered around the fire again to hear news, to tell stories.

Then a man spoke: "I am a traveller who has crossed al Rimal." This was greeted with some awe. To cross the Sands was a great feat. "I have led my caravan through these sands for many years. The route here is long and passes through the territory of many tribes and many families. I have met many people on my journeys. I have met good people and bad, strong and weak, honest and dishonest. My name is Amir."

Abdul Qader, like many of the others, nodded in agreement. Most of them were travellers too; all had seen and experienced the range of possibilities in men. The storyteller began his narrative describing the lives of many of those gathered: the perpetual search for water in the barrenness of al Rimal. Then he told of a caravan that had set out in late summer eleven years before, a group including a young couple, distantly related to him, and their baby boy who was still suckling. He told of how the woman, who was not accustomed to desert travel, had fallen asleep on her camel and lost her child in the Sands.

Abdul Qader sat straighter and looked at the man who called himself Amir more carefully. Much can change in a man in eleven years. He can grow white, can lose hair, can wrinkle around his eyes and his cheeks can form caves. A voice can grow tired and weak, its timbre deepen and tone darken. Rhythms or patterns of speech, though, these are less likely to change. These are reinforced with time, like habits and prejudices. This man Amir's speech seemed familiar to Abdul Qader. Was this storyteller the caravan leader who came to him with the distraught couple? The story of a lost child was a desert tale. But this voice called to Abdul Qader from the shadows of memory.

Aidam felt in the darkness for his father's hand. The boy had heard his birth story before, many times, from Abdul Qader, from Bashir, from Umm Hassan, his mother, from Mahmoud, even though his brother was hardly old enough to have remembered the events. Aidam had never heard his story from the lips of a stranger, however. It felt like robbery. Who was this man to be telling his story? Aidam felt a squeeze and looked up to see Abdul Qader examining the storyteller also, both of them unsure where the story was going even though they knew it by heart.

The men sitting around the fire were rapt. Several nodded, as if encouraging the tale-teller to continue.

Abdul Qader grew uneasy, aware of something outside the campfire, outside the circle of conversation, insisting itself. A threat, a dark lining. Abdul Qader had the feeling of being watched.

"Four months after our passing through this Bedouin trader's lands, we returned. There had been no sign of the baby, he said."

Aidam looked up at his father. Is this true? he seemed to be asking.

Abdul Qader shook his head. This is not true, he wished to say. He held his son's hand tighter, hoping to convey his thoughts in this manner. No such exchange ever passed between these men. I have never told a lie, never deliberately misled another man, Abdul Qader thought, and I have never stolen anything either.

The next day was their third day and after the brisk sale of the remainder of their dates, Aidam begged his father to allow him to go to the sea one last time. Abdul Qader, remembering the words of the storyteller from the night before, fearful against all reason Aidam could be identified and taken from him, agreed and the two of them went to the seashore, where Abdul Qader found the captain of the pearl-diving boat.

"He looks a little young," the captain said. "How old is he?"

"He came to us before Ramadan and we have fasted eleven times since then," Abdul Qader said.

The captain shrugged and shook his head. "He is young. You will have to speak with the owner, Mr. Al-Fahim. It is the owner who decides." He nodded toward men talking on the shore.

Aidam recognized Mr. Al-Fahim as the man in the shirt he'd seen two days before, examining markings on the unloaded crates and barking orders to the numerous workers on the pearling boat and others. Mr. Al-Fahim would look at a crate and point this way or that way and the hauler would take the crate this way or that way. Aidam looked around for the mysterious turbaned man he'd seen, the one who judged the quality of the pearls, but he was not there.

Abdul Qader waited patiently until the men had concluded their business, then he approached with business of his own. "My son wishes to dive."

"And what your son wishes your son receives," Mr. Al-Fahim mused. "Aren't you going to miss him in the desert?"

Abdul Qader saw Mr. Al-Fahim was not among the men who had met by the fire the previous night, so he had not heard the story of the boy who was lost in the desert. Abdul Qader felt he could speak somewhat freely. "My son was a gift of the Sands, *masha'allah*, but not a gift for me to keep. He has worked hard; I will miss him, yes."

Mr. Al-Fahim inspected Aidam the way one checks over a dhow for seaworthiness. After a minute, he asked, "What does he know of diving?"

"What you will teach him, *insh'allah*."

"The season is over." Then he turned to Aidam. "Your lungs must mature. You see these men behind me? On my boats? The least experienced can hold his breath for two minutes without fainting." Mr. Al-Fahim addressed Abdul Qader again. "Come back in the spring when the *ghaus* begins again. Who knows? With God's favour even the impossible may become possible."

When they left to rejoin Mahmoud and the others, Abdul Qader, who was used to spirited questioning on the part of his adopted son, was curious why the boy was suddenly and unnaturally quiet. He turned to Aidam to find the youngster walking beside him with puffed-out cheeks. "Whatever on earth are you doing, Aidam?"

Aidam let out the air in his cheeks. "How long is two minutes?" he asked.

Abdul Qader laughed then. "A long time if you're under water," he said.

When they got to the stall where they kept the camels, they saw Othman and Bashir were just finishing packing the camels. They had salted meats, grains, coffee, spices, a new pot, and Aidam's chickens. Abdul Qader checked the ties one by one and pronounced himself satisfied. Then he went to the fire, which Mahmoud had kept going. "How's the water, son?"

"It's only now come to boiling, Baba," Mahmoud answered.

"A good cup of coffee, and then we shall depart."

"Yes, Baba," Mahmoud said.

"*Shukran*," Aidam said to his brother.

"What's that for?"

"For packing and making the coffee and I didn't help you."

"You can undo it all when we get to the first campsite," Mahmoud said.

Aidam nodded. He crouched next to his brother, and pounded the cardamom with the pestle. "Thank you for not saying anything about my wanting to leave, even though it means you'll be the youngest again."

Mahmoud was silent for a while. He removed the *dallah* of boiled coffee from the heat, then took the mortar of ground cardamom and poured it into the liquid and watched it foam up. When it settled a bit, he returned the pot to the flame. "What did he say?"

"I have to hold my breath for two minutes," Aidam said.

Mahmoud looked surprised. "Two minutes? You'll go mental, or blind, or die! Have you ever seen a retired diver walking around? They stumble, like they drink alcohol or have had too many women."

Aidam started to object, but Mahmoud wouldn't allow it. "Having no air in the head makes you crazy. Even crazier than you are already." He pushed Aidam off balance and his brother fell, causing a puff of sand to rise but Mahmoud was quick and lifted the *dallah* off the fire. "Coffee's ready, Baba," he called, and with his other hand he helped Aidam up and they laughed.

They set off then, in their caravan: Othman in the front followed by three camels, Abdul Qader aboard a white Arabian mare he had won in trading, another camel, then Aidam on his dromedary, one behind him carrying the chickens he had secured, then Bashir, and Mahmoud taking up the rear. It was later in the day than Abdul Qader had wished to leave, but this did not worry him much. Their stay at the *souq* of Abu Dhabi was a day or two shorter than he had anticipated and, with good time, a cool wind and strong, well-watered camels, they could make the journey back to al Rimal to surprise the women.

"Will no one answer me?" Aidam asked again. "How long is two minutes?"

And the men and his brother laughed.

"The length of time it takes Bashir to climb the fourth date palm tree," Abdul Qader said.

"The length of time it takes Mahmoud to pound cardamom for the coffee," Bashir said.

"The length of time it takes for the flatbread to cook on the fire," Mahmoud said.

"And Baba… does he not do something that takes two minutes?"

"Your father is a patient man, Aidam," Bashir said to Aidam, who had slid alongside Bashir in the caravan. "Should something take five minutes, he will not take two. Should something require only one minute, but waiting an additional minute would make it better, he will wait."

The men nodded; the answer satisfied Aidam and he was quiet for some time, on his camel, under this sun. He counted in his mind and held his breath as long as he could, making it to *telatha wa khamseen*. Five minutes later when his breathing had returned to normal, he attempted it again, and so on, sometimes to fifty-four he counted, sometimes to fifty-one, two minutes being a long time, twice as long as one minute, which young Aidam imagined he might never achieve. He persisted the second day, and the third, growing increasingly light in the head, but shrugging it off as an effect of the sun.

It was Bashir who noticed Aidam had fallen silent for longer than usual and when he turned in his seat astride his camel, he saw Aidam's camel was riderless and the beast had begun to stray. Bashir called for the caravan to stop, then reined his animal around back into the wind and raced back along the summit of the dune. The camel protested, but Bashir pushed it forward, his own head and face protected from the blowing sand by his headscarf. Abdul Qader raced in front of him, calling for his son, but the wind stifled his cry. "Please stay with Mahmoud, sir," Bashir said. "I found him once. I will find him again."

"He's my son, my youngest son," Abdul Qader said. "I can't leave him here. I can't lose him."

"We won't lose him," Bashir said. "We will not."

Two times has this boy fallen off a camel, Abdul Qader thought. For Bashir to save him once was miracle enough. Twice would clearly be a sign. Allah, if it be your will, return my son to me. Now, as the sun began to set, Abdul Qader's thoughts darkened. Son. What son? The boy you'd promised to look after until his rightful parents returned for him? I made no such promise. Those were his words, they were not my words. Those people were not good people. They were cursed. It was ordained I should raise the boy as my own when Bashir placed the bundle at my knees. But the boy was marked. It's there. On his chest and over his heart. A telltale mark of birth. A branding.

Hours later, Bashir walked into the tent Othman had rigged. Abdul Qader's heart leaped in his chest. If Aidam was not with him, Abdul Qader would not forgive himself for including him in the caravan this year. If Bashir was alone, Abdul Qader would go into the desert himself to track down the boy. Bashir stepped further into the tent and stepped aside. He kept the flap opened and allowed the apologetic Aidam to pass in.

Abdul Qader showered his son with kisses and Mahmoud was there to greet him with warmth as well. It must be God's will then that this boy is not meant for desert life, Abdul Qader thought as he watched the boys hug. I should let him go to the sea.

When Abdul Qader and his entourage arrived finally at his home on the edge of the Empty Quarter, he saw there were guests. Their camels were tethered to stakes outside the tent where there was grass to eat. There was coffee on the fire. He saw his sons Hassan and Karim busy, sharing the little the family had to offer. He unstrapped the cartridge belt he'd purchased in Abu Dhabi, and his memory began to settle. The head cloths of these men in his *majlis* were wound loosely around the head, almost carelessly, as done by men in a rush; the fold of their saddlebags indicated they belonged to one of the tribes of the deep interior, where everyone was a roamer, carouser, a thief.

Abdul Qader dismounted his horse and recognized how truly unusual the situation was and how Aidam's second fall from the camel had been an omen he had improperly read. Two men sat by the fire with plates of rice and chickpeas in their hands: the traveller who'd told his story the last night at the *souq* and, by his side, the brooding shadow Abdul Qader had sensed around the fire. In the light, Abdul Qader could see him better. He was a man no taller or shorter than any man he knew, but his black eyes moved restlessly in deep sockets under an escarpment of eyebrow. His upper lip twitched. He was not a man at peace with himself. This pair had prevailed upon his house and hospitality before. He'd sworn then it would be the last time.

Hassan rushed to him. "Your news, Baba?" They rubbed noses.

"My news is good, *alhamdulillah*," Abdul Qader said, with brusqueness, dismissing his son in a manner he did not deserve. There was the matter of these men.

"You are the father in this one's story," Abdul Qader said, addressing the one man and pointing to Amir. "You were there last night, hovering around the fire, watching everyone, looking for clues, examining the traders, particularly those with boys of eleven or twelve years. State your case and then you will be seen on your way."

"Is this how you treat guests?" Amir asked. "The last time we were here…"

"Yes," interrupted Abdul Qader, "let us speak of the last time you were here." Abdul Qader stopped there. He knew there had been no return visit. They all knew it. He would not call Amir, the *msaafir*, a liar; for to call a man a liar is to call his mother a bitch. It is not done, no matter how obvious a lie, no matter how often the mother cavorts with dogs.

A weak twist formed on the lips of the traveller. "He is indeed the father. One look at this boy and anyone can see this."

The shadowed man looked at Aidam and Aidam looked at the shadowed man.

"There is darkness in this one's brow where in the young one there is light," Abdul Qader said. "There is anger in this one's eyes where in the young one, there is peace. What resemblance you may see is one of the body, not the heart. The boy is no more a son to this man than a hare should come from the belly of a hyena."

The *msaafir* shrugged. "There is one way to know if this boy is the one." Amir made a gesture toward his chest.

Abdul Qader and the rest were quiet.

"You know the family will want compensation for all the time in which they did not have their son," Amir said quietly.

Abdul Qader poured himself a coffee. "Then I will want compensation for all the time I raised him, as my own, because you never returned."

Amir and the father regarded Abdul Qader. They tipped their coffees, sucking them down to the dregs. There would be no more.

Bashir stood on the edge of the *majlis*. The four boys, who had been brought up as brothers, were close by, listening. Mahmoud held Aidam's hand. They all watched Abdul Qader, waiting for him to speak. He was such a fair and kind father, an honourable man. He always had an answer.

Abdul Qader did not speak for some time. Somewhere, deep within him, he had known the possibility existed this day might come, when all lightness and joy in his life would be quashed. He recalled precisely the conversation from eleven years before, the day these dark and shameless men had entered his life. The *msaafir* had said: "Should travellers who come this way find the child who was lost, I ask that you care for him until our return." Abdul Qader repeated: should the child be found. All those years afterward, he *had* cared for him, and now they *had* returned. He needed to hold up his end of the bargain. What had Amir said exactly? About travellers finding the child? There were no travellers. It was Bashir who went out and found him. Could he argue this point? Could he tell these men no traveller found the child? Perhaps. It felt like an argument for a sharia court, and these men did not act like godly men. They were men who obeyed their own law. He sighed.

All Abdul Qader's life he had strived to do the right thing, by his children whether boy or girl, by his slaves, by his wife; most importantly, by Allah. Doing what was proper had nourished him. Doing so now would do his soul irreparable harm. But it had to be done.

"I will not ask to be reimbursed," Abdul Qader said at long last. "I will insist, instead, when you go, which will be soon, *insha'allah*, when you take my son, that you will also take this man with you." He nodded toward the solid, black figure standing at the edge of the tent.

Amir shrugged again. What was this *kafir* to him? He could insist the whole entourage to follow him. It did not matter to him. He would dispense with them all when the time came.

Abdul Qader looked at Bashir, who would see everything, remember everything, report everything and, when the time came, return everything dear to him.

"With God's favour, even the impossible is made possible," Amir said.

The men stood. What is to become of me, Aidam wondered. Am I really to leave with these people? When shall I see my father and mother again? My brothers? At least Bashir had been part of the bargain. Bashir would accompany them. Aidam would not be left alone. He opened his mouth, about to cry, but Bashir was looking at him and he gained strength in returning his gaze.

"Sultan," Amir said, "you have your son returned to you."

"Issa," the figure hissed as he stepped toward Aidam.

From the depths of Aidam's being, a place he had not known existed, an aural memory reached into and clasped his heart. That voice and that name had the resonance of a nightmare, the prolonged echo of painful memory, and he hated it. He would not answer to it. He would block it from his ears. He would, he swore, answer to nothing but the sea.

"You see," Sultan said, "he recognizes his name." Then he turned away from Aidam and made for his camel.

Amir, the head of the caravan, was already astride his animal. "You are already packed," he said to the boy. "There's no need to wait."

Bashir pushed Aidam forward. "Young master," he said, "we must go."

Aidam looked under the shaded canopy of his father's *majlis*, searching for the familiar warmth of his gaze, but he was not there. He would have liked to see Umm Hassan, and his sisters, but they were in their quarters. Perhaps it was best they did not see what had transpired. He saw his brothers, Mahmoud and Hassan and Karim, staring, confused; but of Abdul Qader there was no sign, as if suddenly Aidam's life had begun to move backward. At first, there had been nothing, then there had been Abdul Qader. Now, at the end, nothing again. Like rain on the dry floor of the desert. There, not there. "Baba," he wanted to shout, but his mouth was parched and he could make no sound.

When they had been gone three nights, and so were deep into the Sands, Amir woke Bashir with the cocking of a firearm. "Wake, you *kafir*, pack your things."

Aidam cried, "No," but Bashir, rising from his palm-frond bedding, told him not to worry.

Aidam again cried out to Amir, who turned and slapped the boy with his open hand. "Get your camel," he said.

Bashir rolled his bedding into his prayer rug and tied it. He watched Aidam, Amir, Sultan and the rest of the small caravan rush breakfast, pack their coffeepot, toss sand on the fire. He had no intention of leaving Aidam to these people. He had given his word to Abdul Qader.

Aidam did as Amir told him. He got his camel and packed his bedding, his rug and his cup. He wiped his face with his scarf, then wrapped it around his head. Fearing the wrath of Amir and the dark

Sultan who claimed his paternity, Aidam did not speak to Bashir. Instead, as he worked, he sneaked glances at his co-conspirator. When he was ready, he got his camel to lower itself. Bashir, Aidam saw, was working even more slowly than he'd been. Bashir was normally the first one up and the last one to go to bed. On trips, it was the same. When it came time for packing, Bashir finished first so he could be ready when someone called for help.

"What are you still doing here?" Amir said.

"It takes time, sir, to pack for such a trip," Bashir answered. "Would it be possible, sir, to have some provisions for my return journey?"

Sultan said, "Leave him to provide for himself."

Amir considered this, but said, "This *kafir's* blood is not worth staining my hands." He reached into a jute sack he'd already placed on his camel and drew out a bag of dates. He threw them to Bashir. "Now go."

Bashir placed the dates in his own camel-pack, lowered his animal and climbed onto her. With a clip of his heels into her sides, she rose and soon Bashir towered over the group. Without a word or a glance back toward Aidam, he nudged the camel forward.

Aidam's heart, which felt lodged in his throat, plummeted.

"Bashir!"

Sultan raised his hand about to strike Aidam, who backed away, his eyes glued to the back of his guardian. Though Bashir grew smaller the farther he went, Aidam's faith in Allah and in his friend strengthened. Bashir was there for me from my first days. Bashir will not abandon me now. Bashir has a plan.

"What are you waiting for?" Amir barked. Aidam got on his own animal and slipped into the middle of the line in the opposite direction of his beloved Bashir.

The former slave waited until he no longer heard Amir's caravan, then he stopped his camel, turned in his seat and looked behind him. The sands stretched out before him were vast and empty, but not as empty as the hole in his heart. He'd known what he was going to do from the moment Amir had aimed his pistol at him that morning and, he presumed, Amir knew as well. It was no show, no game, the dance between the two men. The gun was real, the hatred plain to see, but their movements had been blocked and staged by the wind and sand that had called them to life. Allah himself had written it. Bashir dug his heels into his ride and forced the camel back in the direction of the departed caravan.

After some time had passed, Bashir returned to the site of their overnight camp. With no wind, he could see indentations in the dunes where the camels had rested and the men had slept. The short mound where the fire had been. He passed, following the footprints of the camels of Amir's caravan. Three of the dromedaries were being used as pack animals: their footprints dug deeper into the sand because of the weight on their backs. The remaining six carried riders. Aidam was riding near the middle, Bashir saw; he was the lightest rider, and his camel's prints seemed to barely touch the sand. From the prints of another camel, Bashir determined one leg was shorter than the others. All of them were camels from the sandy desert; their soles were soft and their prints revealed the sweep of tattered strips of skin. After some time, though he could not see them in front of him, Bashir thought they were nearing their home. The camels' scat was pebbly and hard with almost no sign of grass or moisture. Only a caravan leader near home would deprive a beast, knowing his camel would soon have sufficient grasses and water.

Just before nightfall on the third day, Bashir saw the camp, a compound of eight *arysh* houses inside eight-foot-high frond walls with two gates. It was near a grove of palm trees, a small oasis, perhaps the last this far southwest. He settled himself down on the opposite side of a dune, shielding himself and his camel from the sandy wind, and trained his eyes on Amir's camp, looking for Aidam captive in it.

Bashir watched the movements of the men, studied the layout of the compound, found the water well. That night and the following, he slid into the compound and, as a thief in the night, drew water for his goatskin. As he retreated, he swept sand over his footprints. He ate sparingly from the bag of dates Amir had tossed him. He found grass for the camel. Bashir knew he could not keep up his lookout for long. His camel would grow fierce with hunger. He had perhaps two more days' worth of dates. He located the *arysh* house where he believed Aidam was kept. A plan seeded itself in Bashir's mind, a way to steal Aidam away and return him home to Abdul Qader. Bashir was pleased with his thinking, his patience, confident in his plan, and allowed himself to doze in the heat.

"Get up, *kafir*," the caravan leader said.

Bashir, weakened by hunger and thirst, rose to his feet and steadied himself. Then Amir bound Bashir's wrists and ankles and took him and his camel to the compound. There, Aidam was overjoyed to reunite with Bashir, and called out to him, stepping forth before being pulled back and down by the chain at his ankle. Bashir went to him, but Amir struck Bashir in the back of the head and Bashir fell by Aidam's side. The friends, unable to touch or comfort each other, were forced to express their mutual happiness and sadness with their eyes.

For the first week, Bashir was forced to climb Amir's palm trees. Aidam remained at the bottom and collected the baskets Bashir had filled and strapped them to the back of the collective's donkey. It was hard work and the hours long. When the two attempted to speak, one or the other—often both—were struck. They were under guard from the moment they woke and were fed bread with hummus until their last meal of the day, a few dates and some rice and water. When the overripe and sticky dates had been harvested, Bashir, Aidam and several others, dark-skinned men like Bashir, began making bricks from clay, gypsum and sand. They gathered and mixed their ingredients, then poured them into moulds and allowed the mix to bake in the hot sun. They made bricks from morning until dusk, breaking only for prayers, day after day, for several weeks.

"Why do we make these bricks?" Aidam whispered to Bashir as they toiled.

Bashir shook his head. Don't talk, he could have been saying. Or I don't know. "Their intentions will be made clear with time."

One morning, Bashir awoke early and heard a shuffling walk through the sand to their hut. He sat up. At this hour it could only be the tall, thin woman who left Bashir and Aidam their food. Her pigmentation, like his, caged her; but it emboldened her too with pride, Bashir had seen. She did not shy from the guard when she came to their *arysh* and spoke to him as one would a child. Bashir saw in this woman a potential ally, someone he could use to secure freedom for himself and Aidam. Bashir coughed. Aidam woke and sat up as well. He looked at Bashir and with his eyes saluted the morning, his friend, their shared history. Bashir opened his mouth, pretending to take a breath, puffed out his cheeks as if he were holding his breath, and then rolled his eyes to the back of his head and jerked his head slightly, eyes closed, to the right. Aidam did not understand immediately, and Bashir went through the pantomime again.

Why Bashir wanted Aidam to hold his breath, the boy didn't understand. Was he wishing to inspire him, keep him thinking of the sea and his dream of some day diving for pearls? Aidam did not wish to practise holding his breath. Those two minutes of held breath were as long now as the weeks that had gone by since he'd last seen his father. Bashir acted out the breathing again and Aidam saw that Bashir meant for him to hold his breath until he'd fainted. For what reason? That hadn't been a pleasant experience: he'd hit the desert sand hard when he'd fallen off the camel. The frond door opened and the woman with the food entered and gave the plate to the guard to give to his wards, disturbing whatever Bashir had been attempting.

That night, sitting on the floor and waiting for their evening rice and dates and water, Bashir once again mimicked fainting. This time, Aidam held his breath and inside his head he counted *wahaid*, *ithnain*, *teletha*, *arba* until he felt himself being roused by the guard, the woman talking quickly and loudly and Bashir hovering overhead, then the three of them pushed aside by Amir, who was followed into the house by Sultan.

"What is all this crying in here?" Amir asked.

"The boy fainted," Bashir said.

Amir raised his arm as if to slap Bashir across the face. "Did I ask you, *kafir*?"

Bashir did not wish to be struck, so he held his tongue and lowered his eyes. This was not the first time Amir had called him an unbeliever. The woman stepped back, averting her eyes from Amir also. The guard said, "The boy fainted."

"I can see," Amir said. "How did he faint? Has he done this before?" He looked around the *arysh*. "You," he said, as he shoved his chin out at the woman, "what happened?"

"The boy fainted when I passed through the door," she said. Her Arabic was accented; she had not been long in the desert. Though it was not her native language, she spoke it with inflections similar to those of Amir and Sultan. "I cried out and you came."

"Wassan," Amir said.

"It is as she said," the guard said. "It has not happened before."

Aidam was now upright, breathing normally. He examined the room, the faces, some showing concern, some confusion, some anger.

"You, boy, why did you faint?"

Aidam looked at Amir, then to Bashir, who was making motions with his mouth as if he were eating. "Look at me when I'm speaking to you," Amir said. "What happened?"

"Hungry, sir," Aidam said.

Amir nodded. He turned to the woman. "Give him beans in the evening." He started to walk out of the hut, but he stopped when he saw Bashir. "This dark one likes dates. Look at him: flabby in the belly. Four fewer rations of dates per week."

Amir left the hut, followed by Sultan, the man who had given Aidam life but now shared in siphoning it away. Bashir and Aidam ate quietly, the only sound in the hut being their fingertips sliding against the thin metal plate. Aidam snuck glances at Bashir, but Bashir was focused on his meal. After they had finished eating, Wassan nodded at Bashir and Aidam, who got up and followed Wassan out the door, passed the fire in the centre of the compound and out the gate to the edges of the oasis where everyone went to defecate once a day. It was a smelly place, particularly in the summer, and Aidam was always scared a scavenging animal might come after them. When they did their duty, they covered it with sand.

Several times a day afterward, Aidam practised holding his breath, gradually increasing the length of time he was able to quit the rhythm of inhalation and exhalation he was now so conscious of. Because he could not speak to Bashir without punishing blows, he had to smile inside when he passed the minute mark. He fainted again, within a week of the first time in the *arysh*, this time at breakfast. Wassan sought out Amir, who ordered the boy be given more food at breakfast.

When Aidam fainted a third time, Amir stormed into the hut and kicked over Aidam's plate. "What kind of fool do you think I am? You will play games with me?"

He yanked Aidam to sitting. "You will go back to your original breakfast and your original dinner."

Aidam looked at Bashir, whose glaring eyes betrayed the fire burning in his heart. He sat on his hands. Aidam believed he would have to do the same.

Amir slapped Aidam in the face, but the boy did not cry. He faced Amir as a stone faces the wind. Without puffing his cheeks, Aidam held his breath and began to count.

He woke to kicking blows to his belly and chest. "What is wrong with you, boy?" Amir was calling. "Get up!"

Aidam sat. His head felt light and he placed it in his hands. He began his count again, and after a minute, again he fainted. Amir pulled the boy's head with a sharp tug of his long black hair. "Sultan, this is your son. Damaged goods. He has the same sleeping sickness as that wife of yours."

"This is no fault of hers," Sultan said. "This is something new. You saw him the first two weeks here. He was fit as your camel."

"More like a woman," Amir said.

Amir crouched before Aidam. "Once more, Issa. Just once more."

More weeks went by. Aidam sought Bashir's attention, puffing his cheeks slightly. Bashir shook him off. In the weeks following Aidam's beating at the hand and foot of Amir, the sun had begun to descend into the western sands earlier each day and the nights had begun to grow cool. Amir and Sultan spent more time by the fire each night, squatting before the warmth, their palms wrapped around small cups of coffee. Aidam and Bashir slid by them in the silent darkness on their way out the gates to the designated area. Bashir listened with desperate intent each time they passed the fire, for a clue, for any morsel of conversation, of gossip, that could tell him anything, give him something to hang onto. For as bad as it was to work, the toil would not kill him. The silence might.

Yet all was not silent in Bashir's mind. He told himself he was planning, yet he could give birth to no workable idea. He wished he could convey to Aidam that they would find a solution, they would escape. But how? And when? Wassan was with Aidam and Bashir all day and all night. As for their captor, Amir was armed with the pistol he'd once used to threaten Bashir. Sultan was forever by his side. Of the other men in the compound, Bashir could not discern any disloyalty or grumbling. It was evident by the build of their bodies and the colour of their skin and the patterns of their speech they were not of the same tribe as Amir, whom they answered as Wassan did: direct, offering no more information than was required, with one eye to the ground and one eye to the chief.

Bashir gave himself over to the work he was forced to do. The bricks they had spent so many weeks making now had a purpose: a cylindrical building. Bashir, Aidam and four others, always under the watch of Wassan, left in the dark of morning, immediately after the first prayer and walked through the Sands behind camels laden with bricks until the sun had risen, perhaps an hour's trek. Bashir pieced together— from morsels of conversation he overheard between Amir and Sultan about the death of an *imam* named Abd al-Wahhab—the compound's purpose: a watchtower for the men who followed Wahhab, all of them from the lands of the Saud. Bashir remembered the words of warning about the Wahhabis from the Buraimi traveller at the trading post campfire. He was not to trust these men.

It had been months now and Bashir, despite the meagre diet, felt as strong as ever. He noticed too that Aidam had begun to develop into a man. There was a thin, black line across his upper lip. His voice, those few times he was obliged to answer Amir or Sultan, or even Wassan, was low some days, not so low on others. Aidam was changing. When Bashir returned him to Abdul Qader, God willing, Aidam would be ready for the sea. That is if Abdul Qader allowed his son to ever leave his sight again.

Sometimes, Bashir found himself so vacant of thought and hope that he would catch himself doing nothing but counting while they walked from the fire, across the yard and out the gate to the site where they moved their bowels.

And that was how the plan was born. After a day smoothing the walls of the tower with Aidam, anxious for the day to be over and the moon to rise, rushing through his evening meal of bread and dates, gulping the little water he was given, Bashir had to calm himself before stepping out into the night. He took a deep breath and prayed Allah would steady him. He and Aidam followed Wassan the guard into the cool night air and past the momentary warmth of the fire. Here, as close to the fire as he could be without attracting undue notice, Bashir began his count. He did not change his gait, and took the same path the three of them always took. When he and Aidam made it to their designated area, he stopped counting. It was more than one minute. He confirmed the time on the return trip. Bashir passed Amir and Sultan at the fire. He glared at them so intently, he felt they could feel it burn like the flames; but they did not move, did not glance at him. He was invisible to them now, so much a part of the routine he could count aloud their allotted, remaining time and they would not hear him, would give him no more attention than a passing ant.

The next day seemed longer than the one before it. Bashir was aware these were his nerves, and he prayed for evenness and a steady heart. At the site, squatting to relieve themselves, Bashir regarded Aidam next to him. The boy had no idea of what was to come, of the role he was about to play in Bashir's plan, but Bashir was confident Aidam was man enough for it now. The months of captivity had done this. They cleaned themselves and stood. Bashir coughed, twice, and bent over. Aidam reached out to him but Wassan held him back. Bashir stood, raised his hand to indicate he was okay. Wassan left in front of them. Bashir mimed to Aidam once again that he wished for him to hold his breath.

Aidam had wondered when Bashir would ask him to do so again. The moon had come and gone into its fullness two times since Amir had beat him. Aidam held his breath, took a step forward beside

Bashir, and began counting. It had been some time since he'd practised holding his breath and Aidam wondered if he would be able to hold it as long as he once had. But he knew what was required: he had to hold it, keep the air inside his lungs until all thought had left him and his head had become the emptiest quarter of his body. They approached the fire as Aidam neared the limit of his counting.

When Aidam woke from the blackness of his unknowing, Bashir was standing over a lifeless Amir with Amir's gun in his hand, pointing it at Wassan. The air reverberated with sound: of gunfire, of screaming, and was lit up with sparks from the fire. Sultan was shouting, covering his face, yet attempting to stand and attack Bashir, whose back was to Sultan. Aidam, nearest Sultan, kicked the man back to the ground, pulled the man's *jambiya* out of its scabbard, yanked Sultan's head back by the hair and knowingly ran its curve under the man's chin. He wrenched the head back further and the invisible line grew visible and red. Aidam let go the head and watched the body slump to the sand and the blood seep into the forgetful, forgiving ground. He stood reaching for breath over Sultan. There was a shriek behind them from a woman running out of her *arysh*. Alarmed about what the woman might do, Aidam backed away quickly from the corpse at his feet. He tripped and fell and dropped the dagger, which the woman scooped into her hands and raised above her head. Shouting God is great, she brought the *jambiya* to her breast and buried it there. She dropped to her knees and pitched forward, then fell to her side by her husband. Aidam crawled to her side, recognizing in her final act the woman who had given herself to that man and given him birth, yet a woman upon whom he had never laid eyes. He reached around with his hand to feel whether she was breathing. She was still. He touched his fingers to her eyes.

The commotion had brought out Amir's slaves, including the black woman who served Bashir and Aidam their meals. Wassan, now under guard of the armed Bashir, spoke first.

"We have no quarrel with you," he said with care. "We have met your master and we recognize a good man in him, and in you and the boy."

Bashir lowered his arm and tucked the weapon into his waistband.

The woman came forward. "I am Fikre," she said, before she crouched over one body and then the next and began the process of their cleansing.

"Why don't you leave them?" Wassan said.

"Even the bad deserve burial," she said.

Bashir recognized serenity in her movements and kindness in her words.

Around the fire later, Bashir and Aidam, Wassan and the other slaves, came to an understanding: the men and the woman believed they would be at risk of re-enslavement should they attempt to return to their homeland. They would follow Bashir and Aidam to Abdul Qader's encampment and plead for his protection and advice. When they were done speaking, Wassan said to Bashir and Aidam: "You are our friends. The safety of your blood and of your worldly goods is on our face."

The men discussed what to pack and what to leave behind. They decided to leave the forward post alone—"No tower, whatever height, built on these sands will last," Wassan said—but they would take apart the *arysh* and save the fronds to rebuild their lodgings when they had returned to the camp of Abdul Qader. They packed the camels, drank their last coffee, and then stored the *dallah* where the coffee pot could be reached easily.

There was no *dallah* on the pearling boat. There was the fresh water the captain had the men bring on board, but it never lasted long. Much was used for cooking, the intolerable sun evaporated some, and the rest turned distasteful. The crew—this was Aidam's third time out and it was always a different group—drank what water they could. They ate—the captain, the divers, the cook and the helpers—once a day, at night, after their twelve hours of diving. Dates were plentiful; the rice was salty from having been cooked in the same water as the fish. The cook, Musallim, was a boy, perhaps fourteen. The captain was his uncle, brother to the boy's mother, who was not much of a cook herself so had had few skills to pass on to her children.

There were twenty-four young men on board; the oldest almost twice Aidam's age, he being fifteen now. Although he was not quite a veteran pearl-diver, the younger boys emulated Aidam, watching him pass under water, his slight kick or modest turn an expression of strength and reserve. The oldest among them, Yusuf, was slow in the head and had never learned his numbers, so they went on the captain's word that he was twenty-seven. Five times a day, as Aidam prayed with his fellow divers, he thanked Allah, in each of his attributes, with each dive, for the blessing of chasing after the pearl. On the way back up to the boat, with the undulating light in his eyes, Aidam thanked Allah for the blessings of air and sky.

The days were long and divided clearly: working and not-working. There was no ambiguity such as hides in the folds of dusk. After first prayers, the boys tied a rope around their waists, strapped an oyster bag over their shoulders, then clipped a goat horn over their nostrils and, with a cue from their rope partner, dropped into the salty water and descended the twenty metres through the murk to the rocky beds rich with oysters and barnacled mollusks.

Aidam went through the ninety-nine attributes of Allah twice each day, for their diving day was twelve hours, and in those twelve hours, Aidam and his fellow pearlers dove for two minutes, rested for one, then went back down again. After every tenth dive, they rested six minutes, the time calibrated by the captain using a minuteglass with the tiniest aperture through which raced particles of sand finer than the sands of the desert outside Liwa. At the end of the sixth minute, the captain struck the deck with a stick as if calling "Dive!" and the divers dove. The partners loosened their grip on the length of rope to allow the pearlers free movement down, tightening only when a simple tug indicated the diver had reached his destination, and prepared to pull the diver up when next they felt a tug. The six minutes of rest never seemed like enough, and Aidam appreciated the stillness of those breaks, hanging onto the side of the boat, or in the sea, lightly cresting the rocking waves. It took too much energy to clamber back into the boat and find respite amid all the diving gear and crates of food, so Aidam clung to the gunwales for six minutes before heading down again and again and again to the beds, relieved to be back in the water, out of the remorseless sun and relentless humidity.

The captain sat on the bow, cross-legged, naked to the waist like the others, but with his head covered with a scarf. He watched the sun's progress and pointed with a skinny, knowing finger the way to the next shoal. He was known among the owners and diving crews as having the precise sense of where to go next in the reefs. Some said his mother had mated a water spirit. Others said, no, the captain, pleading for his life with a desert *djinn*, had offered it his wife. The *djinn* wondered, "What kind of man offers his wife to another? A man who is no man." So he took the man's wife as his own and sent the man out of the desert, to the sea, where the boatman grew dispirited and mean but good at his job. Unfailingly, no matter where the finger pointed, there would be another bed of oysters.

This particular summer, the one during which Aidam turned fifteen, had begun with hope. The oysters had been plentiful and their pearls lustrous and finely coated. Perhaps this summer, the boat would make a profit. Perhaps this summer, the divers' promised wages could be paid directly from the proceeds of the season and not borrowed against the coming one. The older boys discussed these matters at night, after their work was done and the simple meal of fish and rice and dates taken. Aidam said nothing, a lesson learned during his captivity by Amir and Sultan. He watched and listened.

The profits of the pearlers relied on many factors other than the preponderance of mollusks. There had been a season several years before Aidam came aboard, when the ruling sheikh had called for all boats, even those engaged in pearl diving, to be secured and recommissioned to carry fighters north along the coastline to engage with an enemy tribe. That summer shrank the pearling season to one month from the regular three. Profits were sparse that year, and after the pearls had been sold to merchants from India—Aidam imagined they looked like the turbaned man in the flowing robes he'd seen his first time standing on the seashore—and the owner had taken his ten per cent, the supplier had taken his twenty for supplies, and the captain and the ruler had taken their shares, there was not much left for the divers and their helpers or the cook. The divers' families spent less in the markets consequently and what necessities they purchased were bought on credit. Aidam realized how reliant an entire community was on the divers. If the boats came back dry, the crew had little or no money to give to their parents or their wives to spend at the market and the shop owners had little or no money to buy goods and the suppliers had little or no money to buy from the clothiers or the farmers and no one at all had the money to pay the sheikh his taxes.

The year after the fighting, the story went, there were more oysters. Perhaps it was Allah, blessing them for their service to the sheikh at his time of need or even a reward for the victory itself.

Aidam felt himself lucky Abdul Qader was a generous man. Yearly, during those four months of recuperation after the diving season, when Aidam rejoined the family at the oasis, Abdul Qader refused Aidam's money. "You are my son," he said, applying an herb salve over Aidam's skin, where it was dry and cracking, and to his eyelids and the insides of his ears and the skin between his toes and fingers and the area between his legs. "That is profit enough for me."

Aidam kept his rupees in a pouch along with the blue pearl he had found on the beach of Abu Dhabi on his first visit to the sea. He kept the pouch wrapped inside a white cotton shift, like the tiny robe he'd been wearing when his mother had dropped him in the sands of the desert and upon which a scorpion was crawling when Bashir had found him. Occasionally, Aidam caught a glimpse of the birthmark on his chest, but its shape had changed as he aged and its blush faded. The older he got, the further he was moving away from that child. He hoped he would never grow so old, however, that his love for Bashir and Abdul Qader would fade like the mark. Abdul Qader was growing old now. The time Aidam had been away in the captivity of Amir and Sultan had enervated his father. His beard had whitened and his muscles had withered.

Despite this, in the middle of the night, when the muscles cramped and Aidam jerked in pain, it was Abdul Qader who massaged Aidam's muscles with palm oil and herbs and soothed his mind with kind fatherly words. In the water or on the boat, Aidam missed Abdul Qader's touch. He missed him equally when the sky was still and there was no wind to push the boat, or on those perfect days he imagined his father enjoying, or when the skies grew dark.

Several days a month, the winds were heavy with water and roiled the sea, creating waves that knocked the boat about and made it difficult for the divers' partners to secure the boys. Unable to dive, the boys sat aboard the overcrowded boat, far from the blistering blows of the miserable captain. They mended what equipment they could, but mostly they sat and avoided each other's eyes, for to make such contact, to see into the other's eyes, was a sharing, a telling, and these stormy days were not made for such things. They sat as prisoners and inhaled the scent of the rain.

The day following the storms, anxious to make up for lost time, the captain cut the six-minute breaks to five and pushed the two-minute limit as much as he could. But a diver forced to remain at the oyster bed too long would be tempted to rise too quickly for his one-minute breath at the surface, and rising too quickly from the depths meant potential damage to one's hearing, or one's thinking.

It was on one such afternoon, the day after such brutal weather the boys made not one dive, that Yusuf, the oldest diver, pulled on his rope, telling his partner he needed to come up. The captain saw the partner—a muscled boy named Zia—had begun bringing Yusuf to the surface, hand over hand pulling at the rope one metre at a time. The chief pushed his stick into Zia's back.

"What are you doing?" he asked.

"I am bringing Yusuf up," Zia said. "He is pulling on his rope."

"Are you captain of this boat?" the old man asked.

Zia stopped pulling, but then felt two rapid jerks.

"Yusuf, sir; he is pulling on his rope. He must come up."

"I will say when he comes up," the captain said.

The rope tugged again and again. Zia looked from the captain to the water. Then the rope went slack in Zia's hands.

"See?" the captain said. "He does not need to come up."

But Yusuf did come up. He floated to the surface and Zia jumped into the water to bring him aboard. Zia grabbed Yusuf around the waist with one arm. He made his way back to the boat, where the captain was waiting, stick in hand, to deliver Zia with blows. The stick descended once, twice, three times, but only once made connection with Zia's shoulders.

Zia cried, "He is dead! Stop! Yusuf is dead!" Zia's fellow rope-handlers pulled Yusuf's body onto the boat.

Aidam, like the others, inspected Yusuf's body and said a prayer over him. The young man's chest was covered in red circles and welts, the signature of a jellyfish. He may have survived the stings—plenty of the boys did—but once stung and thus weakened, he could not survive without air.

At the end of the season, having collected his meagre pay, Aidam reunited with Abdul Qader, and his brothers, including Mahmoud, who had come to the sea to meet the boats as they came in. Aidam asked, "How is your news?" and Abdul Qader said the news was good, for it is the will of Allah that all news be good. Abdul Qader asked the same of his son, and Aidam replied, "It is good," and he recounted the story about Zia and the diver Yusuf.

"*Alhamdulillah*," Abdul Qader said. Then he was quiet as the three of them walked away from the sea and along the paths between the stalls of the *souq*.

Abdul Qader made some purchases and sent Mahmoud to make others.

"The story of the diver Yusuf makes me think of you," Abdul Qader confided to his son.

"How, Baba?"

"You were found lying in the sun with nothing but a white cotton shift over your body and a scorpion for company. Had a breeze whispered in the scorpion's ear or had you cried from your hunger and the scorpion been moved to sting you, would the *jalabiya* have been enough to protect you?"

This was no question either could answer. Protection is the territory of God. It is the will of Allah that determines who should perish, like Yusuf, and Amir and Sultan and Sultan's wife, Aidam's birth mother; and who should live, like Zia, Aidam, Wassan and the other slaves, all of whom Abdul Qader had welcomed when Aidam and Bashir had returned from captivity with them. They had worked with Abdul Qader for a year as free men, all the while saving and building up provisions for when they would return home. Only Fikre remained, now wed to Bashir.

Aidam said, "It was the will of Allah that I was wearing that sheath and lived, and I believe it is the will of Allah that Yusuf was not wearing one when he was stung. I do not know whether Yusuf could have been spared the poison if he had been wearing a shift."

There was a shout behind them in the marketplace and Aidam stopped and turned. Mahmoud rejoined them, excited about his purchases, which included a couple of chickens to add to the ones Aidam had gotten four years before and which Mahmoud was raising, having added to the brood with the introduction of a cock. Mahmoud had with him bags of rice and lentils, and a pouch too, which Aidam fingered, marvelling at the tightness of the weave and the lining inside.

"It could be used for grains and legumes," Mahmoud said, "or maybe for salt and spices or tobacco."

"Maybe you will use it for your chicken feed!" Aidam said, laughing.

Mahmoud caught his brother around the shoulders and squeezed. He missed embracing his brother in such a way. "It is good you are home with us again."

"*Alhamdulillah*," their father repeated.

As did Bashir, who, now married, no longer lived with Abdul Qader and the family. Bashir and Fikre, half her husband's age and possessing strengths different to yet complementing his, built their own *arysh* hut nearby, with a small outdoor cooking area protected by a wall of tall palm fronds. Each day he was at Abdul Qader's side at work and each day through the summer diving season he had asked his former master what news he might have heard about Aidam. Abdul Qader would reply patiently that all news was good, though in fact he had not received any news whatsoever.

Now, Bashir rushed out to greet Aidam, who had been first like a son, then like a much-adored younger brother, and then a companion, for it was Aidam whose fainting trick had helped them escape Amir's grasp and Aidam who had, with all the calm of a butcher slaughtering a goat for Eid, dispensed with Sultan, a man more spectre than father.

Abdul Qader once asked Bashir, after they had returned to his fold and been there for some time, what happened while they were with Amir and what precipitated their arrival in the company of Fikre, Wassan and the others. Bashir answered, without elaboration, that Amir had died and the slaves were free to go because Sultan had no say in the matter. There was something in the way Bashir answered his question that told Abdul Qader some evil had passed while his son was away and that he did not want to invoke it now. So while Abdul Qader sensed Aidam was not the same as when he had left, he believed it was by the mercy and will of Allah that Aidam had returned. Only thanks were necessary.

Aidam was no longer the pestering son with a jute sack of questions about date palms and time and the sea. He had matured into a quiet young man with keen, learning eyes who acted with patient, decisive determination. Which is why, when Aidam had returned home with Bashir and their cast of many, there was no question he would go to sea to dive for pearls. And why later Abdul Qader did not question his son when he said he would go to sea no more but would instead make cotton sheaths for the divers to protect them against jellyfish.

Aidam's business began slowly and grew steadily. To diver by diver, and then boat captain by boat owner, he sold his tightly woven cotton sheaths. Within five pearling seasons, Aidam's shifts were worn by divers on more than half of the fleet of boats leaving Abu Dhabi. Aidam shared his success with his family, helping Mahmoud marry a good girl from a good family and establish himself as a poultry farmer. For Bashir and the silently adored Fikre, Aidam planted a date palm upon the birth of each of their seven sons.

He hired a bookkeeper and a seamstress, a modest young woman who was widowed. She moved with the mysterious ease of the moon. Khadra made sheaths that were impenetrable from the outside but allowed the skin to breathe and sweat. As his company grew successful, Aidam hired more seamstresses to help Khadra and an assistant for his bookkeeper.

One day, the assistant came to Aidam and said the bookkeeper was manipulating the sales figures. "I thought you should know, sir," the assistant said. Aidam thought about dealing with the man that day, but he talked about the situation with his brothers and Bashir and, in the end, kept his chief bookkeeper on. Instead, while the bookkeeper continued to fabricate numbers, Aidam sought out someone to teach him the secrets behind the squiggly lines he had seen on the boxes being offloaded from the dhows all those years before. Aidam learned to read and to do math and, when he knew enough, he was able to confront his bookkeeper. "Sir, I have done nothing wrong," the man said. "These are the proper figures." To which Aidam responded with a set of books of his own and let the man go.

It was around this time Abdul Qader grew ill. It had been many years since he had led the caravan to Abu Dhabi. This now was the work of Aidam's older brothers Hassan and Karim. Abdul Qader retired early in the evening and slept late into the morning. Aidam recognized the wet wheeze of his father's breath from his pearl-diving days. Aidam knew that shortness of breath and he knew what would follow.

Still, this did not prepare Aidam for the grief that overtook him when his father passed from this world, and Aidam spent many quiet moments recalling the old man's wisdom, generosity and kind heart.

By then, Aidam was a man in his forties, rich in the happiness of family and friends, all gifts of Allah, but with no one to share the path Allah had laid out for him. This fact gripped his soul in a profound sadness. Why should he have no wife? he wondered. Then he berated himself for questioning: perhaps to be alone on life's journey was Allah's plan for Aidam. He prayed for guidance about how to loosen the leash of this melancholy, for Allah to shed light in this corridor of Aidam's life.

Aidam's days brightened when he was paid visits by his nephews and nieces, by his brother Mahmoud and his soulmate Bashir, who was now an old man, or when Khadra, his chief seamstress, turned her face up and welcomed him at work. He came to realize none are ever truly alone, that the sadness descended on him when he was not in the presence of friends and family. He would keep them by his side forever. He built a compound in the growing village of Liwa and brought Mahmoud and his family and Bashir and Fikre and his growing extended family to live with him and use this place as a base for their respective businesses. Still, Aidam was not truly happy, and still he continued to pray, worrying his beads, polishing them with his thumb.

Mahmoud pointed out to Aidam that his constant rubbing reminded him of the time of Aidam's first trip to the *souq* at Abu Dhabi and the sea there.

"You found a pearl. Do you remember? Father said, 'Some day, you will want to give it away.' Do you even still have it?"

Aidam knew then he would take the advice of his dear, late father, Abdul Qader.

To Khadra, a virtuous woman, Aidam gave the pearl he had found on the beach when he was eleven. "Beside you," he said, "this pearl is but a grain of sand."

"And you are the sun I turn to each morning," responded Khadra, who had waited all these long years for Aidam to come to her.

They were married and Khadra also came to live with Aidam in the compound. When she died, after twenty years together, she left him poor in children but rich in love.

Aidam's grief over her death was immeasurable. Again he descended into despair. His riches could not help him. Many people offered him their girls to take as wives. These offerings only depressed him more, being reminders of the gift Khadra had made of herself. It was Khadra's generous soul that pushed Aidam to act when word reached his ears about a young girl named Fatima, whose family beat her because she desired to go to school like her brothers. Aidam had seen how people who could read and write were of great value to their community, so he paid for Fatima's schooling. When the beatings continued, he paid off the family so Fatima could be at school in the morning and spend her afternoons at the shop, where she could sleep.

One summer, ten years after the death of his beloved Khadra, when the pearling boats were out at sea and the business of making cotton shifts was entering its slow period, Aidam left for the desert. He was now a man of more than seventy years, but he was fit as an oryx and he climbed one hill to the summit of another and yet another again, finding laid out before him a gently unfolding blanket of warm, pale orange sand, fine as fleece. Two hundred feet up, he stopped and turned and there was no one, no thing, no sound. "I am nothing here," he thought. But this did not sadden him. For he saw that even in the wilderness, there was life. There was movement.

Above, circling patiently, was a falcon. It saw movement too. Aidam looked around him, trying to see the land and the sea as the falcon saw it. Tiny grains swept over the sand, pushed forward by an invisible force, forming curlicues at his sandalled feet, then stopping, then rushing straightaway. Although the falcon's eyes were keener than Aidam's, whose eyes suffered from his youthful years as a diver, and Aidam could not see what the bird saw, nor hear what it heard, for Aidam's hearing had also suffered at sea, he sensed what the bird sensed, noticed what the airborne hunter noticed. Aidam tensed. The falcon ripped through the canvas of sky toward something in the sand. Aidam watched the swift death of a desert hare. The hunt was all grace, all natural.

He felt in the moment sorrow for all things that had passed away before him: Abdul Qader, the only father he had really known; Bashir, who understood him without words; his black pearl, Khadra. But he thanked Allah for the life of his brothers Mahmoud, Hassan and Karim, and for Fatima. When her schooling was finished, she had become a proper, reliable and excellent bookkeeper. Aidam had brought her to live in the compound, where he married her and she became the mother of his only child, Bashir bin Aidam Al Ghurair al Rimali, my father.

All he saw in the desert and at sea and in the sky that day filled him with the fullness of Allah. He'd been lost, then found in the Sands; discovered his life's purpose at sea; and probed mysteries of life that were as endless as the sky. All the moments of his life, all the joys and anxieties, these were all there in the dunes, on the waves, in the currents of air, rising and falling, man rising and falling with them.

OIL

I

The radio mourns with the ballads of my childhood. In my seat at the window, open to any suggestion of fresh air, I look out at the road, where the pearl string of cars flows into the city; always someone coming or going, always somewhere, even if that somewhere isn't really anywhere at all. With the music come the memories. Any one of them would be enough to send me down the path I take every night. Always coming or going. Where to tonight? And will you be there?

Maybe it's the music, maybe it's the tea service Whitman has prepared me, but I remember the first time you made me coffee. We were in what seemed to me the middle of the desert. On the ride in, we'd straddled the coast. Das Island was at the edge of our sight, before we turned inland. But what did I know? Eleven years old. We were each part of a much larger entourage. I with Father and my older brother, Bernard, and the falsely deferential British political resident, and the Oil Man, a large diabetic fellow with a cranberry-red face and imperial bluster. You with your elder brothers, the Ruler among them, and others who were subservient to you. Though when it came time for coffee, which was almost immediately upon greeting, it was you who sat on your haunches in front of the wood fire. I'd always meant to ask you why. Youngest son, perhaps, though you had servants, Indian boys. With a large stick as a lever, you raised the charred grate a few inches and moved some of the coal around to bring up the heat and then added a couple of sticks. I remember you were wearing a khaki-green waistcoat, unbuttoned, over a tan Arab shirt coat down to your ankles. You were thin, a live wire. Your brothers wore white, though your headscarves were similar: white, with black cord keeping them in place. The material fell to your shoulders. You lifted your face to me and, without a word, just a smile in your eye, invited me to sit by you to watch. You flicked the sides of your headscarf behind you.

I don't recall how much English you actually spoke then. Certainly more than my Arabic. Father said *shukran* was thank you and *afwan* was you're welcome. And that was all I'd need. I was prepared for those. Maybe there was an interpreter. But no. There was your voice in my ear, confident and cool, mellifluous; even then, at twenty, describing how the Bedouin host must always brew a fresh pot when a guest arrives. You showed me the brass utensils—pestle, mortar, and a pot you called a *dallah*—with such pride they must have been in the family for many years. All this happened while you were roasting the beans in a skillet on the open fire and bringing the water in the *dallah* to a boil. You crushed the beans, then handed me a spoon. Wide-eyed me. You indicated with a flash of your fingers that I should add three spoons of the ground coffee to the water. We waited for the water to boil. I looked up and caught a glimpse of Father in his dark suit coat and tie in deep conversation with the Ruler, Mansour, your two other brothers and the political resident, a Mr. Gilbert Wallace-Humphries. Father happened to turn at that moment and a beam of light shot across his face. Happy I was happy. Lord knows he must have been boiling in his suit. It's no wonder T.E. Lawrence packed his in for Arab kit.

To be honest, I hadn't wanted to go. It was April. I was in school. I wasn't in the least bit curious about the desert. But mother turned ill. One of those periodic afflictions that flattened her. Couldn't get more than a yes dear thank you dear out of her the entire time. Father said it ill-suited me to stay and nurse her when she would be better cared for by Aunt Meredith. So I went. I learned how to make coffee. And drink coffee.

While the water boiled, you showed me how to crush the cardamom. These little shells no larger than a pea with such a foreign nose-burst of spice and nuts. I shrieked when the coffee started to foam and threatened to boil over the pot. You laughed. As unruffled as a camel, you removed the *dallah* from the fire, scooped up a spoonful of cardamom and set the pot to boiling again. When it foamed again, I was prepared, though not for the slightly green hue, like the northern lights we'd once seen on holiday in Scotland. I must have expressed pleasure with the colour or the smell or something. You extracted from a pouch somewhere a couple of wrinkled, dark brown pods. You offered me one, raised a finger and showed me how to split the fruit in two and extract the pit. The fruit was a bit stringy, but sugary sweet. A date. With the *dallah* now resting on the sand, and the coffee grounds having settled to the bottom, you spooned out the fairy-green foam and carefully poured the coffee into tiny cups with no handles. You offered me the first and I looked to Father, who was with Bernard and the other gentlemen sitting around the fire. He nodded and I accepted. I'd never had coffee before. Father says a guest should always accept a Bedouin's offer of coffee, I said shyly. Your father speaks the truth, you said. In that case, one would be expected to accept three such cups. I must have gasped. But we will make an exception, given your novice state, you said. And I realized you were making fun with me and not at me. The liquid was hot and spicy and I sipped slowly and carefully and ate several more dates.

Months before, you told me, fishermen, part of a network of people who came to you with information and requests, had taken you out on their boat to Das. On the ride over, the men sang and you'd joined them. Songs of the sea, songs of the desert: all songs of longing. The fishermen showed you where unctuous water bubbled, then took you along one side of Das, where the beach pebbles and stones were greasy with tar left behind as the tidewaters receded. The air itself smeared your skin, you said. This was 1938, three years after Bahrain and the other Trucial States had signed petroleum concessions. Abu Dhabi alone had refused. What was your older brother holding out for? This was why Father was there: to put pressure on Sheikh Mansour.

I didn't know any of this at the time. Then, I was enthralled simply by how bright everything seemed: the sea, the sky, the sand. The future above all. I imagined a life for myself where I could enjoy all of this always. To hear Father speak of it, however, the future meant oil. All of this is oil, and oil is for always, he said.

Already you could see what oil meant to a country. Schools and health clinics were going up in Manama and in some of the outlying parts of Bahrain. You were jealous and why wouldn't you have been? You wanted what was best for the Bedouin of the peninsula, yet they remained suspicious. The Bedouin saw the sweaty Oil Man and equated that with Foreigner, someone suspect, someone to be cautious around. But the pressure was relentless, like that of the crude below ground, and they caved. The derricks were put in place.

You were at the fire early next morning. I rose and untied the flaps of the tent I was sharing with Father and Bernard. Furrows of blues, greens and yellows as the rays of the sun preceded the orb over the line of the horizon. A *dallah* was on the brazier, boiling. You were bent over on your knees, head touching a rug. I bowed my head and retreated into the tent until I heard you moving about the fire again. When I came out, you indicated I should sit next to you and I should make the coffee. I shook my mind awake to remember what you'd showed me the day before, then, step by step, I prepared my first serving of Arabic coffee. Pleased with you, pleased with me.

Slowly, the other men woke and gathered around the fire. An Indian boy appeared almost out of nowhere with plates of breakfast and another poured coffee for everyone into the handle-less cups. Breakfast was something called *balaleet*, which the Indian boy seemed especially happy with, the way he smiled and pushed the platters at us: You like, he said, you like. A question maybe, or an imperative. This was an Indian pasta dish. Fried vermicelli suffused with ground cardamom and saffron, with an omelette on top. It all felt like… dinner, I said. To which you answered, One must eat breakfast like a sheikh, and dinner like a slave. I didn't much like the word slave, but I understood what you meant. I replied, Then this is a king's breakfast.

I have a surprise for you, you said.

But everything is a surprise, I said.

You are invited to a wedding, you said.

A wedding! I must have shrieked. The men, by now moved away from the fire and sitting on a large rug in a tent Father called a *majlis*, all turned toward me. Father was frowning. The Arab men laughed.

You made the announcement. A Bedouin family, who was close to your heart, close to your family, had invited you to the wedding of their daughter. The family understood you were engaged with business, foreigners among them, but they would be honoured by our presence. They insisted.

There will be camel to eat and much dance and music, you said.

But I have nothing to wear, I said, not even thinking about what you'd said about eating a camel.

You wear a smile as a bride wears jewels, you said.

And I blushed. First time in my life. That I was aware of. No one had ever paid me such a flirtatious compliment.

I smiled. When do we go?

When you are ready, *insh'allah*, you said.

I was ready right then, but we had to wait for the men, whom you joined in the *majlis*. I retreated to my tent, where I changed into the one dress I had brought. When I came out, you were in deep, almost private, discussion with Father. I hovered nearby, close enough to hear, but not privy to the meaning of your talk.

The dress was red with white polka dots and dropped below the knee in pleats from the pinched waist, which was tied with a bow of the same material. The dress wasn't formal in any sense; I was only eleven, after all.

You and the Saudis, Father was saying, you have no industry. Rug-weaving and rudimentary leather-making do not qualify. Neither does the manufacture of ornamental swords and knives. Your state treasury is a trunk. But be assured we can help with this. If you allow it to happen.

The situation with our finances at present is unacceptable, you said. I know you know this. Pearling is not what it once was. The Japanese have learned how to cultivate them. You took a breath. I fully expect Britain will use the situation to its advantage.

Father attempted to object, but you held up your hand, and Father quieted. A man twice your age and you, with gentle respect, reminded him you were the sheikh and he was the British interloper. You continued: Since you are speaking frankly, I shall too. British interests in the Arabian Peninsula are imperial and in complete opposition to Arab national interest, which is to be the masters of our own destiny. Until this state and our neighbours and fellow Arab countries are politically stable and economically sound, until we have governments that can preserve order and improve living conditions for our citizens, you, the British, the Americans, the West, will continue to look on us as impudent women to fool with, playthings. But we will always be a temptation. Now, Ras al Khaimah is receiving a monthly fee of seven hundred fifty rupees. Dubai, I am informed, is about to approve a deal worth one thousand a month. Ajman has a two-year option of five hundred. You have seen our reports. You have conducted your own studies.

You opened your hands. A gesture of openness, of friendship. A challenge too. It's up to you, you seemed to say.

Father nodded.

But let us not settle this now, you said. We have a wedding to attend.

And with that the men turned and saw me standing in my red dress and bare feet. Again, the look on Father's face made me feel I'd done something incredibly wrong, a major *faux pas* that would undo years of negotiations over something called concessions. Was it because

I was listening, or because of what I was wearing? Or maybe Father was upset the deal—with These Arabs, as he'd have said back home—wasn't going his way.

So sorry, I said. Didn't mean to interrupt, I said.

You have done no such thing, you said. And you looked like you'd seen an angel. A rather young one. Or maybe you were unused to having little girls around. You must have had sisters? But who would have known: no one talked about girls in Arabia and the whole time I was there I had met not one. Not even someone's mother.

Rose, dear, Father said, I hardly think this will be appropriate at a Bedouin wedding.

And for the second time in a matter of a couple of hours, I felt the tips of my ears warm and my cheeks redden. Humiliated.

No, no, you said. You are perfectly presentable, Miss Rose. Your presence will honour our hosts.

I smiled.

You are a desert girl.

How so? I asked.

You have sand between your toes.

I looked down. The hem of the dress tickled my knees. My skinny, white English shins, ankles and feet seemed less girlish and more like branches of an acacia tree, digging deep into the sand for coolness and thirsting for water. My smile turned into a grin.

We were separated almost as soon as we arrived at the wedding. The men on one side of a tent the size of half a city block. Me, with the women and girls—finally!—on another, separated by a cloud-thin black curtain. It was a large tent made of hair. Camel or goat, I suppose. Black with geometric patterns of red, blue and white thread. I tried to sit to the edge of the women so I could remain in sight of Father and Bernard and the rest of our group. But two women, in long black gowns or dresses, I would call them *abayas* now, and with brocaded headscarves, took me by the hands and pulled me toward the centre. I thought for a moment they'd decided to marry me off too! But then we sat on goat-hair cushions dyed blue and we clapped in unison to the music. The relatives of the bridegroom were there too, singing and dancing. There was someone with a one-stringed violin and a man blowing into a pipe the size of a clarinet but with a wide range of hollow tones. And drums, big drums, which hung around the men's shoulders. When the family stopped singing, the drums continued, a beat soft and low as the men's fingers trilled and whispered along the top and bottom of the drums. There were two rows of eight drummers, plus four in the centre playing, all dancing back and forth in formation. The longer they went, the louder and faster the drumming and more intricate as well. What had been a three-part beat, a Bedouin waltz almost, became a complex, hypnotic, five- and seven-beat circle of sound. Then the quartet in the middle split and joined their fellows on the sides. A small army of men with swords and whips filled the gap, splicing the air with lightning swishes and thunder cracks.

Next was a woman, dressed in delicately hazy blues and greens, who, with every movement, mimicked the waves of the ocean. Her face was veiled with the same translucent material. But through the veil, we could still make out her dark-rimmed deep-brown, almost black, eyes, like the centres of poppy flowers. She wore bangles around her wrists and biceps that clanged with every arm movement, and resonant metal discs around her hips that jingled and jangled as she twisted and turned to titillate the men, and maybe the women too, with her gyrating bare waist and immodest hips. The mystical stuff of Ali Baba and Aladdin, and I was in the middle of it. Desert romance unfolding before my eyes. The belly dancer made reaching and pulling motions with her arms and hands as if she were trying to entice someone onto the carpeted desert floor. Sure enough, pairs of men and pairs of women joined her, attempting to imitate the undulations of her hips and waist, but failing, adoringly, with humour.

The music stopped abruptly and the dancers returned to their seats on separate sides of the tent. Another song began and a file of girls no older than I entered. They wore a rainbow of *kaftans*, all of them running down to their ankles, with gold embroidery around the wrists, neck and bottom of the dresses. Their eyes were ringed black with kohl, like those of the adult women they were emulating, and their hair was braided and tied above their heads. Drumming started again and the girls untied and unbraided their hair, letting it cascade, long, black as their eyes, wavy where the braids had been, down their backs. They moved in childlike simulation of the belly dancer before them, much to the amusement of the adults, and then began swinging their heads back and forth, creating a pendulum with their long hair. As the music intensified, some of the girls moved their upper bodies in circular motions, their hair whipping around them, while others bent forward, moving their heads to accomplish the same whipping action. The girls' winding hair dance went on for five minutes. I couldn't imagine how they kept it up without going completely dizzy.

I looked behind me to search out Father and Bernard, hoping to get a glance of them through the screen separating us, to see whether, in their faces, there would be a mirror of what I was feeling. Pure elation, giddiness even. Never had I seen such an exuberant display of life. It was fantasy, really. It couldn't be real. I had to have been dreaming. Yet ... the cushion under me was hard and the rug was pilled and the music was loud and the dancing lively. The sides of the tent were rolled up to allow light to enter. The smell of the wedding feast made me hungry. For the repast. For this desert life, this Bedouin dream. Behind me and to the right, on the men's side, Bernard was nodding his head, a slight bounce, so Britishly proper. All around the men was a cloud of smoke and the smell of moist, fruity tobacco.

You were nowhere to be found. And then you were all I heard. I looked right, left, behind me and before me, and could not see you. But your voice was everywhere. Soft and high and sure. The words and melody were unfamiliar to me, yet they penetrated me and lodged themselves in a corner of my heart, long-tendrilled roots of a desert *ghaf* tree that had gone deep and found water. The words needed no interpretation. It was the song of songs, a song of love and intimacy, of honour, duty and loyalty.

From the open sides of the tent came servants carrying *dallahs* and cups to serve coffee and platters of foods for the guests to share. We had roasted hare, chicken rubbed with cumin, turmeric, coriander and cardamom and then grilled inches above the coals, spiced lamb washed with lemon and then stuffed with dates, raisins, pine nuts, almonds, onions, chickpeas and hard-boiled eggs, roasted whole, served on saffron-hued rice. I could have eaten and eaten and eaten; the food was a revelation.

I slipped to the middle of the tent looking for Father on the other side of the curtain. I needed to tell him how happy I was he'd insisted I come on the trip. But he was not with the men. He was outside with Oil Man. Father was agitated, I could tell from his voice, which was pitched high, and strident. Not the most enlightened people, Father was saying. I daresay there's not an independent thought among them. But they want what they want. To which Oil Man responded with his sweaty, overweight wheeze, And who doesn't? Yes, yes, Father said, but I *work* for what I want. These tribals want revenues from oil yet to be found but won't lift a finger to help find it. Don't worry, St John, Oil

Man said. It'll be sorted. We'll get what we need, they'll get a fraction of what it's worth—if it's a quarter of what I'm sure we've got here, they'll all be multimillionaires—and everyone will be happy. Hey, you're at a wedding. Relax. Wedding, Father scoffed. Probably first cousins.

Whooping and hollering stole my attention and I could not hear the end of Father's conversation. I'd had no idea he felt the way he did about the people he was doing business with. Why did he do it if he disliked them so? From one corner of the activity in the tent I could see the groom, a man dressed in white about the same age as you. The groom was lifted by friends and family to their shoulders where he was bounced around in time to impromptu drumming. We never did see the bride.

Although the wedding would continue into the night and much of the next day, we departed shortly after dinner.

Buffeted by a strong, sandy wind, we arrived at our tents and raced inside to escape a severe dusting. There was no more talk of oil and concessions until the morning, when Oil Man, representing Anglo-Persian—Father by his side—and Sheikh Mansour, with you at his right hand, agreed to a three-year option of three thousand rupees per month. I understood now why the deliberations had been so intense, why they'd required Father's presence. The concessions of the other Trucial States were minuscule in comparison, I would come to learn. Should a survey indicate the presence of significant reserves, Abu Dhabi would, in the near future, become a very rich state and you a very, very rich man. Yet all I could see, all I could hear, was you, sitting at a fire, explaining to an eleven-year-old girl with a pageboy how to make cardamom-spiced Arabic coffee, and the honeyed protestations of love you'd sung at the wedding the afternoon before.

Later that day, we went hunting. When I was twelve, you told us, I used to hunt with a rifle. But I was too young to carry the rifle for too long. To shoot I used to lean on something. Then you turned to me and said, Today, I will lean on you. You'd caught me, once more, almost taking you seriously. You and Bernard and Father laughed. It was the most relaxed I'd seen Father since we'd arrived. Deal done. Soon he would want to leave.

Who taught you to hunt? Bernard asked.

There was silence. Father raised an eyebrow at Bernard. I was always surprised by how much Father knew and equally surprised when he reacted with impatience about why we didn't know as much as he. I suspect you caught the awkwardness passing among us and you answered, with none of the drama the answer could have elicited, that it was your father, Sheikh Saif, who'd taught you to hunt, taught you to appreciate the simplicity of rural life. But hunting is not relaxing, you said. It is an education and one must work hard to be educated. The lessons of hunting are patience and perseverance; and, among its joys, being able to traverse large areas inhabited by people one has never met before, to be made welcome by them and to count them as friends for many years to come.

You stopped, raised your left arm to ninety degrees and from who knows where, a Bedouin boy appeared and deposited a hooded falcon to perch on your arm, now protected by a thick leather glove reaching almost to the elbow. We would not be hunting with rifles today. We would be falconing.

With the boy leading, we walked some paces further, a quarter-mile perhaps, from where we could see alteration in the colour and texture of the sand. As we walked, you tried to gauge how much vegetation there would be where we were headed. How much rain? you asked. The boy indicated with his hands about six inches, the depth to which the rains had penetrated the sands. When was this? Last month, the boy said. The terrain changed again as we entered scrub country. Sparse plant life, scraggly bushes, low, insignificant trees, completely shorn of their lower branches and leaves by desperate foragers. They were like a thin green cloud floating above a sandy horizon.

You examined the sands stretching out before us. Listening? Looking? Smelling? I could not tell. Perhaps all these. Then you continued walking, always scrutinizing: here something worth looking at, but found lacking; there something worth stopping for. Whatever it was. Tracks, I suppose. You were tracking something for the bird. You were doing part of its work. Working with it, in a sense. You and the falcon, united in purpose, one and the same.

The falcon on the perch of your gloved hand rested, feathers puffed, one foot up. With your free hand, you untied the hood and tenderly removed it from over the falcon's head. The little hunter was brown, mostly, with some black and white feathers interspersed among the others. The bird somehow made me think of you: strong, intelligent face with steady, observant eyes. You were made for each other. It blinked several times, rapidly, moving its head a degree this way and another degree that way, taking everything in, as you had. Gently, you loosened the leather string from around its ankle bracelets, placed the hood and jess in the pocket of your *thawb*. You spoke to the bird in the same sweet tones you used when you sang at the wedding. Then you extended your arm out completely and, by some signal known only to you and the bird, the falcon was off. It flapped its wings and, without hesitating, entered a current and circled above us, glorying in its brief freedom.

The Arab, you said—and from the tone of your voice I knew you were addressing, almost admonishing, Father—is not an unknown quantity. The desert is not a mystery. *If* you pay attention. You see the desert around you and only see emptiness. The Bedouin can read the sand and the scrub; the Bedouin can read the sun and the stars and the clouds. More importantly, the Bedouin can read a face.

With the falcon above us, we walked down toward the trees. When you spoke again, your voice had softened. Before there were rifles, before there were horses, there was the falcon, you said. The Bedouin and the falcon. The bird continued to circle. Attempting a dive and then balking, returning to its search. You said something to the boy and he handed you a tasselled leather strap, a lure. You made a circling motion with your right hand over the left arm and the falcon descended, talons outstretched, wings pulled back to halt its streak, and landed on your glove.

You have seen how it is accomplished, you said to me. Now it is your turn. As if hunting with a falcon were as easy as making coffee.

Before I could object, the boy handed me another glove, which I put on my left hand. I looked at Father. Though he was watching me, I could sense his mind was elsewhere. You nudged the bird onto my arm. She was light as a teacup though even through the thick leather I could feel pricks from her nails.

Flick your wrist, *habibti*, you said, using a term I'd heard you use with no one else. There had been no women among us. Dear one. If I'd known that then I would have melted. I suppose I did in any case.

I flicked my wrist and up the falcon lunged into the wind, wings drawn out, catching a lift and soaring up and away.

She did not circle long. She had found what she was hunting: the *houbara*, a dim-witted, slow-moving land bird that failed to react in time to escape. We watched as the hunter stabbed the bustard in the breast several times. You raised my gloved hand and placed a piece of raw goat meat in my palm. Your boy called the falcon and it turned. I waved my right hand above my left and the falcon, hunting me, knowing that I, for now, was the source of its food, its reward, without reluctance turned and lifted off, aiming for the tasselled lure hanging between my fingers, aiming directly for my arm.

Keep your eye on the bird, you said.

But I couldn't. I closed my eyes tight as it neared. I heard a thin shriek and a wash of wind by my head. She'd missed my arm, which was now covering my head.

Turn around, you said. Stretch your arm out and don't move it. Let her come to you. *Now*, you said. Do it.

The falcon, in the time it had taken me to do as you'd commanded, was already banking. She landed with grace, talons first, wings folding back to her side. Once again, I was surprised by how little she weighed. And how hungry she was.

You waited until she'd eaten, then placed the hood back on her head and the thin cord around her anklets. You took my free hand in yours. I must have reacted sharply to the familiarity. You let go, then turned to Father, who shrug-nodded. Then you placed my fingers on the bird's small chest. I buried my fingers in the thicket of feathers and felt the quick beat of her tiny heart, a pulse as rapid as my own.

Your boy took the falcon and the gloves away. The hunt had succeeded as exhibition. You had impressed Bernard, thrilled me. And you had in your way told Father we were on *your* land, wild and untameable as it was. What he wanted was yours. What you wanted was yours. You'd seen the desire in his face.

Our walk took us by a semi-permanent encampment of Bedouin, an array of tents and one-storey, flat-roofed houses made of palm fronds. No windows. Two rooms. Two doors, opposite each other. One for men, one for women. When the Bedouin men saw our party, they sent the boys to greet us and invite us to their *majlis*. Even me, though I should have been going to the back door. You greeted the men as *ya aini* or *ya akhi* (my eye, or my brother). We sat, and were offered coffee. With the help of Father's interpreter, I heard you tell the gathered men we had been out with the bird and demonstrated how well I had done falconing for the first time. The men smiled and laughed and congratulated the young miss. Then you asked how the hunting was going, spoke about the amount of rain so far and asked what this would mean for the dates. A Bedouin man sitting on the opposite side of Father leaned over to speak to me. The man told me the Bedouin liked you. He shoots and rides like us, said the man, with a fraying scarf wrapped around his head like a turban, one corner of the material hanging over the left side of his face. His beard wasn't brown like yours, but greying, like Mansour's, a man already burdened by the weight and worries of many.

We sat around their fire until after dusk, the light of our naphtha-fuelled lanterns giving a glow to the faces of the men, these campfire comrades, and reinforcing, too, the emptiness beyond.

At night in our tent, I asked Father what he knew about you. He said yours was like a story from *One Thousand and One Nights*, a tale of treachery and bloodshed and everything one had ever heard about Arabs. You'd grown up in modest privilege as a member of the extended ruling family. Your uncle, Hazza, was a popular ruler at the start of his reign, but he bungled the economy and nearly got the country invaded by the Wahhabis from the western part of the peninsula, the area that eventually became Saudi Arabia. Your father, Saif, and one of his other brothers, Saqr, conspired to have Hazza killed. The deed done, Saif became leader and was able to win the support of the tribal families.

But, Father explained, Saif's days were numbered almost as soon as they had begun. Bernard and I sat, rapt. Once ensconced in the fort at Abu Dhabi, Saif found there was no money in the state coffers. Not a surprise, Father said. And you, upon whom Saif had doted, had taught to hunt, ride a camel, saddle an Arabian, were denied your father's closeness as he descended further into the maw of politics and economic worry. The pearl-diving industry was drying up, depriving Saif of the revenues he needed to pay subsidies to the families.

Four years after the end of the European war, the Ottoman Empire no longer existed, Father said, but you know this; it's not ancient history. Arab lands were broken up and artificial borders created. Abdal Aziz was now a king in Saudi Arabia. And to the north, a new country called Iraq was born, with Faizal at its head.

Then in 1926, four years after the plot to kill Hazza, Saqr turned his aim toward his co-conspirator and shot Saif in the back during a family dinner. Your father! He died instantly and you and two of your brothers escaped with your mother to Buraimi, where you were kept ignorant of many things, though you must have sensed the change. Gone were the games. Instead, you and Mansour and Mohammed were tutored in Islamic studies, arithmetic and Arabic. Another brother, Khalifah, was sent to Qubaisat relatives to recover from wounds he'd got at the dinner when your father was killed.

Outside, I heard the camels snorting. And through the stitches of the roof of our tent entered streaks of light from the moon. A moon that you, when not much younger than I, sat under and silently asked questions. Why had your father killed his brother? Why had another brother then turned on your father and partly orphaned you? The moon pulls oceans and young men's hearts, but it doesn't answer prayers, doesn't take queries. And your mother, if she'd heard your questions about fratricide among the rulers, didn't answer. She was figuring out ways to protect what remained of her family.

Your father buried, Saqr became leader. But he was never trusted. Wrong blood. His mother was an Al-Bu Falasah. Their tribal base was Dubai. More worryingly, because it was the first time a ruler had done so in a hundred years, Saqr offered tributes to the Wahhabis. In exchange, he got their backing. Your eldest uncle, Abdullah, who had previously, presciently, refused to become leader of Abu Dhabi, discovered Saqr was plotting to assassinate him as well, so he made a deal with the Al-Shaar section of the Manasir tribe. He paid a servant from Saif's old household staff, a young man from Balochistan, to kill Saqr. But the servant failed and Saqr escaped only to be caught by the Al-Shaar later and killed.

I do believe Father and Bernard must have heard my heart thumping. But I noticed Bernard, once lying on his sleeping bag with his head propped up, was now fast asleep. How could he have grown bored? I could hardly bear to hear more about the grisly endings of these men, almost the entire generation of men before you, but I had to hear the rest. This was you we were talking about.

Your uncle Abdullah could have taken power for himself, but he did not wish it. Instead, he quietly admitted to masterminding the plot, then exiled Saqr's children from Abu Dhabi. To this day, Father said, no one in the ruling family is allowed to name a child Saqr. Next came a gesture of some humility, genius really, which you must have observed and absorbed. Instead of passing the leadership to his son Hamed, Abdullah restored Saif's bloodline to the throne by naming your brother Mansour ruler. Mansour, I realized that night, was the very same person Father had been negotiating with. Mansour returned to Qasr Al Hosn, the Ruler's fort, in Abu Dhabi, where you and your brothers had lived for four years as children. You all swore an oath of fidelity to your mother—being a Qubaisat, a well-respected family, instrumental as kingmakers—to support Mansour and not resort to fratricide.

The next morning, again at the fire together making coffee, we spoke quietly until the others rose for breakfast. You imagined what oil would do for Abu Dhabi, for its people. We live in the eighteenth century, you said. *Habibti*, you have seen our Bedouin tents and *arysh* houses. Our outdoor kitchens, our four-legged transportation. The rest of the world is now thirty-eight years into the twentieth century. Of what interest is Abu Dhabi? There is nothing here anyone wants. We have sand; we have camels and goats. We do have palm trees. Maybe you want some dates? Once, we had pearls. But they are hard to find. We no longer have anything here worth exporting. So we are poor. We are illiterate. We suffer bad health. Mothers die as they are giving birth. Infants die before they can walk.

There is a seam, you said, that runs south from Iraq. It is a vein full of oil, black gold, that will lift the people of Bahrain, Kuwait, Saudi Arabia, Qatar, Abu Dhabi, all of us here in these desert lands, out of poverty. You stopped, looked up and around at the tents, the dunes farther off, the sky. When you return, you will not recognize us, *insh'allah*.

You said this with sadness. As if you knew the cost of progress even then. When you return, the barbaric splendour with which the West associates us will not be so barbaric anymore, and splendid Abu Dhabi will be as indistinguishable from a British village as these oilmen are from the agents who accompany them.

You stopped. Then you looked at me as if I, an eleven-year-old British girl of no consequence, could understand all your worries and more: the apprehensions and anxieties of an entire nation. There was such trust and confidence in the way you looked at me that for a moment I believed I could do just that. Your lips spread in the slightest of smiles. You offered me my cup.

I have something for you, you said after taking a sip of your coffee. You reached into your pocket and came out with a jess. You tied it around my right wrist. The leather was rough against my skin, but the gesture was smooth and kind.

We do have hope, you said. We have tomorrow, *insh'allah*. And we have Allah.

Alhamdulillah, I said.

You must have caught my delighted surprise in myself. You laughed. I laughed. Then you poured us a second coffee.

II

BOAC flew into Sharjah regularly, a stopover along several of its long runs, to Brisbane, Delhi, Singapore or Rangoon. There was another flight to Dubai, a boat-plane that came in from Bahrain and landed in Dubai Creek. How exciting that would have been, though it was not an option to me at the time and the opportunity never came again.

Travel to the Orient was such a different experience in 1948 than when Bernard and I had visited with Father ten years before. We'd come into Dubai by steamer. It wasn't air-conditioned and the cabins were unbearable with the din of people, the tight, cluttered confines, the rocking of the ship and the smell of Indian cooking. I'd spent as much of my time as possible on deck, breathing the cool and salty air and enjoying the occasional spray of water.

Given the late hour the aeroplane landed in Sharjah, we overnighted in the Rest House, part of Al Mahatta Fort, which, thankfully, had showers and acceptable beds. We were to be picked up the following morning for our trek to Dubai, the neighbouring emirate. I dreamed sweetly of climbing aboard a camel again, wondering if I had forgotten how to ride, trying vainly to recall the feeling of sitting so tall and so high. I needn't have worried. There were trucks now in the Trucial States, a fact I would have thought unimaginable when I was eleven. Even at twenty-one, a truck seemed impractical to me. How on earth could a truck cross those dunes? Again, I needn't have worried. The truck itself was a U.S. model, a Chevrolet, what one calls a pickup, much smaller than a British lorry. From Amrika, the driver said, eliding the "e." Then, with a kick of the tyres, he added: brand new. The nicks, scratches and dents belied that notion. Like all around it in this desert, his truck had not had an easy life. There were no roads of bitumen. No graded tracks.

As a peregrine falcon flies, the distance between the Sharjah airport, where the RAF had maintained a base during the war years, and the Dubai Creek is about thirty miles. But the route was not a consideration for us. Instead, we started out north by northwest toward the Persian Gulf. This Al Bidayer, the driver Ali said, pointing toward a large mound miles off on the western horizon. Big Red Dune. We avoid, he said. It looked formidable even at a distance. There were nine of us altogether. The driver and his young son, perhaps ten, and me in the cab and six men in the back with tow ropes and jacks, a shovel, their luggage, plus mine, which the driver insisted on inconveniencing the gentlemen with because it would not do for a lady to have her bags at her feet in the cabin of a truck. I'd told the men, four of them foreigners like me, I didn't mind riding in the truck bed, but they'd insisted, even though it meant covering their faces with headscarves.

I was glad I acquiesced. The bumpy ride was hard on the coccyx. Not five miles out, zigzagging along the hard-packed sand, we hit a patch of porridge-like softness and, given the weight of nine people and all their luggage inside a two-ton pickup truck, we promptly got stuck. Everyone out! Ali called. He started grabbing at the luggage and tossing it into the sand. When the men realized what he was doing, they gave him a hand. One picked up the shovel and commenced digging out the rear tyres. Once they were exposed, Ali lowered the pressure of the tyres.

Miss, you drive, Ali said. Men push.

I shook my head. I don't know how, I said.

I can do it, one of the men said, stepping toward the cab.

No, miss do. Ali said, motioning me forward.

I sat in the seat. Ali turned the key. Right foot gas, he said. Left foot clutch. Same time. Right hand gear. Move to number one. Let go clutch same time gas. *Yallah*!

Okay, I said. Though, I—

One two three, you go right foot gas, left foot—

Clutch, I said.

Ali smiled. Teeth white as salt. Eyes as full and black as a desert night, face covered with fawn-coloured sand.

The men pushed, I ground the gears down to nubs, I'm sure, but we got out of our sandy trench. We drove ten miles or so, got stuck again, got out again. Turned left at the Gulf—the water green and clear as sea-glass—and Ali pushed us on toward Dubai along the salt flats, the *sabkha*. We got stuck one more time, though by that point I had timed the movement of the clutch and gas and gear-shifting to avoid the crunch of metal on metal. It was my reward, on our final stretch, to see my first desert rose, a cluster of large petals of crystallized gypsum and sand. They are formed, I discovered later, when the winter rains percolate and the hard, salty beach sand absorbs the water. Deep inside me, I'd known. The rains had started ten years before, on my first trip to the desert. And I was back now to absorb it all.

I was back, breathless, on my own. No Father, no Bernard, no Oil Man. I had returned to Abu Dhabi to brush up on my Arabic, for one; and to study the water distribution system, particularly how it affected or had perhaps changed the lives of the Bedouin of the eastern Arab peninsula. Your people. This was all for my degree at the University of London's School of Oriental and African Studies, and that was what I told the border people. I couldn't very well tell them I was hoping to see you again. No guarantee of course, since you hadn't responded to a single of my letters.

We slept in a Somali-run guesthouse. It was too late to eat though we were all famished from our excursion; instead, we were ushered upstairs to the sleeping quarters, three rooms for the men at two per room and one, slightly smaller one, for myself. Ali and his son slept elsewhere. I had thought to ask where, but I realized doing so might highlight the differences between us: the hired and the hirer. Embarrassing, though perhaps more for me than him. The bed was a poster bed of dark-stained cherry wood and the bedding was a thin cotton duvet with a flowery blue and white pattern cut from Damascus cloth. None of it mattered. I was asleep the instant I lay down.

I slept through the first call to prayer, but awoke a short time later to the cacophony of the nearby market and the smoke of food grilling in the restaurant below. The food won out. The guesthouse was a large concrete-block building, plastered, painted white, with large wooden beams in the ceiling, dark stained like the bed I'd slept in, the floors white tile. My God, had Abu Dhabi changed like this as well? I glided my hand along a wooden banister as I descended the tiled stairs. The businessmen who'd come in with me from Sharjah were already at breakfast, at a table set for eight. I had my hand on the back of one of the two open chairs at their table when a waiter, half-bowing, never looking me in the face, said, Here, mum; here, mum, and steered me to a small round table behind a wooden lattice-work screen. I sat and my heart sank. I was more than aware of my status as a single female traveller. I took pains to be prudent. But this felt like overkill. The men were as much foreigner as I.

We were in the Deira neighbourhood on the east side of Dubai Creek, our guesthouse standing at the end of a street near the *souq*. After inquiring about the suitability of walking through the warren of streets to the market—much too hot for a woman was the consensus—I ventured out. I had a free day in Dubai before going off to Abu Dhabi and my ultimate goal, the oasis villages of Al Ain and Buraimi. I'd made my arrangements beforehand, using some of Father's connections—though he failed to understand what I was doing or why I persisted.

I carefully donned black cotton slacks and a sheer white blouse. Long sleeves. In the coastal towns of the Arabian Peninsula, there's a balance between one's comfort in the heat and humidity and respect for the culture. It was thus in Gertrude Bell's time as it was for me in 1948 and forever shall be, amen. But my, was it hot. One hundred and twenty degrees Fahrenheit with humidity reaching fifty per cent. And no air-conditioning! In the *souq*, the temperature dropped. There were two main arteries off which short, narrow capillaries darted into darkness. Each artery or alley was like a tunnel, covered by a thin, light-coloured fabric roof designed to reflect the heat away from the marketplace. The merchants were grouped by wares. One whole length of the *souq* was given over to fabrics, large bolts of colour arrayed like paint on a palette, the material splayed out for all comers to see; across the way were tailors and clothing shops, bold *kaftans* and starched *thawbs* and white *kandouras*, sandals, scarves, *kaffiyehs* and *sheylas*. Seated cross-legged on a dusty rug in front of each shop was a seller— Indian or Arab or Persian, rarely the owner, I guessed—idling quietly waiting for a customer or sitting in chitchat over tea (Persian or Indian) or coffee (Arabic) with a friend or neighbouring vendor. Around the seller would be his newest or freshest goods. Other goods, maybe not as popular, or perhaps less in demand, hung in darkness behind him, like clothes in the back of a wardrobe.

I thought I'd had a good-sized breakfast, but the smells of the *souq* prompted me to follow them. There were stalls selling various produce—tomatoes and aubergine and onions, dates, figs and pomegranates—and others selling pistachios and walnuts and peanuts. I found lentils in an array of colours and sizes. I could identify very few of the spices, though the smells, separately and together, were tantalizingly aromatic. The cardamom I did recognize, however. And it brought a smile and, surprisingly, tears to my eyes. I'd written so many letters! Ten years I wrote letters. Most of them in the first year or two. Drifting off the older I got. Until the last two. I wrote to tell you I'd begun reading Arabic history at SOAS. No response. Why would that have been different, I guess. And then the month before I arrived, to tell you I was returning.

Casting a smoky pall over the entire area were the stalls selling grilled meats and vegetables, and curries. All of this was mixed with the sharpness of *narghile* tobacco. The odours put me in such a pleasant mood, as in a daydream, that I was startled to find myself being nudged at the back of the thigh by a hard, insistent object. Maybe the Somali hoteliers were correct in their estimation of my safety outdoors. Men. Could they not leave a girl alone? I picked up my pace, annoyed at having had my peaceful morning walk through the *souq* disrupted by some... I couldn't imagine this happening in London. A catcall perhaps, but reaching out to touch me as if I were Aladdin's lamp to be rubbed? What cheek! I swatted at it, whatever it was, only to strike something hard, curved and metallic. When I heard the honking sound of a car horn, I jumped and turned.

A car! In the *souq*!

Everyone had scurried to other aisles or tucked themselves into shops except me. My, did you have a laugh. As did I. Once over the shock.

Had I been eleven again I might have jumped into your arms I was so happy. My heart did, that I know.

Instead, you opened your car door, nudged against the palm wall of the stall where you'd stopped. So tight against the *souq* you had to close the door to come to me. You crossed your right arm over your chest, hand on your heart, and bowed your head. So proper you might have been Victorian. I felt like curtsying. When you looked up, I stuck out my hand. You grasped it in yours and with your left hand covering our joined hands you pulled me an inch closer. I can't imagine how many laws of etiquette we'd broken, but it didn't seem to matter. For as public a venue as we were in, we were inhabiting a private place.

Asalam aleyikum, I said, by way of formal greeting.

Aleyikum asalam, you answered equally formally. Your Arabic has improved greatly.

I grinned. Then said *kayf halek*, the more informal How are you? Though I could tell in any case; I could see it in your face: eyes brimming with joy and a smile wide as the Gulf. More handsome and finely chiselled now than when we'd first met. As if some painter had finally figured out what to do with your face and put all his life there. You'd grown a beard. It suited you.

And me, you must have noticed the changes. Still the short, wavy black hair, the constant, curious gaze of dark brown eyes. Still thin. But womanly slender, not the flat biscuit of my youth. Did it please you?

All is well, you said, thank God.

Which I understood to mean all was well because Allah had willed it so.

I asked after your family, your brother the Ruler.

You asked after Father, Mother, Bernard.

And all was well.

There was the slapstick attempt to open the passenger door for me in such narrow quarters, but soon enough I was seated next to you. Decorum kept me from sliding all the way over in the seat to sit by your side and have you drape your arm around my shoulders, as in some Hollywood movie. Instead, I parked myself on the passenger side and couldn't keep my eyes off you.

You inched us out of the *souq* and along the side of the creek where it seemed dozens of large wooden dhows were docked. They came in from Iran and India, you said. Boxes and crates of varying sizes piled in front of them. The dock smelled of fish. The sand we drove by was littered with goods dropped from spilled boxes or produce left to spoil, deemed not good enough for the *souq* merchants. Yet men and covered women were negotiating to purchase even these paltry items.

But tell me about you, I said.

You shrugged. Another time, *habibti*, you said. There is much to show you.

You took charge then, and I obliged. Back to the Somali hotel, toss my bags in the boot of the car, then back to the Dubai Creek, where you said we would lunch across the water. I imagined having to drive to the mouth of the creek and cross over, or ford through in the Mercedes. Rather, we got out and left the car beside an official-looking two-storey mud-brick building. Official, meaning the only one with windows and a door. I tried to look at the buildings and streets the way you did. You'd spoken with some pride about what was happening in Dubai, but I detected envy as well. Abu Dhabi was not Dubai, and where I was headed—Al Ain and Buraimi—were not Abu Dhabi. They were oasis villages, tiny, the last signs of life before the Omani mountains. We walked down the pier, where dozens of oversized, covered boats, twenty feet in length and eight feet across, swayed at their moorings. We sat in the middle, on a long wooden banquette. Seats ran around the edges too. Everyone sat, their knees touching someone else's. Smiling shyly. Or not glancing at all. At me at least, being the lone woman in the company of a couple dozen men of the Subcontinent and the Peninsula. Examining the waves in the water, or the chips of blue paint of the *abra*. Bounced and jostled as roughly as the next. We couldn't speak over the rough whine of the outboard motor for the ten minutes it took to be ferried across the river. The men stood to let us off first.

The *souq* was smaller, darker than the Deira marketplace, only about two hundred yards in length, but constructed in like manner: rectangular shops on either side of a central aisle with an employee seated on the ground at the front of the shop displaying his freshest wares and eager to ply a buyer with tea or coffee and conversation before getting down to the business of bottom prices. You steered me here and there, your hand at times at my elbow to indicate a turn. I wished your arm around my waist. But such a gesture wasn't likely. You and I had known each other for such a very short time and such a long time before and I was only eleven at the time. Still, I was twenty-one now. A woman, and independent.

You never answered my letters, I said.

I apologize for this lack of manners, you said. I should have written. But I did not know what I could say.

Anything would have been fine, I thought. I told you everything, I said. Thinking, maybe this was the reason he hadn't answered. I'd written whatever drivel popped into my eleven- and twelve-year-old head. And he was a man ten years older than I. Would I write to a teenage boy with a crush on me? Precisely.

You're forgiven, I said.

But, of course, you said, then stopped and put up your hand. Wait here, you said. I won't be a moment. You disappeared down an aisle of the market. I remained where you left me, looking about for a place to sit. It was chilly in the shade. I put on my cardigan and the full weight of what I was doing here, back in the Orient, descended on me. Yes, I had my research work, more than enough to busy me for a summer, but what was I doing? Father had asked the same when I'd made my plans known.

What provisions have you made for hospitality? Have you a driver? An interpreter?

I said I had made such arrangements. And my Arabic was good enough to do without the added expense of a translator thank you very much. Besides, I'd written you, I said.

And he never responded, Father said from behind his *Times*.

He will come through, I said, with all the conviction of a convert.

Maybe Father was right. Maybe I was behaving like a dreamy schoolgirl, holding my heart out to you. All those letters and no response. All the time, and money, we'd spent looking for a qualified Arabic teacher for a twelve-year-old girl. What did I think? For all I knew you were married. Most Arab men your age would be. And an Arab man of your stature? It must have been arranged when you were a child. Was she a girl from the same tribe? Or was it a marriage of expediency, mutually advantageous to Abu Dhabi and Dubai or some other emirate? Tall, like you. Dark, it went without saying. Modest, probably not as educated as you. There to bear your children.

Then I saw you walking back, a package in your hand, a smile on your lips. Two packages. Both in brown wrapping paper. I'm sorry, you said. This took longer than I had expected.

It is no problem, I said.

These are for you, you said. You handed me the larger of the two packages. I unwrapped a gorgeous silk scarf, a blue-white background with purple jacaranda blossoms. This is beautiful, I said. For me?

Yes, of course. To protect you.

Then you shoved the second package into my hands. And these too, you said, for the sun.

A pair of dark-rimmed sunglasses.

I put the scarf over my head and tied it under my chin, then slipped the glasses on. What do you think? I put a hand on one hip and thrust out the other arm, flicking the wrist like a dancer.

Your eyes widened.

I realized where I was. It was as if I was still that girl, stepping out of her tent with a red polka-dotted dress to wear to a wedding. Oh, God, I said. I can't believe I—

Your laugh told me it was okay, but for propriety's sake I looked around at the shops and the shopkeepers. No one was watching. We were invisible.

You are always a surprise, Miss Rose.

We headed for a guesthouse in the Bastikiya neighbourhood of Dubai, named for all the traders from Bastik who had come seventy years before. They made the area their home, you said, and they built houses like the ones they'd left behind in Persia. Usually coral stone. Usually with panelled doors and filigreed screens. You pushed the door open, held it for me to enter. A hush descended on the room while we were observed. The diners, the waiters. All eyes on me. Partially obscuring you behind me. The talk recommenced as if we weren't there at all. But then you stepped to my side and it was as if we were back on the *abra* that had carried us across the water and everyone had allowed us to disembark first. The owner hustled to join us, hands extended to you in greeting. How good of you to cross our threshold, Your Excellency, he said. How is your health? Before you had time to reply, he was onto the next question: How is the health of your brother? Your family, the Sheikh? All is well, you said, *alhamdulillah*, praise be to God.

The owner bowed slightly at the waist and, with his open palm gesturing to the left, offered us a table behind a wooden privacy screen. We crossed the length of the dining area, passed a hollow room with water on the floor and a ceiling that soared several storeys high. Wind forced down from the top entered into the room, cool and moist.

I placed the sunglasses in my purse and unknotted the scarf. I was about to remove it from my head.

You raised your hand. You'll want to keep that on, you said.

I didn't understand. I hadn't ever veiled myself before in your presence. But I did as you asked.

The owner returned and placed a basket of two puffed-up flatbreads fresh from the oven in front of us. Your Excellency? I whispered as he retreated.

You opened your hands. My brother has seen fit to entitle me with leadership of Al Muwaiqi, our ancestral home.

If you were now referred to as Your Excellency, I thought, you *must* have a wife, someone to bear heirs to the Ruler's representative in Al Muwaiqi.

I remember it, I said. I remember an oasis, palm trees, a few houses. The wedding was near there, right?

You smiled in memory. I am often told, you said, when I meet that Bedouin family, how honoured they were by the presence of your father and brother and yourself at the wedding of their daughter. It is a rare occurrence, such a guest, they say.

It was a highlight of my time here, I said. That and learning how to make coffee.

And not the hunt? you asked.

Ah, the hunt. A bit frightening. My brother, Bernard, has told the story many times.

You will join us again, *insh'allah*.

We ate bread. Then came *shorbut addis*, a lentil soup, perfumed with ground cumin and coriander and made slightly yellow by turmeric. It was spicy and it was good and after one spoon I hungered for more. You said, On the hunt, do you remember I asked the boy when it had last rained in the area?

I nodded. One month.

This is the length of time the bud of many desert plants takes to bloom.

I hoped I understood what you were saying. You were paying me a compliment. I smiled. I would have blushed, but I'd left those days behind. Maybe you hadn't married. But so what if you were or weren't? I was here to work, I had to remind myself.

The owner came with a round tray of more more more, none of which I'd heard you order. There were parsley and bulgur salad, fattoush, with its sharp sumac and chips of crisped pita, plus skewers of grilled chicken and lamb, grilled onions and tomatoes, hummus, falafel, nutty tahini and garlic paste, a feast for a family. Which is what we soon became. We were joined in short order by one of your brothers and two men whom you identified as brothers as well. In a way, they were. Bedouin tribesmen; my eye, my brother. The Manasir. They looked at me briefly, muttered greetings to which I answered with a polite smile, then they sat and absorbed your attention.

You had killed two birds with one stone that day. You'd come to Dubai to retrieve me and take me back to Abu Dhabi, but more importantly, I understood from your discussion, you'd come to broker peace between your state and that of your marauding neighbour. And the Manasir were there to present their concerns and remind Dubai its raids had cost the tribe more than fifty members.

The last member of our party came in after the Manasir. He was dressed in a suit coat and tie and held his hat by the folds in its crown, tapping it against his thigh. We were introduced. I've forgotten his name. He said, How do you do? British, like me. The political agent? I didn't much care. When he had arrived at the table and plopped his sweaty, meaty body in the chair next to mine, I'd felt my shoulders droop. I believe I sighed. But it was he who explained—he rattled in a surface manner befitting what he assumed was a young woman with no apparent knowledge of Trucial State affairs—how the war, which began shortly after our European one had ended, had transpired and how British attempts at mediation had thus far failed. I sighed, I hoped quietly enough only a small amount of exasperation was perceptible.

These federations have not proved to be durable, he said.

And the British have earned themselves a dismal reputation recently as the architects of those federations, I said in Arabic, which took the Manasir by surprise.

Federation was not the issue, you said, in English so the British agent could understand. But a wise father knows when to let his children settle differences between themselves.

The agent looked into his plate of meat and rice and shook his head. With his mouth full, he let the matter drop.

You rose and we rose and we were off. We walked through the *souq* again, where you left me to browse. Your next stop, the final one in Dubai, you said by way of explanation, was the hospital; as a woman, I wouldn't be allowed in where you were going and there was no place to wait on the grounds. You said that here at the hospital bed of Sheikh

Fallah bin Sultan, your brother Sheikh Mansour was to be reconciled
with the ruler of Dubai, of the Maktoum line. There would be no more
war, you said. You and the Manasir and the political agent were there
to witness the agreement. When I tired of walking through the *souq*, I
went to the creek to take the *abra* back over the water, accompanied the
whole time, unsuspecting, by one of your servants.

That evening, we left Dubai in a Chevrolet truck. You'd given up
the Mercedes, the gift of an American oil company in competition for
your favour with the British and of absolutely no use where you lived.
With the money you got selling the car, you bought two pickups. All
this had been done while I had breakfast in the guesthouse the day
following our meeting with the Manasir. It never ceased to amaze me
how you worked. People made room for you, did things presumably
without being asked, anticipating requests.

We went directly to Al Ain without stopping in Abu Dhabi,
sticking to the flats as much as possible, sliding down the occasional
dune. The trip was too much for one day, so we overnighted in the
desert. I looked forward to this, with such keen and happy memories
of my first time in the desert, but we did not luxuriate here. I wasn't
asked to make coffee. It was a brisk setup of the tents, one for me,
one for you; the driver of the second truck, Fahdi, a youth about my
age, who was the servant who had kept an eye on me the day before,
and the two Indian boys he had with him slept under blankets near
the fire. At dawn we were wakened by Fahdi while one boy made
coffee and the other made a flatbread. While we ate the boys took
down our tents.

It's not like the first time, is it? you asked.

No, I said, hoping my voice did not give away the desire I felt for
that time gone by, for the girl I was then, for the man you were with
that girl. Maybe Father was right: What *did* I know about you? And
what did I know of the people I was here to study? Only what I'd
learned in books and concocted in girlhood daydreams. I was as bad
as the Orientalists I scorned in university. I was hopeless as a cultural
anthropologist. Worse: I was a misguided scholar infatuated with
her subject. For as much as I loved having been swept up by you in
Deira and brought to your luncheon with the Manasir and now being
escorted to your desert home, the feeling didn't seem reciprocated.

I understood now the need for my presence at lunch with the
political agent and the Manasir. I was there to defuse tension, keep
the men from the harsh words they might have been tempted to use.

No one would have done so in the presence of a woman. And the scarf hadn't been a gift, not really. It was a way to get me to cover up in the company of male strangers. And you knew, from the letters I'd written, my Arabic would surprise them, put them at ease.

I tried to smile. You tried to smile. Then the boy came by and rinsed out the *dallah* and poured the water on the coals.

Houses in the village of Al Ain were familiar to me from my previous visit: *arysh* houses of palm fronds with flat roofs made of palm trunks. There were others, though, newer ones, of mud bricks. Again, flat-roofed. No windows. The same mud bricks were used in the construction of the simple market, two rows of little bays, niches cut into the narrow covered pathway. Dates and dried fish and flies buzzing around meat, skimpy bolts of dusty cloth, the needs of an impoverished people. Outside the *souq*, camels kneeled at water's edge. Their owners, the Bedouin, bargained inside for the few essentials they needed before leaving at sundown. This was not Dubai, not Deira.

Fahdi took us to your compound, where I was surprised, and elated, to find you had arranged for me to stay. The house was built of the same material as the others in the village, though it was larger and more commodious. Yours, across the courtyard from your mother's in the compound, was larger still. When you visited your mother, you sat in the public room, separated from the back of the house where the women slept. In most other houses, modest ones, I came to discover, an internal door separated the men's and women's quarters. I imagined your own house had a similar setup, though I was never invited. There seemed no point. Most of the action in the compound happened in the public courtyard or the *majlis* of your mother's home.

Your gracious mother, Sheikha Maitha, kept to herself initially, quiet but observant. I felt studied, which was natural and even to be expected. Such was the segregation of the sexes, Sheikha Maitha had probably never encountered a foreigner before, even when her husband had been ruler of Abu Dhabi and you had all lived in the Hosn Fort on the island. Your beautiful sisters welcomed me like a sister. They tried on my clothes—they couldn't believe a woman wore trousers—and passed some on to me, including an *abaya* and *sheyla*.

One morning that first week, I woke on a large woven palm-straw mat in my room. I could hear birds and an odd noise, like a pulling or stretching. I sat up and cracked open the front window. I was immersed in lushness, in greenness: the palms, and gardens of trees and flowers. A bougainvillea heaved its brash colour over the compound's mud fence. The birds were arranging and rearranging themselves in the trees. My eye was caught by the motion of a pair of oxen plodding around in a circle. The noise I'd heard was the rope the oxen were pulling around the well. There was the answer to a question that had crossed my young mind ten years before: Where do they get water from in this endless desert?

At first, you insisted on my not walking through the village unaccompanied. Being busy, you insisted I go out with your sisters, which I did. And they were sweet and took me to visit with neighbouring women, female cousins and aunts. We ate dates and figs and pomegranates and drank tea with milk or tea with saffron, or coffee with cardamom. We made the same circuitous trip the next day and on the third we stayed home and the neighbouring women and female cousins and aunts visited us. We ate dates and figs and pomegranates and drank tea with milk or tea with mint or coffee with cardamom. I was beginning to think the order was less circuitous than circumscribed and I longed to get out to explore the village and the surrounding area on my own. I was aware of how short my time among the oasis-dwelling Arabs of the eastern peninsula would be and how much I needed to know to write my thesis: living conditions, what people did for work or amusement (an odd concept I would have to explain), what they ate, where water came from, how they prevented disease, what the men did with their time and what the women did with theirs. When I asked how many people lived there, I was met with curious looks, until one of your sisters lucidly and plainly said, Enough to live.

I broke free on the fourth day. Rising early while everyone was at prayer, I opened the compound's wooden gate and escaped into the village for my own look-see. Even at dawn, the *souq* was a hive. From the camels sitting outside by the water, I knew I would find the market full of Bedouin traders. Sure enough, they were there, many of them buying large quantities of dates. Even with the Arabic I had learned at university I could not understand the dialect. Though, listening in here and there, I understood some were buying for themselves to take back into the desert and others were traders, middlemen, who would be taking a load of dates to the north, to Abu Dhabi, and elsewhere along the Persian Gulf coast, where the water was too salty to support palm tree farms.

This is what I had wanted to do since I had first come and here I was doing it. I was in Arabia, meeting Arabs, learning Arabic. Thank

God the villagers were patient as I stumbled through their verbs. I had two goals, other than researching the *falaj*, the gravity-based aqueduct that brought water to town. I wanted to meet more Bedouin, like the ones you'd introduced us to at the wedding and after our falcon-hunting. Not because I wanted to meet what an explorer in an earlier time would have called true Arabs. That was a Victorian concept, a Gertrude Bell notion. Nineteenth-century travellers descending on the East seeking an idea of purity the West had packaged and sold. Such views were Orientalist. Like the poet Wilfrid Blunt, who wished to cast off the slough of Europe, to have done with the ugliness and the noise… bathe one's sick soul in the pure healing of the East. The mere act of passing from one's graceless London clothes into the white draperies of Arabia is a new birth. Yes, he wrote that.

Nor was I Freya Stark, intent on discovering treasures and illegally crossing borders to find Luristan or Shabwa. I wanted to find a traditional culture on the brink of a sea change. Because that was about to happen. Oil was here. And it was coming out of that ground, come hell or high water, and nothing was going to be the same again.

You came and went during the month I spent in the village. A curiosity for many at first, I was part of the matting by the time I left. I was made welcome in your home among the women and continued to visit with the neighbouring women, the female cousins, the aunts. I helped a young mother, Umm Saleha, care for her mother-in-law and two sick children who had caught an infection after ingesting fouled water. The men, I think, begrudgingly accepted my presence. A foreign woman, someone sincere and respectful but who moved and acted independently, dirtied her hands, covered her hair with a scarf but wore trousers. I was identified as the daughter of the British envoy who had negotiated the oil concession, and a student at the big university in England who wanted to learn about the life of the Arab. I was to be treated with respect, in other words. The men nodded, a couple even smiled.

I went out with you and some of the men from the town to look at the *falaj* system. We drove out in your two Chevy trucks. You drove one, with me in the passenger seat. Fahdi followed in the other. The beds of both trucks were filled with men, their head scarves flapping in the wind. You took us up into the hills, perhaps two thousand feet above sea level. We stopped at a spring, a *wadi*, bubbling and gurgling through and over rocks and stones. Grasses, bushes and small trees dotted the landscape.

This is where it begins, this is the source, you said. The men had gathered around us. You crouched and put your cupped hand into the water, then drank a mouthful. You addressed the villagers. Join me, brothers. Drink. It has been a long ride.

As the men drank, you said the water was a gift of Allah no different than a camel or a child or a wife. Such a gift is meant to be protected. We are entrusted by Allah to shelter our wives and children and livestock. We must protect our water as well.

You got up and we walked along the dusty trail paralleling the spring, weaving and dodging as it meandered down the mountain toward the villages below. I asked questions the village men eventually grew comfortable answering when they saw how at ease you and Fahdi were in my presence. At some point, one of them, a boy of perhaps sixteen or seventeen, ran ahead down the trail, then shouted out Miss Rose!

The men laughed. He is eager to show you the work he did last year, said one, who, given the brow-shape they shared, could have been his father.

The boy pointed to the channel, where the spring officially became part of the *falaj*. The aqueduct was lined by large stones, its bed the same sand and pebble as further upstream.

I built this, Miss Rose, the boy said. With my own bare hands. And he lifted them, calloused palms out, to show me.

You did a superb job, I said.

It is a primitive system, you whispered in English.

I didn't think you meant primitive. I disagreed. It shows how much our modern technologies are based on the old ways, I said.

Perhaps, you said, then switching back to Arabic, we are losing a lot of water through percolation and absorption.

The men made suggestions about filling in the cracks between the stones with mortar. Another said the whole conduit could be made of stone and plaster, like the forts at Al Ain and Abu Dhabi. A third put forth the idea of concrete, something less permeable, like the buildings going up in Dubai.

We drove to a second site. No one had worked on this channel yet. It was a natural spring weaving down from the mountain, lazy as a snake. We followed it. The men talked about straightening out the course of the water. As we walked, we noticed the ground had turned soft in some areas. We stopped when we saw the reason: the stream had become completely filled with silt. The sediment—fine sand the water had carried down from higher up for years and years—had built up so much it blocked further progress. The water no longer flowed and couldn't percolate through the riverbed, so it overflowed its tiny banks.

This will have to be dug out, an older man said.

I can do it, volunteered the boy who was so proud of his earlier work.

Of course, you can, Sayed, you said. Of course, you can.

And the men all laughed.

You proclaimed our inspection over and that you would take up the subject of the *falaj* again with them at the next *majlis*. We walked back to the trucks, then drifted homeward, gravity pulling.

When you convened the *majlis*, I was invited to observe. Not quite sit in. Despite the manners the men who'd gone on the *falaj* inspection displayed, inviting a foreign woman to be seated among the men, as an equal, would have been one step toward modernity the men were not willing to take. Instead, you allowed me to listen and watch from the opposite side of a screen. You were in your element, at the centre of a horseshoe of men who, one by one, wished Allah's blessings on you and thanked you and asked for this or complained about that. One by one, you asked for Allah's blessing in return, and listened to each man in turn.

Here, I learned that the oil concession which Mansour, the Ruler, had finally signed a year after my first visit, was to last seventy-five years. Many of the men in this room will be in heaven when this concession expires, you said. But our children and our children's children will reap its benefits and from the concessions for oil yet to be found, God willing. I noticed you did not say how much the concession was worth. And no one asked.

But the European war came, you continued. It has been over for three years, but we had our own fighting with Dubai in the intervening years. Now this too is over and the drilling can begin.

These benefits of which you speak, Sheikh, what do you mean? a white-bearded man in a sun-faded black *thawb* asked.

Someone said he heard big buildings were coming for schools and hospitals run by foreigners. It was too much. Their people had survived for hundreds of years without hospitals and schools. Our happiness is God's business, not the business of foreigners and oilmen.

You listened, still as the night.

You are a strong man, the old man continued. Talk to them like a man. We don't wish this.

Someone else, a younger man about your age, said he envisioned terrible things happening to the village. To their trees and livestock. To their water. To their women. These are the things that matter to us, he said. Not these concessions, not these benefits. Then he backed down. But you are the sheikh. You will decide.

A craggy-faced man with deep-set, dark eyes asked about the new state of Israel and what this would mean for the village and for the ruler in Abu Dhabi.

Only when everyone felt they'd had their say, did you reply. The benefits are wide and will affect all, you said. No one will be left behind. We will march forward together toward prosperity.

First, we must repair the *falaj* system. It is no longer adequate for the needs of a growing community. Several of you have seen the *falaj*. We are losing water or, in some cases, not getting any, and what water we have is contaminated by our waste. By the will of Allah, this must end. Second, you continued, we have no medical clinic. A clinic, however small, with properly trained staff may have saved the lives of Abu Saleha's mother and his son, Kamel, this week. As for a school, we will require educated people to run the companies and businesses and understand the contracts associated with this oil. We could use another mosque. Repairs to the *souq*. More palms. There is much to do and with the help of God it will be done.

As for the Zionists, we pray for the families who have been forced to leave their homes. We look at this situation as an opportunity for Arabs, from the Maghreb to the Levant, from the Arabian Peninsula north to Iraq. We will build consensus and we will have unity. *Insh'allah.*

God bless them, the men listened. For you talked like a man sure of himself and his position among other men.

When the *majlis* broke up, I waited behind the screen until all the men had left before entering the compound. You were there, near the fire, with a man I hadn't seen before. You introduced us. It was Umm Saleha's husband. I said I was sorry about the death of his mother and son. He looked to the ground, said he was thankful for the work I was doing studying water and the care I had taken with his wife and family.

I said it was my honour, then good night and continued to my room in your mother's house. Before I entered, I turned to look for you.

Abu Saleha had left and you were making your way to your house on the other side of the compound. Did I detect a hesitation in your step? A sigh in your voice when you'd said good night? Dreamer, Father's voice whispered in my mind. Were you going home to someone? I heard your sisters' and mother's voices inside. I wiped my eyes and brought out my best smile and went in to have tea and wish them a peaceful night.

It was time for me to go home some days later. I was confident in the interviews I had eventually conducted with the women of the village—outside of the excursion into the mountains near Oman, only two or three men not related to you consented to speak with me and only in the presence of their wives—and in what I'd seen of the *falaj* and the oasis that I had enough material to finish writing my undergraduate thesis.

You would not take me to the airport in Sharjah because you had business with your brother in Abu Dhabi. We said our goodbyes the day before I was to leave. It was friendly, as warm as could be, I suppose, given who you were, the public role you had and the cultural traditions of your tribe. Don't forget to write, you said, as you got behind the wheel, your gear in the bed of the truck with the boys. I won't, I said. You put the truck in gear and I waved and the boys waved. I stood there in the sand watching for a while, then felt a gentle hand at my shoulder and your sister guided me back into the compound.

I spent the rest of the day preparing for my own going-away and thinking how I'd come to be a twenty-one-year-old girl packing a suitcase in a desert *arysh* house thousands of miles from home, speaking Arabic more fluently than I could have thought imaginable when I'd left school in May, full of love for this place and these people. Of course, it all came down to you. You had given me this. You had befriended a girl ten years before and opened her up to life. That this eleven-year-old then fell in love with an idea and with you as the emblem of that idea was forgivable, predictable even. The twenty-one-year-old she became realized how still in love with the place and with you she was—in fact it had deepened with respect for you. I could see how wise and caring and passionate you were. I was not too young or too in love to notice the irony. The more I loved you for who you were and what you represented the more likely you and the role you had to play would prevent you from returning that love. It was no one's fault. This was who we were in the place and time we were living.

The night before my departure, the sheikha, your mother, presented me with a leather box. Inside was a necklace of silver medallions. Pounded Maria Theresa silver thalers that had made their way down from the Habsburg era of the mid-1700s. I wouldn't have known that—the dollars had been hammered out of recognition—without your telling me. I did recognize them as similar to the bangles I'd seen on some of the Bedouin women at the wedding ten years before. The necklace was gorgeous. I put it around my neck immediately and cried. *Shukran*, I told your mother. You are beyond generous.

She looked surprised. All gifts are from Allah, she corrected me. He is the generous one.

III

Bloomsbury in the rain. Incessant. And what a day for it: June 2, 1953. I suppose it's like what they say about rain on a wedding day. It's a cleansing, a way to start anew. What better way to crown a queen than with a steady spring drizzle. May your reign be long, Elizabeth. And new.

For now, it was a public holiday and the shops were closed even though it was a Tuesday. No going out. And no excuse to go out. Instead, I would sit at the foot of the television box with Mrs. Firth-Heyward—our landlady, whose husband, a low-level administrator at the university, had died two years previously and left her the house—and the other boarders: Janie Bolton, Elizabeth Rillington, and Laura Lindsay. All of them secretaries at the university, though Janie was also reading English. Laura had a few years on us and was stepping out with a Mr. Frankie Taylor. She'd asked Mrs. Firth-Heyward permission to invite him and another friend to watch the Coronation.

The more the merrier, I always say, Mrs. Firth-Heyward said.

In that case, Laura started, wickedly, did I tell you Frank's brother is the famous footballer? They're in town for the Arsenal game and the club haven't a place to watch the telly.

You know what I always say, Mrs. Firth-Heyward said, two's company, three's a crowd.

And we had a nice laugh at that one.

Frank did bring a friend over after all, but it was not his brother and certainly no footballer. Mr. Ian Bentley was tall, thin as a rake, dark brown hair with a curl over his left ear he couldn't flatten, and a winsomely half-crooked smile. It did not hurt the portrait of the man that he was in uniform. He was recently returned from East Anglia, where his unit had been continuing to work on flood relief. He'd been on his way to his sister's, where he had intended on watching the festivities, he said, but the road was blocked by well-wishers and procession-watchers. It was on his way home that he ran into Frankie, who had insisted he stop by to meet Laura.

Mrs. Firth-Heyward invited Frank and Ian in, but Ian, who hadn't even come in from the foyer, attempted to apologize. I am grateful for the invitation, but I really must try to get to my sister.

Inside, we heard hissing and popping and scratching from the living room. We rushed into the room to find Janie fiddling with the antenna of the television. The image on the screen flickered in and out of focus. Is it supposed to look like this? she asked. None of us had any way of knowing. Mrs. Firth-Heyward had bought the set, like so many other Britons, in the two weeks before the Coronation. The box, a yellowy-brown polished to a high gloss, had been delivered the day before.

There! There! Mrs. Firth-Heyward cried. You had it.

Janie moved the antenna ear back a notch, to no avail. Oh, heavens, she said.

Here, perhaps I can be of help, Ian said, stepping forward. He shut the television off, counted to ten and then turned it on again. There was a scratchy sound, and then the unpleasant noise stopped and the picture, black and white and a little grainy, appeared.

Oh, you'll just have to stay now, Mr. Bentley, Laura said.

He scanned the room, smiling shyly, and hesitated. I might still have time to make it to my sister's.

No, no, I insist, Mrs. Firth-Heyward said.

We saw masses of people lining the street near St James Palace. They looked like wartime refugees, blankets over their heads and shoulders, and wrapped around their torsos and legs. Mugs of tea in hand. Look, Elizabeth said. Can you see the steam?

My, don't they look uncomfortable in the rain? Laura said.

Frank said they didn't seem to mind it; cold rain was worth the trade-off. This could be the only Coronation they'd see in their lifetime. He was sitting on the arm of the chesterfield. Ian Bentley had backed away from the set and stood at the threshold between the foyer and the sitting room.

We've seen two, Frankie, Laura said. We were ten when her father was crowned.

True, he said. And then: I forgot to say Ian has brought us some news.

What is it, Captain? Mrs. Firth-Heyward asked.

Only something I saw in the *Times* this morning, Ian said. The British expedition led by Edmund Hillary succeeded in conquering Mount Everest.

What a fine present for the Queen, isn't it? Elizabeth said. We all agreed.

Onward and upward, I always say, Mrs. Firth-Heyward said.

And Everest is certainly upward, Ian said.

Please don't humour her! I said.

And we all had a good laugh at that too.

On screen not much seemed to be happening. The news camera was focused on the front door of the Queen's residence. All of England waiting for her to make her grand entrance.

Oh, do come in finally, said Mrs. Firth-Heyward. And Ian, glancing at Frankie, then Laura—and, oddly enough, me—said, You know, it's probably for the best.

Then Ian pulled out from behind his back a paper bag and presented it to Mrs. Firth-Heyward. I had intended on giving this to my sister, but I'm pretty certain I won't be going there now.

I won't tell if you don't, I always say, Mrs. Firth-Heyward said, peering into the bag. Then exclaimed: Humbugs! We haven't had humbugs in donkey's years.

Rationing had lifted earlier in the year, but the horehound mints were still rare. What a treat these would be.

And then there she was, gliding out in a white dress, radiant as a bride. She *was* a bride in a way. Our early-summer Queen about to be married to a nation, an empire, one royal hug stretched from Hong Kong all the way around to New Zealand. She was followed by her husband, Prince Philip, and they slid into a two hundred-year-old Cinderella coach drawn by six regal white horses.

The camera moved away from the Queen and Prince and showed the couple's two children in the window of the palace. Charles and Anne.

It would seem the younger generation aren't invited to the party, Laura said.

Shame, I said. It's their mother, after all.

Oh, I don't know, I wouldn't want children at my wedding, Janie said. All underfoot. Or crying. Or needing their nappies changed.

Out of sight, out of mind, I always say, Mrs. Firth-Heyward said.

It must be a cultural thing, I said.

What do you mean? Ian asked. This *is* our culture.

That's Rose's Bedouin thing, Elizabeth said. All flying carpets and big baggy pants, that one is.

We think she's got a beau, Janie said.

Beau Bedouin, Elizabeth joked.

I tried to defend myself. I can't imagine a Bedouin wedding where the entire family wasn't there, I said. It's just not done. Family is all-important to them.

The carriage carrying the Queen to the church passed under the Admiralty Arch. Affixed to the rise was an oval disc with the letters ER.

Elizabeth Rillington! Laura shouted.

What?

Oy, Frank said, you missed it. Your initials were on the sign on the arch.

Elizabeth said it was one more thing she would have to share with Elizabeth Regina.

And what is the other? Laura prompted.

Stunning good looks, of course!

Janie shook her head. You are to die for.

I saw Laura elbow Frank, who was sitting next to her, and nod her head toward Ian, and then Frank rap Ian's knee with his knuckles and raise his chin my way. Ian shrugged. What were they on about?

Conversation was light, and rose and dipped to fill in the lack of action on the tiny screen. We were in front of the television for more than an hour, during which my eyes tired. The Archbishop of Canterbury laid the blessings of the Church on Her Majesty, now seated in King Edward's chair, the crown in her lap, the weight of all the countries under her rule, the lives of all those people pressing on her. Yes, I did have a thing, a romantic connection to the desert. Watching the Coronation, I couldn't help thinking of you. What was it like when a sheikh was chosen? Like your brother years ago. Then I remembered the family history Father had recounted fifteen years before in our desert tent. Maybe a bit of ermine and a fairy-tale coach weren't so bad. Though we Britons certainly weren't immune to family feuds, even spilled blood.

The Queen's horse is running the derby tomorrow, Frank said out of the blue.

If I were a betting woman, I always say—

You would bet on Aureole? Frank asked Mrs. Firth-Heyward.

It would be her day, her year, she answered. The Coronation today, reaching the summit of Mount Everest, then those two lovely doctors who discovered the whahoozit.

DNA, Ian said.

What a stroke of good luck! Mrs. Firth-Heyward said. I would take that bet.

She does seem to have the halo around her today, doesn't she? Janie said.

Though she can hardly take credit for Dr. Watson and Dr. Crick's work, I said.

In a manner of speaking, perhaps she, or at least the monarchy itself, could, Ian said.

How so? I asked, sitting up.

By laying out the conditions allowing for such research to be done, Ian responded. He pointed to the television with the hand in which he was holding his cup. We live in a democracy where education and research are vital and respected. Not some backward land run by a potentate high on hashish and susceptible to baksheesh. It's why we went to war.

It was a direct challenge to a direct challenge and I was about to respond when we heard the fanfare of trumpets. Oh, how wrong he was. Such a patronizing attitude. Then the discharge of the great guns in the Tower of London and it felt as if we were hearing it twice: live, outside, from three miles away, and then a second or two later, on the television.

Ian left not long afterward, hoping to make it to his sister's as the procession wound down and the throng of people dispersed. Frank left with him.

When the door closed behind him, Laura was at my elbow. Well?

Well, what?

What did you think of him?

He's still the same old Taylor, I said.

Not Frankie! Ian Bentley!

Ian? I wondered. We hardly spoke. We shared two words about Bedouin culture, then almost got into a row before Her Majesty interrupted.

Yes, but what did you think?

Why are you pestering me? Wasn't he here to meet you?

Oh, Rose, I'd already met him. The whole sister thing was a ruse. I had Frankie bring him 'round to see you.

You mean check me out, I said.

I wouldn't have put so crass a word on it, but, yes, to check you out. He's a catch! He's entering the diplomatic corps. He's perfect for you. Travel, adventure... culture.

I raised an eyebrow and smiled. Well... I began... he'd have to change his way of thinking about the Orient.

Brilliant, Laura said. We'll go 'round the pub tomorrow night.

Thursday mid-morning, in my room, deep into writing my doctoral dissertation on democratic institutions in the Middle East. Mrs. Firth-Heyward came knocking. There's a gentleman here for you, she said. Odd voice, as if she weren't sure if he was really a gentleman.

Would it be Ian already, I wondered. We'd gone out for drinks just the night before with Laura and Frank. He'd said he'd pop over soon, but this would have been a redefinition of soon. Welcome, certainly. We did have a brilliant time, and he turned out to be an amusing, interesting man. And cute, even without the uniform. He told army anecdotes this side of being off-colour for mixed company. His impish smile gave him much leeway. He was a bit vague, mysteriously so, not cagey, about his work in the corps. I dismissed it as his not wanting to bore us with the details. As he said. Even though I'd assured him, with all seriousness, that I didn't find it boring at all. I found it exciting he was off to the Middle East. If so, he said, then perhaps we can talk about it some more. The men walked Laura and me home from the Imperial Hotel and as Frank kissed Laura good night, Ian said he'd enjoyed my company and would it be okay if he came around again, alone perhaps. We talked so much about me; I want to know more about you.

I was flattered. I had, indeed, enjoyed his company, and I said yes, of course. I wondered what kind of relationship he expected us to build in one week. If a week was all we had, perhaps that was why he was at the door now, the very next morning. Hoping to squeeze in as much of me as possible. And despite the work I needed to do on my dissertation, I would accommodate him. Why not? Handsome, ambitious, intelligent, slightly irreverent: all qualities to be admired. And to be investigated further. His comment on Coronation Day about drugs-smoking, bribe-taking Middle East rulers was not my experience of Arabia, though there were certainly leaders in those countries who fell short on the morality scale. Anyone can change, I thought. I drew on the jumper hanging on the back of my chair and rushed down the stairs.

To find, in the foyer, a fish out of water.

I hadn't ever seen you in a suit and tie. For a moment, I wasn't sure who you were, but you smiled and laughed and said *Marhaba* and I knew it was you. I hustled down the last steps and took both of your hands in mine. You must have been taken aback—we'd not yet had that kind of physical contact—but I couldn't contain myself. I felt my smile would crack my face and my heart burst from my breast. You're here?

Aiwa, you said. Yes, you said. Yes.

The way you said it, in your Arabic—not the classical Arabic of my teachers, not the street-scrappy Cairene dialect or one of the squeaky Maghreb tongues—but in *your* Arabic, that of the sand-softened Gulf, the *khaleej*. I thought I should melt, or cry, or laugh. A whirlwind of thought and emotion.

Wahlan as wahlan, I said. A phrase meaning Welcome, but so much more as well. You are safe and welcome in my country, it implies. And to me at that moment, Welcome to my heart.

By now the girls were hovering. I made quick introductions and you sat for tea and told us you had come to the U.K. to represent the Trucial States at the Coronation. You had a series of meetings planned for the next week and thought, with your free time, you might pop in to visit an old friend.

You were at the Coronation? Elizabeth said.

Janie: Did you meet the Queen?

Laura: What was she like?

Mrs. Firth-Heyward: Let the man speak.

You laughed. What a sound. I hadn't realized how much I'd missed hearing it. Open, friendly, the way I remembered you in the *majlis* of the Bedouin men after our day of falconing, the day you surprised me with the car in the Deira *souq*. You were by nature gregarious, comfortable in the company of others. But you squirmed a little in your western garb. It didn't suit you.

Yes, you said, I met the Queen. She is lovely. Pause. And she sends her regards.

Oh, and didn't the girls love that.

Who knew you had perfect comedic timing as well?

You looked at me then as if I were the only person in the room and you were performing for me.

Meanwhile, Laura was examining me as if she were wondering who I was. I don't know what I would have told her if she'd asked. The girls and Mrs. Firth-Heyward all knew about my studies and what I hoped to do with my degrees and research, but no one had ever got around to inquiring about my heart. How, despite the passing of the years, my love for you remained, suppressed and perhaps unrequited, but there, like a living thing itself. In the five years since I had seen you last, in the lush oasis village of Al Ain, I had written intermittently, telling you of my studies, inquiring after your mother and sisters and for news from the village. You wrote once. Or perhaps someone had written it for you. It was early on. Fahdi wanted to learn English, you said. Work was steadily progressing on improving the *falaj*. One of your sisters had married.

It was almost a full hour before I had you to myself. I want to show you around Bloomsbury, I said.

You held the wrought-iron gate open for me and I stepped out onto the pavement. You stayed at the gate, swinging it open and closed a couple of times. Knowing I was on the other side of the opening, you said, was like entering the gates of heaven. I'd felt the same in Abu Dhabi, passing through the gates of your village compound five years before.

You looked up at the house as if committing it to memory. Our building, four storeys, attached in townhouse style to homes to the left and right, had exited the war unscathed except for some shrapnel now pocking the white brick façade of the ground floor. Mrs. Firth-Heyward said several of the windows had been blown out and had had to be replaced. The tarmac where the bomb had fallen—what could the Germans possibly have been targeting in Russell Square?—had long been paved over and the zebra crossings painted. You closed the gate. Show me, you said. Show me everything.

I took you around the neighbourhood where I studied; I talked about the construction and the Blitz and showed you the library building where I spent so much of my time. The building had been hit in September 1940, when only half-completed, but who could tell now? So much damage and hurt; all of it now invisible. You asked a question here and there, but I could feel myself filling the silence between us with idle chatter. So much of this was outside the frame of your life, yet silence wasn't shameful or awkward in your Bedouin heritage. Rather, the silence was your complete absorption of everything I said and everything we saw and heard and smelled. Admiring the speed and efficiency with which reconstruction had happened (particularly the library), appreciating the architecture—the Russell Hotel, Christ the King Church, the functional and beautiful design, chromed cars on rivers of asphalt, the formal postwar dress of men and women and the vibrant colours of their children's jumpers. I saw you looking around and sensed vulnerability and strength, longing and resolve.

You brought me back to my accommodation and you sought me there bright the next day, returning me to my quarters so I could complete my day's scheduled research and writing. On our third day, we entered the Underground at the Russell Square tube station on the other side of the square from Mrs. Firth-Heyward's flats. You were impressed so many of the stations had been used as bomb shelters during the war. I took you on our double-decker buses. We passed bicyclists, men in suits, women in dresses and skirts with a modest length of leg showing, street sweepers wheeling their bins, delivery trucks and taxis. Alighting from the bus, we joined the people working or shopping or browsing, milling and teeming without aim except the desire to be outside. The air smelled of coal, and the colours of our days were earthy browns and pale blues and whites, the shades of the buildings and the sky and the clouds.

When the forecast one day was for rain, we visited the British Museum. The full collection was back now after having been dispersed during the war in secure basements, the National Library in Wales, the Aldwych tube station; I suspect the homes of museum directors as well. We sat in front of the Rosetta stone. Quiet mostly. You were thinking. The longer the silence, the deeper my self-consciousness and my self-doubt. I was one long string of worry beads. What were you thinking? Was everything okay? How much of it had to do with me? Fifty per cent quickly grew to one hundred in my self-absorption. I had been too talkative, not talkative enough; I had dragged you around, tired you out, forced too much on you, I hadn't spent enough time with you in my need to be home early to study.

I could read you no more easily than I could read the hieroglyphics on the ancient black slab in front of us. You had always been my Rosetta stone. It was through you, through your eyes, that I saw Arabia. The desert. The Bedouin. But at that moment, the two of us seated and staring at the stone, you were a puzzle, and I had no key with which to enter your mind. You alone would have to tell me what was going through your head.

The West, you finally said, has always looked down on Egyptians and Arabs as a lazy lot, unwashed, prone to lying whenever the opportunity arises. It is your prime minister, Mr. Churchill, who said Britain had a moral obligation to occupy Egypt. Presented in this way, it must also be an obligation to pillage a country, rob it of its resources, and at the same time despise as morally inferior the people whose resources and treasures one is stealing. Is the Egyptian morally inferior to the British? Am I? This stone in front of us was removed from its rightful home. Those items from the tomb of Queen Pu-Abi belong in Ur, in Mesopotamia, in Iraq, in Arab lands, the land of Ibrahim the prophet. For Arabs to enjoy and learn from.

I was stunned. This was not what I was expecting. Yet I knew to say nothing. You were right.

Yet, you continued, I am embarrassed to say the Rosetta stone and the great Sumerian treasures belong here. Here, in England, these items may endure. For the entire world to see. Home, in Egypt or in Iraq, we have not the wealth yet to protect them. There is too much instability. Witness the unrest in Egypt at present.

I was about to comment, about to disagree. No, no, these items belong to the Arab people. But you stood then. God, you were tall, right and straight as a god. And I was so happy, felt so privileged to be with you. Brother to the ruler of a Gulf Arab state; a first man among men; a rich man; a smart, intelligent, caring man; a good-looking man. You put out your hand and without thinking I took it, and felt a frisson, a shudder of electric excitement, as you helped me to stand. With reluctance, I let go of your hand and smoothed my skirt. Something to do while I calmed my nerves. I touched my hair. Still there. Unlike my mind. I'd let go of my senses. I picked my purse up from the bench and we left the museum.

We took a long walk around Russell Square, the leaves of the trees still glistening from the morning rain, the pavement damp, the birds chirping, then another turn and a stroll through the park itself. People turned their heads when they saw you. I was so happy. And why not? Handsome, tall, well dressed. And they were seeing just the outside. What did they know of your royal origins and the power and respect you wielded in your country? Millions had witnessed the Coronation of our Queen. And you'd *been* there. An emissary, equal, almost, in stature.

But when people turned their heads to look at you, they were looking at me too, and the question in their heads was what I was asking myself: what was *she* doing with him? Short, brown-haired waif, underdressed for most occasions, not of the same class. At all. Not dowdy, for God's sake. I did try to keep up. But on a student's budget. In postwar England. Did any of this matter to you? I guessed not, since you'd visited me daily. And you wouldn't have met me in Deira that day.

And your hand, the surprise of your touch and what ran through me. I thought of the first time you'd taken my hand. In the desert. You'd taken my hand and glanced at Father, all of us knowing the boundary you'd crossed, and guided my fingers into the feathery breast of your falcon to feel its tiny, rapidly beating heart. Now my heart was fluttering like that bird's. I was as hungry for you to touch me again as that bird of prey was hungry for meat. Carnal. To devour and be devoured. And if you'd asked me—no, if you'd taken me—to your hotel room, then I would have lost myself to you. Indeed, I already *was* lost.

Did any of it—your visits, your hand, your smile and laughter and kindnesses—mean what I hoped they meant? Dared I hope you felt the same way about me that I believe I'd always felt about you? The reality—you a sheikh from a country thousands of miles away, me a shy scholar—was too much to contemplate. Still, I let myself hope.

On the Thursday afternoon, on our return to the house, you on my right nearer the automobiles and me on the left, daydreaming my fingers along the iron fencing in front of my neighbours' homes. And there was Ian Bentley standing in front of the building. It must have looked like I'd seen a ghost. In the mist of the past week, I had forgotten Ian, even though daily, upon my entering the house, Mrs. Firth-Heyward would inform me Mr. Bentley had called, or rung, or dropped by the apartment and stayed an hour over tea. I hadn't taken in the news. If it hadn't been for Ian's uniform, there's a good chance you and I would have walked by him and I wouldn't have recognized him or given him a second glance. We stopped. I made the appropriate introductions and Ian said good day and you said goodbye and I stood on the stairs wondering which way was west. Had you suspected Ian was a prospective boyfriend? Had he assumed something was going on between us?

Ian came around again a half-hour later. He was visibly upset. I thought we'd got on, he said. We did, I said. Of course, we did. But who is this guy? What's he to you? And I tried to explain about the little girl in the desert and you being my Rosetta stone to all things Arabian and how if it hadn't been for you and my experience of the desert, I probably wouldn't be at SOAS, which meant I wouldn't be in Mrs. Firth-Heyward's house at that very moment having a talk with him. To his credit, Ian listened without interrupting. But who is this guy? Ian asked again. And why is it when I watched you walking around Russell Square—yes, I was there—and then through the park for an hour, you were looking at him like he was Christmas pudding?

I was at a loss. No fidgety prattle now.

I'm leaving for Bahrain in two hours. I like you, Rose. I meant it when I said I wanted to get to know you better. You're smart. You're pretty. I think we'd be some good fun together. I'm telling you you've no business with a guy like him. He'll chew you up and spit you out.

I started to object. I wasn't in business with a guy like him. You were a dear friend who had meant much to me for over half my life. But Ian wouldn't hear it. He was solemn in his protestation about the kind of man he was and the kind of man you were.

If you think so little of them, I asked finally, why are you going to Bahrain?

It's where the work is, he answered. When you're in the diplomatic corps you don't ask for placement. You go where they tell you.

The answer was similar to one Father had given me years before when I brought up the ugliness he spouted about Arabs. My portfolio is oil and gas, Rose darling. I didn't choose to put the oil under the desert sand.

I had best be leaving, Ian said. Can I write you?

I failed to grasp how he could ask this considering his obvious anger and disappointment. But there were many things I failed to grasp in my youth.

I shrug-nodded. It was a motion I'd seen Father do hundreds of times. Committing without committing.

Good, Ian said, then he took a step closer, stooped and kissed me on the cheek. I walked him to the door and he said goodbye and walked down the stairs. I watched him go, unconsciously wiping my cheek where his lips had pressed against me, and looked out at Russell Square, the waves of ornamental grasses and round bushes, the grand Scotch elms and yews and the evergreen holm oaks. Who was he, and who was I to him? We barely knew each other, yet he said he liked me and wanted to write me? But you. You and I had history together. We understood each other. Dare I think we loved each other.

IV

I am thinking about our land catching up with the modern world, but I am not able to do anything because I do not have the means in my hands. One day these dreams will be realized, *insh'allah*. And I should like you here to see it happen.

You wrote that. Though the letter, from the salutation *habibti* through all the description of what you saw in Europe and Turkey, flowed in Arabic script as graceful as calligraphy, you wrote that in English. You wanted to make sure I knew what you were saying.

You were inviting me back to Abu Dhabi.

Ten words to dispel any doubts I had about what you might feel toward me. Ian Bentley? The name didn't cross your mind. No jealousy there. Why would there be? You knew you had me. And then you resumed in Arabic, allowing me to see what you were thinking, what your concerns were for the future of your country, and of the region. The overthrow of Prime Minister Mossadegh in Iran was worrying. You were inclined to believe in the correctness of what he was doing in auditing the accounts of the Anglo-Iranian Oil Company. The terms of the contract favoured the British, and nationalizing the company's assets was the right response in light of the company's refusal to comply. You believed the coup held lessons for Abu Dhabi, Dubai and the other Trucial States. Although the British had had their feet on Arab soil for two hundred years, they'd never laid a brick, you wrote. No schools, no health facilities, no *masjid*. Perhaps, you said, the contract should be re-examined. Perhaps we should insist on local investment. Perhaps we should convince the British oilmen they need to keep the natives happy.

I couldn't agree more, I wrote back. When do you want me?

I returned in December, six months after we'd seen each other in London, persuading my dissertation supervisor to allow me extra on-the-ground research. I said I wanted to see first hand the successful reconstruction of the *falaj* system you had undertaken in 1949 after my last visit and the cholera that had claimed Abu Saleh's mother and son.

But the flight to Dubai passed through Bahrain and a desert storm grounded us overnight. I made a call to the one person I knew in Manama.

Overjoyed, grinning, Ian called me an early Christmas present. He took me to the restaurant of the Sheraton Hotel for dinner, the only place on the island where people were allowed to drink alcohol. I said I was surprised to see local men at the bar drinking. No religion is devoid of sinners, Ian said; it's why religion exists. I was never much of a drinker myself, so between the dehydration from flying, my disorientation between time zones and general fatigue, I found myself carried away on the bubbles of champagne with which we celebrated.

What are we celebrating? I asked.

The desert rose, of course, Ian said.

He looked at me so sweetly then. There none of the disappointment in me or disgust with you he'd expressed when I'd last seen him in London. Instead, it was a display of the decorous charm and intelligence, the pleasantness and amiability he had expressed in letters written me these past six months. There was none of the animosity and prejudice he'd spouted in June. He seemed happy with his work, with his boss and colleagues in the diplomatic corps. We talked oil, of course. And Sunni-Shia relations in light of what had happened in Iran over the summer. It was foolhardy of Iran to do what it did and Mossadegh got what he deserved, Ian said.

I could hardly have disagreed more, but I kept my opinions to myself. Britain oversaw defence and foreign policy for Bahrain, Qatar, the Trucial States and Oman, Ian said, as if I needed reminding. These little potentates—that word again!—should appreciate what they have, he continued. I am of the profound conviction only the steady hand of the British Empire can hold these countries together. We are a paragon of progress, tolerance and freethinking, the hallmarks of good governance.

And this was a man who said he was enjoying diplomacy! I dared not think what he'd be like if he disliked this work. I thought of an article Freya Stark had written after she visited the Druze in Lebanon. It was a twenty-year-old article by the time I'd read it, but its truth was everlasting. She wondered if men, particularly those attracted to the Middle East, were not all slaves of Aladdin's lamp, drawn by its shiny quality, its mystery, the potential danger. Itching to rub it. But the lamp had to be handled gingerly, she wrote. One hasty wipe by some plainspoken but tactless junior envoy—an Ian Bentley, or even a more senior one like Father—and the genie of Arab nationalism would rise from the lamp. And all the efforts of all the emissaries to push the genie back into the lamp would be like trying to force steam back into a *dallah* of hot coffee.

It was time for me to go. He walked me to the taxi, stepped away an inch as if to look in my eyes before kissing me. And then an inch more. He must have sensed that more than mere inches separated us.

An hour later and I was gone. I had a flight. I had you to see, and weeks of work ahead of me, pleasurable work, but work nonetheless. When you had started refurbishing the aqueduct in 1949, only four of the fourteen known *falaj* were functional. Three were badly silted up. But now, less than four years later, eleven million gallons of sweet water were flowing into the Buraimi oasis near your home every day. The area was a palette of colourful trees and grasses. There were livestock and cattle grazing. New lands, rich lands opened up and distributed free of charge to farmers. All due to you.

You even were able to persuade a few Bedouin to give up their nomadic lives and get behind a plough. You had the successful example of Abu Saleha and his goatherd.

In twenty years, you said, this whole area will be irrigated by the waters of the Hajar Mountains. The desert will change colours the way the moon changes faces. What is brown will be green. What is barren will be full of life. *Insh'allah.*

It was all so fragile, this dream. The ecosystem. Everything here— from the aqueduct to the *arysh* houses to the palm-frond *souq*—could at any time succumb to the elements, revert to sand.

But you didn't express doubt. You dreamed the dreams of a visionary. I could not connect the man I saw making these changes to the man Ian Bentley saw, someone who needed guidance and a firm hand like a child. Was Ian representative of the rest of the starchy British diplomats and oilmen? As there was no political resident in the Trucial States, diplomatic work of the type Ian and his office conducted was done out of Manama. Did everyone else in his office feel the way he did? It couldn't have been worse if he'd said you wore bed sheets.

The man I saw, a week into my trip, seated at the head of a semi-circle of men in the *majlis,* wore the dress of a rich Arab male: a white *thawb*, a thin gold cloth hanging from the shoulders edged with gold embroidery, a gold-and-white checked headcloth hanging over the shoulders and kept on the head with a black *egal.* This was not your ordinary dress. Today was special. Your brother, the Ruler, had arrived the day before to pay his respects to your mother and later was coming to meet members of the extended family and to be among fellow tribesmen. He seemed surprised to see a foreigner in the home. You had to assure Mansour, who always needed a reintroduction (even though we had met several times, all the way back to when I was an eleven-year-old girl in a polka-dot dress), that I was trustworthy and not a British agent. It was a privilege, to be sure, to be allowed to meet the Ruler. Most local women would not have been afforded such an opportunity. Mansour nodded and said not a word. I doubt he'd remembered me, or would again.

After your family meeting, as the local *wali*, you led the meeting with the tribal chiefs. And when the men were satisfied with what they heard about subsidies Mansour had promised them, they left as well. It was late now, well after the last prayers of the day. The sun had receded long before. The moon was in its crescent phase.

Every time I see the moon in this shape, I feel I understand its centrality to this place, I said.

Every time I see the moon like this it reminds me of a woman heavy with child, you said.

You were behind me then, a few feet away. I wished to feel your breath on my nape. To have you drape your arms around my front, my belly. I was flowing over with such longing for you I could have taken you by the hand and taken you to the room the women had set aside for me in the compound. But we were distracted by a light extinguished in your house across the courtyard.

Thank you, I said.

You looked at me, puzzled.

For everything, I said. Hoping I could convey in these simple words the everything I was feeling.

It is me who should thank you, you said. Then you looked again across the way. Good night then.

Yes, I said, good night.

In the morning, a slight scratch at the door before a woman entered. Immediately, though we had never met, I knew who she was. The woman was tall and thin, with skin the colour of lightly roasted sesame and with dark, searching, intelligent eyes. A thin downward pull of her mouth and eyes resigned to some sadness. A veil covered her hair. Almost perfectly. There was a strand or two peeking out, showing themselves to be as black as her eyes. She brought water, in a clay jug, which she placed on the ground by my head. I sat up and wordlessly she lifted the jug and I placed my hands over a nearby bowl and she poured the water over my hands. Though I was not Muslim and not obligated to clean myself before a prayer I did not perform, she saw to it my morning ablutions were completed. Saw to it that I, a foreign woman—not equal to men, but above her in my freedom to move between the worlds of men and women—had freshened up before breakfast. I wonder, too, whether she was there not only to serve but inspect, pass judgment, indulge her curiosity. Dark and dignified, she disappeared as silently as she had appeared. And I did not see your wife again.

For breakfast, I was summoned to Sheikha Maitha, your mother, who, I remembered from my previous visit, was a fount of stories and anecdotes. In the traditional way of greeting, she asked about my health and that of my father and mother. I said Father still worked for the government and Mother had died. She'd been ill, I said, for many years. The sheikha said she was sorry to hear that. She must have been a beautiful woman, she said. You are a beautiful girl. I said thank you. Then Sheikha Maitha lowered herself to the carpet and I sat by her and we began to eat.

She recounted a two-hundred-year-old tale about a mother who fell asleep on her camel during a long ride and dropped her baby from her arms into the burning sands of the Empty Quarter. By the time the woman realized what had happened, it was too far to go back and the baby was left for dead. But the child was found, and raised by a good man of the desert, and the boy grew up to be a prosperous man, rich in wisdom and love, fathering many sons even in his old age. My Arabic, as good as it was after many years of study, was perhaps still too rudimentary to grasp the full meaning of the story, which had all the feeling of a fairy tale, particularly since Sheikha Maitha began and ended it with the phrase *kan ya ma kan,* maybe it was, maybe it wasn't. Like saying Once upon a time.

Then she began another story, about the Prophet Mohammed, peace be upon him. After his wife Khadija's death, Mohammed, who was a shrewd businessman, flexible yet decisive, entered into marriage contracts with several women to ally himself to the important Arab tribes. His favourite wife, the one he loved the most, was Ayesha, who was so young when Mohammed married her she was still playing with puppets and dolls. Because she was so young, she lived for many years in her parents' home and Mohammed visited her there but he did not have her until she was old enough to move from her parents' home and live in one of the apartments of the *masjid.*

Although Mohammed had many wives, and he was careful to lie with each one in turn, he spent many evenings at Ayesha's side. There, he did household chores and mended his own clothes and shoes. He tended their goats and ran footraces and played games with Ayesha. She spoiled him.

It is because of Ayesha that in Islam women are equal to men. She was not submissive. She was not shy. She drank from the same cup as her husband. She was also sensitive to his moods and perceptive. One evening, while sitting together in contemplation, Ayesha noticed Mohammed had grown very quiet but his face was lit, reflecting the generosity of thought passing through him. Ayesha said, Husband, you seem bright and happy tonight and I thank you for bringing this light and happiness into my humble hut. But Mohammed leaned over to kiss his young wife on the forehead and thanked her instead. May Allah reward you, dear, for the joy you bring to me outshines the joy this old man can bring you.

Sheikha Maitha clapped her hands and her attendant entered the room. The woman took away the breakfast and then returned carrying a silver platter with a box on it, which the sheikha then took. She held it out. For me? I said.

I opened the box and found the most exquisite pearl and diamond necklace I had ever seen. The pearls were in three strands and to one side was a diamond-encrusted silver rose. I gasped. From the sheikha? I could not believe it. These are for me? I said.

My son wishes you to have this.

You had given me the jewels. Pearls, the lifeline of Abu Dhabi for so many hundreds of years. And the rose.

He wishes you as his wife.

I must have shown my surprise and my disbelief. You had given me no indication you thought of me in this way, as someone to marry, someone to claim as yours. Or had you? My mind raced through various encounters. Had I missed signs of your feelings for me? Any flirtations were mild to the point of being careful, culturally circumscribed, I'd even say. The closest we'd been had been those few short days in London after the Coronation.

The jewellery was beautiful. And the man I loved more than anyone in the world—yes: I had eyes for you and you alone—was asking me to marry him. I was crying now, but I was not answering. Why? What was going on in my head that I couldn't pronounce what my heart so wanted?

My morning had begun with the ministrations of your wife. I would be the second. Would you treat me as fairly as you treated her? She was so stunning. This morning I felt so naked and vulnerable in front of her. Would there be others after me? Would I be called on to wash their hands? Their feet? Would I be your Ayesha? Perhaps this was the reason your mother told me that tale. I was the young one. The one you knew as a girl. And the first story? A man of sand, sea and sky. Wise and loving and rich. Like you.

I would have to convert to Islam, which I had never considered before. I wore my inner conflict on my face. Sheikha Maitha said, You do not have to answer now.

But I do, I said. I cannot let him wait.

Everything came back to me, in a jumble of memories, shards of thought and emotion. What about my studies, my dissertation?

That was the final step toward what I'd assumed would be a lifetime of travel and research and writing and lecturing. Would I be allowed these? Or be forced to give up my career and dream in exchange for a life of visiting neighbouring women and aunts and cousins or having them visit me in return? To be attended to? The meeting between the brothers the day before: their wives weren't there. Your sisters weren't there. Would I be allowed to such a gathering if I were your wife? No more *majlis*? Ayesha may have been the impetus for Mohammed's declaration of sexual equality in Islam, yet more and more women were covered; women served and were subservient. The reason I'd never seen you with your wife was she was never at your side. But I was. I was more equal as a foreigner than your own wife.

I closed the box and slid it along the rug back toward Sheikha Maitha.

She raised an eyebrow.

I cannot marry, I said. I must return this.

She slid it back.

A gift is worth giving only if there is no obligation attached to it, your mother said. This is a gift. These are yours, daughter. You do not need to answer now.

Then I burst into tears and the sheikha leaned forward and kissed me on the forehead. You bring much joy to our household, she said. More than you know.

I did not see you that day, nor the next. Business had taken you to the desert. It would be several days before you returned and by that point I was due at Sharjah to make my aeroplane. I left. Only by putting distance between us would I be able to see, hear, and think clearly. And then speak.

V

If you were visiting London, you came to me. If Europe, I went to you. You did not press me to marry and I never answered your mother's offer. The necklace was the first gift of many I received without obligation. And the first of many I wore when I accompanied you to dinner, the opera or the ballet, or any of those western things you felt you needed to appreciate, those things expected of you as you spent more time in the public eye.

In 1954, my book *Greening the Desert: The Falaj System of Eastern Arabia* was published. I was lecturing in Arab political geography and Bedouin culture at SOAS. I was a contributing writer to the *Journal of Middle East Studies* and had a regular newspaper column in the *Times*. My Arabic continued to improve. My Bedouin and Arabic teachers' patience was immeasurable. But you were my best teacher, my vocabulary now extending to words of love and sexual desire.

Our first time was in a suite in the Europa Hotel in Heidelberg. The German translation of the book had recently come out and I was on tour. I'd flown into Frankfurt. You had a limousine pick me up at the airport and drive me an hour to the hotel. I was no sooner in my room than there was your knock on the door. I cast it open and you cast me on the bed. I removed your headscarf and pulled you down on me. Then your arms were tight around me as we kissed, long and deeply. I was conscious of nothing but you. You filled me, as you filled my thoughts, my heart, my world. With every movement of you on top of me, I grew more aware of myself and of you and what you were doing to me. Your hands on my hips, your lips on my breasts. I felt your hair brushing my breasts as you kissed my belly and then your hair on my belly as you kissed me between my legs. I wanted you inside me and me inside you. Then it happened. As I had wanted. I would be your lover. I didn't need to be your wife. This was what we were meant to be, something free, conforming to no rules. You and me. Filling each other. No distinctions. No boundaries. And above us, against the ceiling, the crescent-shaped shadow of the lamp.

So our lives went on, separate and together. And Abu Dhabi continued as well, token steps, some small, some like leaps. Off the tiny rock outcrop of Sahoot Island, high tide struck in the middle of an exceptionally violent storm in the spring of 1956, destroying the harbour front, sinking a tanker and flooding the desalinization plant. Five hundred workers were left stranded. With no radio communication and no regular flights or sailings to and from Sahoot, officials in Abu Dhabi did not know about the incident for days afterward.

Protests materialized in the city when news of the storm damage made it to the mainland. Everyone had heard stories of black gold coming from the ground and from the ocean that would make them rich. But no one was rich. The local people the British oil companies hired barely eked out a living. The companies had established their own supply chain and brought in their own contractors. Any locals were hired hands and poorly paid to do drudgework.

Meeting in Cairo, the newly formed Arab League began calling for the expulsion of the British from Arab lands, particularly the oil-producing Gulf countries. This didn't sit well with you, nor with your brother the Ruler.

It felt like the right time for me to return to Abu Dhabi and I told the *Times* my next columns would be from there. I felt my skin heating already—from the desert sun, from your touch.

I am coming back, I wrote. And again, I received no reply. Yet someone would be at Sharjah airport to greet me and take me to Dubai and then on to Abu Dhabi.

What I found in these cities, three years after my last visit, was a people on the edge of modernity. One foot in a life caught in the slow-moving sands of time. It is easy to romanticize the old days. But they were also days of penury, hard work, sometimes little food. The other foot was in a future full of foreign promises. In between, an abyss. Still, there didn't seem to be much choice but to move forward. The doors to the outside world were cracking open. Oil was seeping out and another way of life and doing business was seeping in. The Bedouin life was under threat. As bad as salaries were for locally hired workers, and as dismal as their opportunities for promotion, the oil and gas industry provided a better wage, a better way of life, than farming dates and raising goats. New ideas. New industries. Material goods. Yet a life sapped of spirit, I was observing.

I met the oil company representatives, with mid-level administrators in the office of the Ruler. You were busy. You would come to me the next day or the one after. *Insh'allah.* I went to oil sites and spoke with workers. I heard the word exploitation. I heard the name Nasser. The people need schools and hospitals, almost everyone said, counting off the list of needs. You yourself told me once before: Wealth without health is death. But they were few who counted the cultural cost.

This visit was so unlike my others, so unlike our trysts in the capitals of Europe, where I would fly out, take a cab to the hotel and find you in the penthouse. Here I was, in your country, in the place of our meeting, and where were you? Was it business? Was it domestic life? Your wife? By now, maybe a child or two? To protect my nerves, I dove deeper into my reporting.

The British oilmen and their managers have no interest in whom they work with, whether Bani Yas, Manasir or Bani Qitab, a subcontractor from Dubai told me. He had a Pakistani mother and had gone to school in Lahore. Now he was back in the Gulf where his father lived. They might hire a man from one tribe, he said, and ignore a fellow tribesman in favour of someone from a feuding tribe. They don't realize the closed world many Arabs still live in, the ancient allegiances. And in their ignorance and arrogance, there are troubles.

Yet the greatest struggle was within the culture itself, the rootlessness encroaching western civilization was creating among the Bedouin and the seafarers and farmers. The chains binding the past to the present were straining and breaking.

We're like foreigners in our own land, a friend of the subcontractor said. Like native aliens. I'd met them in Dubai and shared a ride to Abu Dhabi with them when I'd first arrived. I'd told them what I was doing in the Gulf and they agreed I could interview them, as long as I didn't use their names. They were concerned what they said might get back to their bosses. I interviewed them at a table in the back of a stall in the *souq*, one of the only places to eat in the city—still a village in so many respects: hard-packed dirt roads, lots of one-storey *arysh* homes, two guesthouses for the public, one school, one pre-fabricated clinic staffed by one Indian doctor.

In the *souq* came static-filled music of *oud* players and singers. I recognized Umm Kalthoum. Then the radios grew quiet and someone called out a number and people fidgeted with the radio dials. Crackling to life was Sawt al-Arab radio station, from Egypt. It was Nasser saying, in an effort to end European imperialism in the Middle East, he was establishing Egyptian cultural missions in every country in the region to promote Arab nationalism. Sellers and buyers returned to their negotiating, but I had a sense they were conferring over the finer points of Nasser's speech.

Time was shrinking, said the contractor. His friend, whose family raised camels in the desert between Dubai and Abu Dhabi, agreed. They both pointed out that for all the money supposedly coming in, few buildings had been erected yet.

After several days on the ground, I had a chance to see you, but it was in a public room in one of the guesthouses where the British oil men stayed. Officially, it was an interview, replete with interpreter and oil company representatives. I hadn't disclosed our relationship to the editor at the *Times*. You had not changed since we'd seen each other in April, at the former San Giorgio monastery near Venice. Thirty-eight, trim and fit, with only the slightest laugh lines in the corners of your eyes. In public, you carried yourself regally, *comme d'habitude*.

You said no projects would be undertaken simply for prestige. History is full of examples of cities built on the sands of hubris, you said. Empires brought to their knees like camels. The black banner of the Abbasids flew over Baghdad for hundreds of years when they moved there from Damascus. They grew a city of glory, grander even than Constantinople, which shivered in fear. The time of the Abbasids was the zenith of Muslim intellectual and scientific exploration and art. But the court of the Abbasids was sick with the cancer of corruption. Baghdad was a woman who had lost her modesty and pride. The Mongols fell on her and raped and butchered her. And for six hundred years it was a ruin. A dusty and pale, neglected hag. This, I will not do, you said. The projects must be simple, they must be aimed at meeting the needs of our people.

By this you meant a hospital, a water distillation plant, electrical power, residential areas, drainage, sanitation, schools, infrastructure. Stuff English politicians find too boring to bring up on the campaign trail.

Too many generations have been lost to illiteracy and a devastating lack of education, you said. Never again. And it was in this way I quoted you, the *wali* of Al Ain, when I filed my four hundred words. Minus the stuff about rape. It was the *Times*, after all.

You visited me at the guesthouse nearly every remaining night of my stay. Often, it was two, three or four in the morning before you left. We made love every one of those nights, two, three times, with hours talking between. Those nights, I felt like a cabinet minister, a confidante, though anyone keeping watch would assume I was your mistress.

I worry whether my brother will ever pull his head from the sand, you said. There is no convincing him investments are required.

But his heart is in the right place, I said.

Yes, you said, with a smirk. He did not bury that.

The nascent nationalism upset you because you felt it wasn't purely Arab, purely Muslim. It was mixed with communism and radicalism. It felt, in some ways, like a western idea. You were worried about the Suez. If Nasser were to go ahead with his threats to nationalize the canal, what would that mean for trade here and in the Subcontinent? Would the British and the French fight over this? Could the Middle East afford another war so soon after the Nakba?

The Arab League has its uses, you said. We should not discard it. But nothing ever is solved. Sister Egypt, Sister Iraq. There is much quarrelling. There is not much unity. Except we agree Zionism is an abomination. As is colonialism. Which go hand in hand. But this disunity and disagreement are no surprise. It has almost always been so.

You had been lying on your side as you were saying these things. Your index finger was tracing the halo around my nipple. You stopped, then you bent over and kissed it, and then tugged at it gently between your teeth. Then you kissed it again, and the other, and we made love again, and you left me to go home to Al Ain to your wife.

The next night, eating in the guesthouse restaurant, your concerns were local.

I have spoken, at great lengths, you said, about our plans for health care and education for all. Yet to most people it seems far-fetched. They see oilmen come in, they see oil go out. But they have not seen the benefits.

I said things take time. The payoff will come. *Insh'allah.*

We have ex-army trucks and we have four-wheel-drive trucks. We have no roads. We have put the cart before the horse. But people are demanding goods from the cart.

I wished to take you by the hand and take you upstairs to bed, to comfort you with pears and apples, wash you in rose water. Instead, I gave you succour the only way I knew how, in my words. You will give them what they want. Not now. Perhaps not tomorrow. But the day after. It will be done.

By the grace and will of God.

Yes, I said.

Sometime in the first week after my arrival, the protests died down and work and life returned to normal. *Times* readers had grown bored with the story in any case. There was Manchester United's winning of the First Division title to celebrate, and worries Anthony Eden would not last even one year as prime minister. But I didn't go back to London. The semester was over. I decided to stay, and return to London before the humidity descended on Abu Dhabi in June.

I remained at the guesthouse. You visited. I walked around town. After I'd requested it, you arranged for Fahdi to drive me to Al Ain, where I visited for several days with your one still-unmarried sister and your mother.

One morning, in the compound, I saw a toddler playing in the dirt, naked, throwing pebbles and chasing after the chickens. He had to have been yours. There were no other men living in the compound to explain the boy's presence. I spotted, outside your house on the other side, an unfamiliar woman. Somewhat shorter than your wife, a little chunkier, perhaps pregnant. Was she wife number two? I imagined she could have been me had I said yes.

I felt your mother at my side and we watched the boy.

What if I changed my mind now? I asked. Would he still have me? I don't know if there's protocol for such a change of heart.

She held my hand. Is it a change of heart? she asked. Or is what you are feeling brought on by the sight of the boy?

I don't know, I said. I am so at home here. All my life I've felt this contentment here. I told her what you'd told me eighteen years before, when I'd come out in my dress for the wedding and you said I had sand between my toes. I looked down. I was barefoot. I hardly felt the heat of the sand.

And yes, I said, the boy is beautiful, so good humoured.

She waited. I waited. Then she prompted me, But?

But I am equally happy doing what I do. I teach, I write, I travel.

You see my son when it suits you, Sheikha Maitha said.

I winced. She turned to face me and took my other hand. You don't have to be ashamed, she said. I know who he is. Then she brought me in close and hugged me and I cried into her shoulder.

I went out to the desert for several nights. When I came back, you were upset.

I am not your wife. But I couldn't say that. I had come to the desert. I thought I heard you calling and I came. But it was not your voice I heard in the wind. Nor your brother's nor your mother's. It was my own.

Instead, I said, I am my own person, *habibi*. This is one of the things you say makes me me. You have said so.

You said you felt you were losing me. It may have been the closest you ever came to saying you loved me. I recalled all those nights over the past three years—Abu Dhabi, London, Zurich, Paris—when I was oil in your hands, viscous and combustible, but it felt you were telling me I was oil slipping away from you.

This was now my third extended stay in Abu Dhabi and I was growing comfortable travelling on my own. Yes, I practised a certain amount of circumspection, but I had *wasta*, a lifesaving connection to someone of influence, someone with power, protection. Besides, men tended to leave women alone. A veiled woman was invisible to them. And when I went out on my own, I veiled myself.

I'm sorry, I said. I shouldn't have gone without telling you. It won't happen again. You were worried. You want nothing more than to keep me safe.

Yes, you said. To keep you safe.

The success of my desert excursion—that I was able to do it in the first case and, in the second, that I'd met people on my own and conducted interviews exclusively in Arabic—and your reaction to it proved to me that, increasingly, you were no longer the Rosetta stone you had once been for me. I could move freely, speak freely. I felt no threat from men; I was accepted by women. Through the month of May, I travelled about the state, going to Dubai and Sharjah and Ajman on the northern coast. Always giving you notice. Always receiving your blessing.

Everywhere I went—from Liwa to Al Ain and Buraimi, from the beach at Tarif to the foot of Jebel Hefeet—I met people who told me they knew oil was being exported and the country was bringing in revenues. There was money in Sheikh Mansour's trunk at Al Hosn, but their daily lives had not changed. They had not prospered.

They called you the creator, the caregiver, the emancipator, the architect, the ecologist, the visionary, the avenger who would wrestle with the British spectre and create a country of which all desert people could be proud.

They expect me to bring water and bread out of the desert, you said. It was a rare moment of doubt in your abilities, shared when you were most vulnerable, naked, in bed with me.

You *have* brought water from the mountain, I reminded you.

We were silent. I don't believe you were seriously contemplating the various *kunya* the Bedouin had applied to you. Honorifics meant nothing to you. Rather, you heard what they were saying underneath the words. They were expressing their displeasure with the present leadership. And you knew this would be a problem if their voices grew louder and clearer. Abu Dhabi did not need more protests.

Mansour has banned new construction in Abu Dhabi, you told me. He says we must not have construction without a proper plan. The government might be held liable to building owners if construction went ahead and then plans were enforced resulting in the demolition of the buildings. I believe he is correct, but it has been too many years without planning.

What is your brother so worried about? I asked.

As always, you took your time to answer the question. My brother saw our father kill his brother to become ruler. It was an unfortunate necessity. But it has not happened in many years, *alhamdulillah*. Mansour is worried about threats. So the money coming in from oil concessions and sales he stashes away in case of emergency.

This money should be freed up for construction, I said. The longer he keeps his eyes at the back of his head, the longer he will be blind to the future.

Yes, yes. Construction. For schools, for hospitals, for mosques. We can give financial support to the people. They can rise out of their poverty.

And they'll be forever grateful, I said.

You nodded. It is a way to protect ourselves. From elements within. And without. The West needs Abu Dhabi to triumph over these threats, even Nasser's ideas. I believe in the Arab world fully. But not at the exclusion of our friends in the West. We have greater threats in our own house, the religious zealots who are the powerbrokers of Riyadh, for example.

Every trade-off is imperfect, you added.

What are you going to do when the money really starts coming in? I asked. Right now, it's a trickle. But soon, soon, you will be rich like Saudi, like Bahrain and Iraq, or Kuwait and Iran. How will you manage it?

I will visit you once a week. And call for you every other week.

I'm being serious.

I am a serious man.

I rolled my eyes. You are a tease, I said in English.

Explain tease.

I kissed you and touched the tip of your penis, then stroked the shaft until you were hard.

This is tease? you asked.

Yes, I said, this is tease.

You were gone again the next day. To your Bedouin brethren.

I understood. I knew what the desert offered. I had seen how men were when you were with them and, more importantly, how you were when you were with them. You were the prodigal. You were the falcon returned to the warmth of its aerie.

Then you were back. In my world. In my room. In my bed.

Afterward, we spoke about your time away. The Bedouin knew their days of nomadic freedom were coming to an end. If not in five years, then in ten or fifteen. What would they be given in exchange for that liberty? You shared their concerns with Mansour and were able to persuade him to pay for agricultural projects. He knew well enough Dubai and Sharjah were on their way to developing farms for self-sustenance. You were so proud of yourself. You'd also got him to agree to build trial stations on Saddiyat Island where desert-resistant crops could be developed. As importantly, you'd persuaded him to cough up money to build a new port. Trade would help the Bedouin maintain their traditional routes and freedom of passage. And agriculture would give them a base of income when trade was slow.

I poured us glasses of lemon water from a pitcher.

I said I was proud of you. Happy for you. This was your dream and, bit by bit, it was coming true. It was my dream too. My dream for you. For us. For I was a part of this. I said this was a compact between the generations. This was a pact indicating you, the tent generation, knew what was important to the oil generation and you were giving them the means to succeed, and to write a pact with the *third* generation, the generation of commerce and productivity.

You said you hoped so. Yet pacts are so easily torn. It is best to rely on the word of a man you can look in the eye, you said. I fear the fourth generation will still be searching for its identity.

It's any country's national obsession, I said. Identity. Who are we? What are we doing? Where are we going? But the country you can build here, with this money, this oil, will be one many will want to emulate. I took a sip of lemon water. Can you imagine? I asked. The world's first Arab democracy? Where the poorest of the poor and the richest of the rich can be equal and share in the rule and wealth of the country?

You almost smiled. Oil will not make us a democracy.

I nodded. Of course not. Oil is just oil. But it will grease the political machinery.

We have no political machinery.

True, I said. You have British advisers, political agents, who, when you order them to, will leave. As they did from India. And if a country like India can become a democracy, surely... I opened my hands. An offering.

Oil will bring us wealth. Like Saudi Arabia, like Iran and Bahrain, Iraq and Kuwait. Like Qatar. We will share that wealth. Our tribal system is old. And though it is old, it is not febrile or senile or broken. Everyone will be better off than he is now.

Now it was my turn to express perplexity. You mean you'll keep the same system you have now?

Insh'allah.

A tribal patriarchy. Nothing democratic.

The tribal system *is* democratic. Everyone has a say in the *majlis.*

Every *man* has a say in the *majlis.*

A woman is equal to man in the eyes of Islam, you said.

I couldn't believe what I was hearing. It was so… so… male! It couldn't be a man equal to a woman, could it?

This is the time, I said. Look at what is happening in India. In Egypt! The king is gone. I know the military basically runs the place, but he is promising elections. I'm not suggesting the Arab nationalism Nasser would impose. You're not even inclined that way. I'm saying a democracy, with a *shura,* but elected. Like our Parliament or the Congress in America.

You shook your head slowly, and your face betrayed a half-smile, half-frown. Rose, these are naïve propositions. What we have here works for what we have here.

What you're telling me is that the largely tribal, largely unenlightened masses have no independent opinion and will just do what you say. I could feel myself heating up, my pulse quickening. I thought we'd been in agreement all these years. And I couldn't let the matter drop.

Not at all, *habibti.* The men who sit in the *majlis,* from the richest of the rich to the poorest of the poor, as you say, rarely share the same opinion. They are capable of independent thought.

But how can they be? I shouted. They're a bunch of uneducated goat-herders and camel jockeys who'd do anything you or your brother, the ostrich, tell them!

I'd never spoken in this way before. I'd never raised my voice to you. You were shocked. I'd lost control, composure. I'd lost face.

Oh my God, I said. I'm so sorry.

You stood. You placed your glass of water on the table.

I believe you must be tired.

Yes, yes, I said. I had a long day of reading and interviews. I was out in the sun a lot of the day. I'm sorry. Please forgive me.

Then you stood in front of me. You held me, by the elbows, in both hands and brought me forward gently. You kissed my forehead. One doesn't walk through life without being betrayed, you said. And one cannot love without forgiveness.

I nodded and wrapped my arms around your waist. You allowed the hug for a moment, then stepped back just enough to indicate I should let go. Then you left. That was it. It was you who was the oil. And I let you slip through my fingers. I would not see you again.

In the ruins of the hope I had for you and the country lay the ruins of our relationship.

I cried myself to sleep.

The return trip included the stopover in Bahrain. I most fervently did not want to see Ian Bentley again, but there he was at the airstrip. How the hell did he know? While the aeroplane took on extra passengers and extra fuel, he took me into what constituted an airport lounge: a few chairs and tables and a counter where they served juice.

He could see I was upset.

Listen, Rose, Ian whispered.

Yes? I asked.

I need to apologize, he said.

Whatever for, I wondered. What had he said or done?

I was a bit of a cad that afternoon in London, he said.

When he saw my quizzical look, he clarified himself. The day I saw you walking about the square with your Arab friend. I shouldn't have said the things I said. Even when I saw you here last, on your way to Abu Dhabi.

I nodded.

I didn't realize who he was, Ian said. He's an important man, your friend. It's good, useful, to have such important friends.

Useful? I asked. How was my knowing you useful to Ian Bentley in Bahrain? And how would I tell him I'd so recently lost that connection? I was dead in your eyes.

Then he tried, in his way, to change the subject, lighten the mood. Telling me stories about his work. Something about a man and his family, none of whom had papers, all wanting to emigrate. Bidoons, Ian called them. Stateless. Not like Bedouins. And then: wogs.

Wogs!

Yes, dear. Like the ones in Abu Dhabi. There's not a clear-headed person in this room right now or at the consulate who wouldn't wonder why you'd gone off to that hellhole, just because you want to learn Arabic, really? But I know what you intended to do there and it had nothing to do with your studies.

Then Ian Bentley finished his juice, placed the glass on the table and grinned.

I assured him I had no idea what he meant, what he was suggesting. And I take issue, I said, with your use of pejoratives to describe people whom I've known for a good portion of my life and whom I've come to love and respect.

Why, you had sex with that towel head, didn't you? Ian said. Now that *is* useful. Someone like you close to someone like him.

And it all came clear to me: the way we'd been introduced in Mrs. Firth-Heyward's flat. Secretive Laura and her boyfriend Frankie Taylor. The vagueness about Ian's work. Diplomatic corps, my arse!

You're a spy! I said. You were sent to recruit me, you bloody bastard! Ian Bentley, I will be a happy woman if I never see you again.

He remained seated. And you, he said, you'll get what you deserve.

I strode from the room and returned to the aeroplane, where passengers were now reboarding. Waiting in the queue. Walking across the tarmac. Up the stairs. Into my seat. Thinking: What a racist, slanderous bastard. But wasn't there something truthful too? Didn't I, in my heart of hearts, desire only you? I'm going to be unpacking my bags again, I thought. In less than twenty-four hours. In my tiny room on Russell Square. Whereas my heart wanted to be flying the other way. Return to the guesthouse in Abu Dhabi. Where I would change everything. I would marry you if you would have me, wipe out those twenty-four hours already passed, my last two minutes with you, relive them, do them right this time. I would lay my dreams at your feet and have you tread on them as softly as you would walk on a carpet.

The flight was long. I had time to go over and over my embarrassing explosion in front of you and the row with Ian many times, especially the last, veiled threat he spoke: I would get what I deserve. I had no idea what he meant. Yet, I did. I did know.

VI

I have been practising Tagalog with Whitman, the houseboy. After French, Arabic, Kurdish, Urdu and Farsi, I'd say I have some facility with languages. Or maybe Whitman is being kind. Sometimes I see him smiling as he's pouring tea and some expression I've made ricochets off its original meaning.

Whitman shuts off the radio and removes the tea service from the table at the side of my chair. Cars have slowed. Traffic has built up. I finger the pearls at my neck. Whitman brings me my afghan and holds my book while I fix the knit the way I want. I've been reading a book about Syria. I've been so heartbroken about what's happened there these past few years. And I have been less than happy about what I've read in the newspapers about the reluctance of Gulf states, including the U.A.E., to take in refugees from the civil war. Too concerned about radical elements, the papers say. Quoting some minor minister. A family member, one of your grandsons, probably. I remember what you said about the West needing Abu Dhabi as a buffer. I don't see Abu Dhabi playing that role now. Shameful.

I am glad you're not around to see what's become of the country you built. I once watched you dismiss your entire entourage so you could sit in your *majlis* with the Bedouin, so their tongues would be free. You told me this was the only way to prevent what you feared the most: losing touch with your people. You would not be happy now. The obscene wealth rising cheek by jowl with the abominable working conditions and camps for labourers from the Subcontinent and maritime Asia—all of whom replaced the working-age local population; the imprisoning of people if they speak freely; and the Federal Council, that rubber-stamping council of men, and a few women, elected from a group of government-moulded nominees. And if you'd thought we Britons were numerous then, you should see them now. Not a one of them giving a farthing for what you created, as long as they get theirs tax-free.

While you lived, there'd been years of splendour. You removed your brother Mansour from power. No blood. Waited for him to go abroad one weekend. In on Wednesday, gone on Thursday. And then the money flowed from the treasure chest. You did as you had told me you would. You built a nation within forty years what took others two hundred. At the centre of it all, still, is you. You are no longer a dead president. You are an icon. Revered. Posters and paintings and photographs of your profile are in every corner shop and *souq* stall in Abu Dhabi.

To the end, you took little credit. These achievements surpass everything we imagined possible, you said toward the end of your life. But this has been possible by the grace of Allah and a sincere will to serve people.

You didn't mention oil.

Oil is what got you where you wanted to go. Sheer will and camel milk would not have done it. Oil made you money. Oil lubricated the wheels of international relations. You made friends of presidents and prime ministers. The next time you saw the Queen, it was she who visited you. In one photograph, from that 1970s visit, skulking in the background is the consul general Ian Bentley. Never left the desert, poor, pathetic man.

Of course, in my own way, I never really left it either.

We are a complex species, aren't we? Full of contradiction, inconsistent, and shifting as the wind. But time isn't like that at all. Time is black and white. Conveying the present into the past even as we're living it. What's done is done and there's no changing it. Henry needed a divorce and Edward abdicated for the woman he loved. I took a walk around Russell Square. You negotiated a bloodless palace coup. One makes a choice. I lived with mine for the rest of my life. The words I said that night that could not be retrieved, I doubt you remembered them, or me, at the end of your years. You were the sheikh and I was, perhaps forever, the English schoolgirl.

Where I live now, there's no alternative universe where the schoolgirl chooses Abu Dhabi. No parallel life where I choose days of sand, and pack animals, tents and cardamom-flavoured coffee boiled on an open fire, veiled dancers, falcons and bustards, grilled lamb and long walks.

There is no place where I can choose you.

Though I do, I do. Every day. I do.

IDENTITY

I

"Is he talking much?" Hamsa feels compelled to ask. He picks up his grandfather's meagre hand, feels the slight bones move under the rubbing pressure of his thumb. He scrutinizes his grandfather's face for the slightest expression or gesture, any external hint of his once-vibrant interior life.

Corrie shrugs. "He always has a story."

Hamsa doesn't correct her. Corrie uses the present tense, even for events that have happened long ago. He knows for her it's a language thing, though in some cultures, including his own, the past is forever present.

She nods. "Always the baby who is lost and found."

Hamsa smiles. Sets the hand on his grandfather's lap. Unacknowledged.

"He tells his story to anyone who visits, Sheikh Hamsa," says Corrie. "He tells me, he tells the newspaperman."

"Yes, it's a good story," says Hamsa. He is no sheikh, only Hamsa Al Ghurair al Rimali, a grandson, come home to check on the health of his father's father, his *jiddo*, because his father has left the nursing in the hands of a Filipina, loath to enter what he continues to consider his wife's side of the villa.

"The boy goes to the sea and when he comes back from diving for the pearls he is kidnapped and then he escapes with his faithful friend, what his name…"

"Bashir," says Hamsa.

"Yes, thank you, sir, Bashir. They escape and, oh, wait… he is kidnapped before he goes to find pearls."

"Yes, I believe that is so, Corrie."

They speak in English, which is the common tongue of Abu Dhabi these days. Hamsa had never heard his grandfather use more than a few words of it, and wonders what his *jiddo* grasps when Corrie talks to him. For some of the simpler commands or phrases—sit, eat, sleep, toilet—she uses Arabic, but when they're alone and Corrie talks to him, no doubt regaling him with her own tales of her university-bound daughter, her brothers in Cebu, the husband she calls her "bad man," does he comprehend?

"I hear so many time I know story in my heart," she says.

"Yes," Hamsa says.

Maybe she resorts to Tagalog. That would make sense. The language closest to one's heart should be the conveyor of stories.

"Sheikh Rasul mix sometimes," Corrie says.

Hamsa's grandfather is over ninety, closer to a century, so what if he did muddle the chronology?

The room is bright with the morning sun. The old man is a propped-up figure in his wheelchair. The television is on and his chair is in front of the screen, but the light from the window overexposes the image. In any case, he's not watching. No one is. Not the news. Not sports. Not *Million-Dollar Poet*. Not the interminable Egyptian soap operas broadcast during Ramadan to get everyone through the long hours of fasting. The elder Al Ghurair has fallen asleep.

Hamsa rises, twists the rod to close the window blinds, then returns to shut off the television with the remote. When they were younger, the family parked his young brother, Zayd, in front of a television like this at Ramadan. Hamsa wonders if he had followed the storylines. His brother has always had a high emotional intelligence and soaps are downright emotional.

In truth, the focus should be on God during the Holy Month, but Hamsa is aware the thoughts of even the most religious of men can deviate from their proper course. Unflinching concentration, focus, is almost impossible. There are times when he's flying, with the blue of the sky extending two hundred and seventy degrees around and above him, with all the dials of his jet stable, when he, too, gets distracted. Head in the clouds at those moments. His father always said he was the flighty one—"takes after his mother, that Canadian goose"—and had enrolled him in the air force academy in England

and then more training in Al Ain to try to focus what he saw as his elder son's inattention.

Hamsa would be the last to define that as a success. He thought himself a decent enough pilot, and even though he is a commander, but not of his own wing, he doesn't foresee the military as a career. Too much focus on focus. Not enough attention to the things that don't demand attention. Like whether the lost-and-found boy, Aidam, was kidnapped before or after he'd gone to sea to dive for pearls. Whether Grandfather Rasul was comfortable in front of the television. Whether tahini is required in hummus. Yes, it is true: some people make their hummus without tahini. And it is also true: When Hamsa goes off like this, he sounds like his grandfather in these last years. The loose tongue partner to a rambling mind. Granules of sand driven by the wind in winter.

"Your father no help." Hamsa snaps to. He doesn't know whether Corrie means his father is of no help because he can't do the work or because he *won't* do the work. Regardless, his father is no help. Nor has he been for a long time. Corrie says she's tired and hasn't taken a day off in months. She's afraid to leave the old man alone. That's why I'm here, Hamsa thinks.

"I like your *lolo*," she says, using the Tagalog, and reaches for the old man's right hand, which has slipped from the armrest of the wheelchair. She lifts the hand and places it in his lap.

Hamsa looks at his grandfather and smiles. "Yes, I like him too," he says. "Shall we move him to his bed?"

Corrie shakes her head. "He sleeps here. For snack, easier in chair. Already sit."

Hamsa watches Corrie watching his grandfather. The old man's head droops to the left with his mouth open; his lips are fissured and dry. The beard is as patchy as it ever was, whiskers like wispy filaments of cloud at thirty thousand feet, but now as white as the moon. White, the presence of all colour. As much fact as metaphor. Knowledge and wisdom and love and passion and caring and kindness accounted for the white of Rasul's beard.

Hamsa is grateful for Corrie's care of the old man. It's evident she is fond of him, even though she's been in the employ of the Ghurairs only seven months, since Rasul had a fall and fractured his hip. She hadn't known him in his prime.

Rasul, the storyteller. Rasul, who exited his mother's belly with stories on his lips. No cry, just words; no exclamations, just recollections of his tribe and those of his fellow Bedouin. Rasul's tales about life in the desert or on the waves, about date farmers and goat herders, falconers and hunters, shopkeepers and pearlers, camel ranchers and caravan drivers, were accounts of Bedouin living the life of good Arabs, good Muslims. The way his grandfather used to recount family history made sense. Of everything. But not in a moralizing way. Rather than lessons, his grandfather's stories were suggestions of what it means to be who we are, the multiple ways our universal condition can be lived, all the different roads one can take yet arrive at the same destination.

"Right then, Corrie," Hamsa says, confident his *jiddo* is asleep. "Can you call me when it's time to feed him and to put him in bed? I want you to show me what you do."

"Yes, Sheikh Hamsa," says Corrie.

He's about to correct her. But in Corrie's mind, Hamsa surmises, any man in a starched, white *kandoura* is a sheikh. Plenty of them are. On the plane over from Manila—Hamsa pictures row after row of Corries—her recruitment agent in all likelihood drilled in the necessity of showing respect to the people she served. To do her job well, she calls them "sheikh" and "sheikha"—whenever his sister is around—even if they aren't. To point out the error would embarrass her and debase her in a way, even though she does so unwittingly when she refers to them by these puffed-up titles. They differ from her only by accident of birth. What would *Jiddo* think of this and that tale of the freed slave, Bashir? he wonders, then drops it.

He goes to search for his father.

Hamsa pursues the sound of a television on the other side of the villa, a ten-bedroom affair, small as villas go. From various viewpoints in the house on Al Muzoon peninsula—whether bedroom windows, balconies, decks or walkouts—one can see Al Gorm resort island to the northwest, the fortress-like U.S. embassy and the Sheikh Zayed Grand Mosque on the main island, Hodariyat island across the Khor al Bateen and, to the south, mangroves. He's flown over the palm-tree hidden house dozens of times en route to base. That high up, the villas of Abu Dhabi are squares of tan Lego blocks masked by feathery palms. He distinguishes his from others by the swamp around it. Hamsa's father had threatened to have the mangroves removed because the trees prohibited easy access for his yacht, a monster of a boat the size of five dhows. But the mangrove removal was blocked, not by environmentalists tormented over what removal of the trees would do to the fragile Gulf ecosystem, but by a prince of the ruling family who fancied himself a birdwatcher and was inclined to observe the flamingos attracted to the swamp. Hamsa recalls the pleasure he felt hearing the mangroves would stay; as children, he and his sister had skimmed in their kayaks like stones over water, thrust through the thicket along the tidal shores, marine explorers, pretend adventurers.

Hamsa walks through the grand foyer with the four-foot-diameter Waterford crystal chandelier no one has ever turned on, except Hamsa and his sister when, as children, they would send Morse code messages to each other, Hamsa dotting and dashing, his sister transcribing and mapping coordinates for rescue ships. No one sits in the living room or in the *majlis*, where male guests once gathered for entertainment or meetings. No one is in the dining room either except the Filipino gardener, Thomas, dusting window valances the maids aren't able to reach in a room where no one has dined since *Ommi* decamped to the other side of the house. Thomas isn't much taller than the maids and cooks, but he's "the man," he says, and so gets to mount the stepladder.

Hamsa slides his hand along the balustrade as he climbs the staircase to the second floor. The sound of the television is louder here, as if the white noise of the villa has swelled. He passes several bedrooms until he finds the source of the din. He pushes down the handle and shoves open the door.

Before Hamsa, on a divan and on his cellphone—despite the blare of the television—reclines his father, Nadim bin Rasul Al Ghurair al Rimali, the fourth generation to carry the family name and the *laissez-faire* majority owner of a company built on cotton sheaths for pearl divers but which branched out after the Second World War and the collapse of the pearl industry into swimwear and outerwear. Also, amateur day trader, father of three, divorced husband.

The room is dark. Hamsa pulls back the drapes, locates the remote on the coffee table under empty paper cups in a large, velvet box of chocolates and mutes the television. His father squints, looks up. "What?" he says.

Hamsa picks a blanket off the cool tile floor and tosses it at his father. "Cover yourself," he says.

"What's your problem?" Nadim says and sits up.

"You're naked. What if one of the maids walks in here?"

"They know what to do."

Father and son regard each other for a moment. Neither says a word. Then with a huff, Nadim cradles the phone between his shoulder and ear and says, "I gotta go. Hamsa the steadfast and pure has darkened the door." He listens for a moment as he searches for his boxer shorts. His nod is automatic. He says "yes, just sell it" into the phone, then "*masha'allah*," pulls on his pants and presses the button to disconnect before he tosses the phone on the couch.

"To what do we owe this visit? You scare away all of Bashir Assad's bad bad soldiers?"

"You read the newspapers," Hamsa says. "You have as good an idea of what goes on as I do."

"Oh, yes, I read the newspapers all right," his father says, then reaches under his shorts and scratches himself. "And I watch the television news. I know the longer the French go on about burkinis, the more I sell of them. And, more to the point, yes, I have an idea as to what you're up to. Proud as a cock on the walk in your uniform and all the talk about service for the country."

"It wasn't my idea to go to Cranwell and join the air force." Hamsa remains erect, hands behind his back, feet shoulder-width apart, at ease, as if he were in uniform and not his *kandoura*.

"Of course, that was *my* idea," Nadim says. "I sure as hell didn't expect you to lounge around the house like your indolent cousins. But I sure as hell didn't think you'd be bombing Syrians. They're Arabs, for God's sake. Muslims!"

Hamsa rolls his eyes and sighs.

"What?" his father asks.

"Shall I describe what Muslims do to each other in Syria? You want me to tell you about that butcher?"

"Don't believe everything you read, Hamsa."

"I'm talking about what I've seen, Father."

Nadim lifts his hand and brushes the air. "Believe what you want to believe."

The phone chimes. The men consider it.

"Have you heard from your sister?"

The phone chimes again. The ringtone is an Arabic pop song, a different one than last time. A different caller. How to keep them straight, when so much music sounds similar now?

"No."

The conversation never changes: Nadim expresses disappointment with Hamsa's career choice. Hamsa points out his father pushed him into it. But this is as far as it goes. Neither keen nor prepared to push the argument further. Hamsa suspects there won't be too many more flights over Syria. There wasn't much appetite for it in the ruling family and, based on recent articles in the newspapers and discussions on television, not much stomach for the bombings among the general population either. For show or for real—and in Abu Dhabi sometimes it's hard to know which is which—the perception is Emiratis are dropping ordnance on Syrians, fellow Arabs, fellow Muslims. This claws at Hamsa. His father could be right.

The pop song intones a third time.

"Go ahead," Hamsa says. "The world of high finance mustn't wait."

While his father in equal measure counsels and berates whoever is at the opposite end of the mobile phone, Hamsa walks around his father's bedroom, a cavern of more square footage than Hamsa's former quarters on base in Al Ain, and that room accommodated four airmen. To about the height of a short man, the walls are painted in gold which fades as it rises to white like the ceiling. The marble floor tiles are eighteen inches square, the shade of the dunes. The effect is of seeing the Arabian sunrise over the Sands. Against the shorter wall, furthest from the door by which Hamsa entered, is his father's bed, a rococo-style gilded frame with a tufted black leather headboard and red satin sheets, limned in gold. At the foot of the bed, a black leather, gold-framed settee. The end tables are similar: lacquered gold and black. And above the headboard, between two black drapes (behind which Hamsa knows there to be no windows), are abstract paintings that bring to mind the gold-drip chandelier hanging in the middle of the room. Across from the bed, the television, a third as large as a cineplex movie screen. A smaller one hung in its place the last time Hamsa visited, two weeks before.

Against the long wall of the room, opposite the windows and the French doors and the walkout balcony, is a large topographical map of the country, in high relief, so, if one runs one's hand over it, the height, depth and breadth of the mountains and valleys can be felt. Hamsa turns. By the door, his father catches his eye and holds up a finger. "One minute," he mouths, but turns back to the conversation and heads out onto the balcony. Hamsa faces the wall again, remembers hours seated in front of it as a child. The map in its vitality has never failed to mesmerize, though this morning, creeping into afternoon, Hamsa can pick out only the faults it represents. No map, however vivid the details or accurate its features, can be a faithful portrayal of what one sees from the sky. As no word can describe the thing it is meant to depict with absolute precision. A chair may be a chair, but what does that mean? What is a chair?

Five minutes later, Hamsa hears his father's voice deepen and slow as it does when he's angry but doesn't want to let it show. The conversation doesn't seem to be a minute from ending. He leaves the room and returns to his grandfather's side of the villa.

The query about his sister unsettles Hamsa. He's felt it in his bones for a while. "That twin thing," his father used to call it. Something has felt off. She was usually in good touch with their father and their mother, had managed for all their twenty-eight years to maintain neutrality between the two war parties, to observe the situation with objectivity, as if from a distance, though, in private, the separation and subsequent divorce caused her endless worry. His sister had shut down emotionally. She'd focused at the time on her schoolwork, let go of her friends, then gone off to McGill to study English literature and journalism. After an internship at the newspaper in Montreal, she'd landed a job at the new paper in Abu Dhabi. Since then, she's seemed brighter, cheerier. It's a significant change and Hamsa is happy for her, whatever the source of her joy. The family was proud to see her byline, one of the few recognizably Emirati until the government went on a program to put local university grads to work. Males somehow ended up with the government jobs. The foreign and private sector companies were all too happy to hire the young women seen as hard workers because this was their sole window to accomplishment before marriage shut them behind closed doors. Now everyone at the mosque seemed to have a friend or a family member with a kid who wrote for the paper. But only one byline read Hadeel al Rimali.

Two years into her job, Hadeel was rewarded with a foreign assignment, as the Bahrain correspondent, based in Manama. It had helped that Hadeel knew how to shoot photographs, always at the hemline of their mother in the darkroom. Then Hadeel was off to Syria. No one has heard from her in a week. Was that so unusual? Hamsa wasn't sure how newspapers worked. Hadeel could be on an assignment requiring her to be away for some time without internet access. Given what he's seen, Hamsa figures that could be pretty much anywhere. So many Syrians had left their farms because of the drought, only to end up in the middle of civil war and blast-site cities more dusty and more dead than the countryside they'd vacated.

Their mother's family was from the Rawda neighbourhood of Damascus, a district of natural beauty and man-made splendour.

When they were children, Hamsa, Hadeel and their parents would fly into the capital from Abu Dhabi every winter and summer and, in a rented Mercedes, drive down wide boulevards lined with trees that shaded villas and apartment structures of various heights, the more magnificent ones dating from the French colonial era. Their mother said not much had changed since the sixties, when she had lived there. The buildings, the ones most Damascenes lived in—minimum four stories, many much higher—were pale concrete and steel, almost Soviet in style. But to Hamsa, on a visit as a boy, these edifices were magnificent giants, skyscrapers taller than any building in Abu Dhabi, except the hotels, and cleaner too, as if the wind swept the sand away rather than plastering it against windows and concrete. Perhaps it seems this way because of the feelings Hamsa attaches to that city of history and magic. It's certainly not the case now.

Hamsa remembers walks with his mother's father, his grandfather Elyas, along the Barada, along the sidewalk by the river for several miles. They would then cross a bridge and drop down through some small trees and brush to sit on the riverside. "Our people have lived by this river for thousands of years," Elyas explained on one such excursion. "At first, here in the delta, where the river expends itself, but then the family grew large and split and some went higher, to Lake Barada up in the Eastern Lebanon Mountains. They hunted and fished there for many years, while the remainder stayed here, below the gorge, which is narrow like a throat, where we also hunted and fished, and later farmed."

"We have family in the mountains?" young Hamsa asked.

"We have family everywhere, many many cousins and brothers," his grandfather answered.

Elyas would sneak Hamsa and Hadeel treats before they set off for the airport to return home, little candies wrapped in a rainbow of metallic cellophane. They always gave the children presents, which, Hamsa realizes as an adult, is what grandparents do. They give without reservation ... and sometimes without parents' permission. Everything, anything. Mostly love.

That excursion on the Barada was early in a month-long visit with his grandparents. The family had gone up after school had let out and when they were ready to decamp back to the humid soup of Abu Dhabi, Hamsa had pleaded to remain. Elyas and Grandmother Amena were more than willing to accommodate, and the boy—Hamsa thinks he was about five at the time—was overjoyed. Hadeel would have none of it.

"How come he gets to stay?"

"He's your brother."

"So what! He's the same age as me!"

She was pacified with a gift, a clear plastic maze with three ball bearings. In her child hands, she balanced the toy, manoeuvred the tiny silver globes a bit here and a bit there until each entered a hole. The holes were apertures in a red mouth and eyes with thick black brows in a clown's face. It occupied her all the way to the airport and much of the flight back.

Hamsa scrawled his first Arabic words that month; he also picked up an assemblage of French words from the grocer, and learned how to ride a bicycle. They went up into the mountains in search of the source of the Barada River and had picnic lunches on Saturday afternoons where his grandfather fired up a compact charcoal brazier to grill meat, onions, tomatoes and capsicum and to warm bread while his grandmother spread a blanket and set out hummus and *moutabal*, *labneh* and juice. Afterward, Hamsa kicked a ball about and Elyas and Amena smoked from a waterpipe, sending fruit-scented smoke to hover in the air above them.

Now Elyas and Amena live in Canada, in Montreal, with Hamsa's mother. Elyas, who was a pediatrician, is a counterman at Marché Adonis. Too young to retire, a degree and practice that meant nothing in their adopted home. Amena manages a store in Villeray whose specialty is Middle Eastern antiques and she mounts shows of her daughter's photographs. In Abu Dhabi, Hadeel writes for a newspaper. Their father, Nadim, sits naked in his bedroom selling stocks, and Hamsa flies bomb runs over al Rawda, where the presidential palace sits more or less vacant as Assad moves among residences.

In his father's villa, Hamsa slips into the kitchen and takes three butterscotch sweets from a ceramic bowl on the granite counter. One for Corrie, one for himself, one for the old man. There's a pot of lentil soup on the stove and the smell of cumin fills the room. Hamsa covers the pot, checks the burner, then picks up a turmeric-stained wooden spoon from the counter, washes it and runs a sponge over the yellow smudge on the granite.

Jiddo is awake when Hamsa arrives on his mother's side of the villa. Corrie spoon-feeds his grandfather. The television is on again. Is it for Corrie's pleasure or does she think the old storyteller will absorb it by osmosis? There's a yellow dribble at the corner of his downward-turned mouth and Corrie dabs at it with a tissue.

"I can do that," says Hamsa.

"Okay," she says, then puts the bowl, spoon and tissue on a tray. She gets up, points the remote control at the television to mute the volume, then moves toward the door, where she stops. "I come to help him to toilet, then he naps."

With Corrie gone, Hamsa pulls a stool closer to his grandfather's wheelchair and picks up the bowl of soup. He dips the spoon into the bowl and brings it to his grandfather's lips. "The soup smells wonderful, doesn't it?" Hamsa says.

Rasul neither nods nor parts his lips.

Hamsa places the edge of the spoon on the bottom lip.

Rasul moves his head. Imperceptible but undeniable. No.

No to what? No to soup. No to TV. No to being toileted. No to sleeping most of the day. No to life?

"Grandmother Baheera made wonderful *shorbut addis*, didn't she?" Hamsa says.

Rasul's eyes flicker at the mention of his wife's name and his lips turn up in a tight almost-smile. She's been gone twenty years. Hamsa and Hadeel were in grade school when she died. Zayd didn't even exist yet.

"You were with her a very long time, weren't you, Grandfather?" says Hamsa, and he squeezes a trickle of soup through the old man's lips. "You told me many stories about your wedding. You remember the stories? About your wedding?"

Rasul swallows and licks his lips as if he's about to speak, but he can't.

"You were a young man and she was a young woman and your families arranged the marriage," Hamsa begins. "The wedding was traditional Bedouin, held in a large camel-hair tent in the middle of the desert. You had musicians and drummers, singers, and there was a small army of men with swords and whips."

His grandfather's eyes focus on a middle space between Hamsa and the television behind him, but the distance the tale seems to have taken Rasul is long, measured in years marked by loss. Hamsa knows the details, but his account of the wedding pales against the florid, expansive tales of his grandfather. On the other hand, he reassures himself, his purpose here isn't to mimic, but to engage with a mind once as quick as a desert hare.

"After the dancing you drank coffee and ate chicken and lamb. And the sheikh sang. The sheikh was a guest. The sheikh was a cousin,

I think, of Grandmother Baheera. He was a very important man even then, a young man like you. And he brought with him foreign guests, right? There was the British agent and an oil man, and a little girl too who danced with the women and thoroughly enjoyed herself because who doesn't enjoy a wedding?"

Corrie returns and together they take Rasul to the bathroom, help him onto the toilet, care for him there, then brush his hair and his teeth, change him into pajamas and lift him into bed for his afternoon nap. A nap that might extend deep into the night if not through to the morning.

Hamsa feels Rasul's hand on his forearm, a weak wrap that slips to the wrist. His grandfather's eyes want, they yearn, though Hamsa doesn't know what it is, how to satisfy the craving, and Rasul is incapable of expression. His wishes will rebound in his mind, in his skull. As Corrie fluffs the pillow under Rasul's head and neck, Hamsa bends over. He hears a rasp from Rasul's throat and mouth, an expulsion of air and sound that is part-word, part-sensation. An utterance. The cry of a man who can no longer cry.

"What is it, *Jiddo*? Do you want something?"

The noise from the part in Rasul's lips stretches and thins in the air. It is Hamsa's name. Hamsa is sure of it. Although he has heard it ten thousand times in his life and may still hear it twenty thousand more, he has never heard it spoken in quite this way.

"He says goodbye," says Corrie.

She can't know that. Besides, who is she to assume she's the one to interpret?

"Yes," Hamsa answers after a moment, though what he wants to say is please leave me alone, please leave me with him. He looks up at Corrie and his anger slides away. Corrie has been faithful and her heart will know deep grief when the old man goes.

And as the old man goes, so go his stories. So go his words, which have meant so much to him. Words, upon which he built a life, to which he clings even as illness deprives him of their use, steals them away one by one.

Rasul falls asleep. Corrie tucks him in, adjusts the pillow again, uses the bed's controls to raise the upper part a smidge. Then she turns off the television.

Hamsa twists the rod to close the blinds; afterward, carries the bowl and spoon and tissue into the kitchen. The tissue goes in the trash. The bowl and spoon he rinses then puts in the dishwasher. He hears the television in his father's bedroom. In all his life, Hamsa had never seen his father carry a dish away from a table. This was left for others to do. They did their jobs well. His mother oversaw the workings of the household, of course, and she paid generously. Everyone wanted to work for the Al Ghurair family. Emirati women scolded her. "You can't pay them so much. They talk, you know. Among themselves. Word gets around. They'll start asking us for the same. Just because you did this in Canada... blah, blah, blah."

Rasha would raise her hands in a sign of defeat. But then she'd get up from her seat and pick up their plates and utensils and balled-up tissues and walk them with all the dignity and humility of a servant into the kitchen. Oh, she loved to throw it right back at them. She did it with the children too. "Misery loves company," she'd say when they would whine about their gloomy, wretched lives, "here's a mirror."

Hamsa knows his mother's story. He knows her people, where she came from. He's been to Syria. He's been to Canada. She had no servants anywhere she lived until she came to teach photography in Abu Dhabi and his father accidentally on purpose bumped his grocery cart into hers in Spinney's and they got married months later. She has no servants in Montreal. She hadn't fleeced his father in the eventual divorce, but she'd taken enough to force him to worry his investments like beads.

In addition to running the family businesses, Nadim became a bit of a day trader. Out of boredom as much as necessity, Hamsa supposes. The Ghurair al Rimalis are part of the renter class of Abu Dhabi and Dubai, families who went from camels to cars in one generation, who don't work, but rent to businesses or housing and hotel developers the land they were allocated when oil bubbled up out of the ground and the sheikhs felt obligated to share the wealth. The rulers paid for projects to burnish their reputations as generous and benevolent. What they'd really bought was peace. To Hamsa, it was the worst move the sheikhs could have made—giving away land and riches made most people both wealthy and lazy—but Hamsa holds counsel with no one. Thoughts such as these, should they be spoken, can be dangerous to one's health. Can land one in prison, like his father's cousin, the professor, who, in the middle of the Arab Spring, signed a petition demanding the U.A.E.'s Federal National Council, a sycophantic body of government appointees, be given more autonomy, more authority and more accountability.

On the other side of the house, Nadim is shouting. He's lost it. Whoever is on the receiving end will receive a basket of chocolates the next day by way of apology. Sometimes it works. Rasha threw the chocolates back. The roller-coaster of venomous bellowing followed by spineless grovelling got to be too much for her. She moved to the other side of the villa and brought everyone, Grandfather Rasul included, with her. As impermanent as marriage can be, and how easy it is in Islam to annul one, Nadim would never voice the words "I divorce you." Pride, vanity, who knows. Men love without knowing how to show love. He continued to shop at Spinney's. But when her parents left Syria in early 2011, after Assad had those young protesters killed, Rasha decided to join Elyas and Amena in Montreal. It was only then, though she had lived apart from her husband for ten years, that she initiated divorce proceedings.

It's all transient, isn't it? thought Hamsa. All built on sand, from marriage to malls. The rulers can sit in their palaces, but those palaces weren't built any sturdier than the apartment complexes disintegrating around the city. Nothing in Abu Dhabi was made to last. The heat and the cycle of humidity and extreme dryness were ill-tempered twins flattening sand castles on a beach.

Hamsa thinks of his sorties over Syria. His explosive payloads have helped those twins do their work. Bombed-out shells of buildings, where the Assad government kept munitions or repaired tanks and planes, stood side by side with hospitals and apartments Assad had destroyed. All of it crumbling to dust. Assad. Clutching at anything if it could cement his hold on power. Like Putin. Another one who thinks power lasts. Nothing lasts. We went from camels to cars and we'll end up back on camels soon enough.

Hamsa finds himself in the living room. Leather couches. A stupid idea in this environment. Now dry and cracked and peeling. They were meant to last a lifetime, but are tossed as soon as they show signs of shabbiness. Hamsa pushes through the room and plops himself down on a floor-level, cushioned seat against the wall of the *majlis*. This is where the men gathered in the house, when men used to gather here. As a boy, Hamsa loved coming into this room the morning after the men visited, sniffing out the smoky flavour of the *shisha* in the pillows, picking up the odd dirham coin that had slipped out of someone's pocket into the gaps between the cushions. He'd found a twenty-dirham note in the cushions once. So long ago. When his father was a younger man and other young men gathered and smoked and talked with animated hands about business and football and the state of the world. Nadim would listen, and then he'd talk a little. Never raised his voice if he was angered or displeased or if he was trying to make a point. Hamsa isn't sure when the men stopped coming, but they did. And Nadim withdrew into his work—swimwear and biking shorts before he also began buying and selling shares. He grew louder and larger.

Hamsa tosses one of the cushions aside and moves a pillow so he can lay his head down. The house is silent. The maids, Corrie, Thomas, are resting or working outside. From his father's rooms upstairs, Hamsa hears the pneumatic wheeze of a CPAP, the breathing machine that keeps apnea from killing Nadim in his sleep. Nadim *had* been warned. Plenty of people—the children, his wife when he had a wife, his own father, the doctors he chose to ignore—had said, "Lose the weight, Nadim. It will kill you." He's huge now. Sleep apnea is one result of his weight. Another is diabetes. Billboards around the city every Ramadan warn not to binge at *iftar*. Nadim manages the diabetes, takes pills for a heart condition. The prostate was removed the year before amid a cancer scare. Nadim could die before his own father, but Hamsa does not really believe this will be the case.

One hundred is creeping up on Rasul. Soon, he will be gone. Nadim will hear of it when Thomas or someone enters with tea. Hamsa himself will not be present. He'll be in Syria. Not over Syria for a run this time, but on a personal errand, one that tugs at him. And when Hamsa returns home, it will be Corrie, who will have given notice and asked for a job reference now his *lolo* is with God, who will tell him what happened. Breathlessly and speaking in the present tense, she will unwrap the story of Rasul bin Bashir Al Ghurair al Rimali's death as if the details were chocolates. She will say she's sorry over and over, and Hamsa will wish she would be quiet, though he'd never say that, and she'll say how much affection she has for his grandfather, whom everyone said Hamsa took after, right down to the way they walked. Hamsa will allow Corrie to continue with her story, and when she's done, she'll wrap up the box of chocolates, the gift of story, about one teller, and from one teller to another. She will pass it on to Hamsa. He used to think, when time finally catches up to a man, all memory dies with him, leaving an empty quarter in the next generations, an omitted piece of identity like a birth date not filled in on a passport. But he will accept the gift of Corrie's and Rasul's stories, and accept death simply as the way stories must end.

II

What Hadeel wouldn't do for some poutine. It must be the most unhealthy, most cholesterol-laden dish known to man, but for the love of Allah, she wants some. It's so unhealthy, in fact, why hasn't someone begun selling it in Abu Dhabi or Dubai? Any proper Emirati would eat it right up. Inhale it at an *iftar* buffet at one of the downtown hotels. The fast-food burger joints that serve poutine in Canada are all present and accounted for in the U.A.E. You'd think one of them would have thought to add it to the menu. And then some fancy Montreal-trained hotel chef would class it up, add foie gras as they do at Au Pied du Cochon, though Hadeel dismisses the thought. Pâté from a restaurant devoted to all things pork is not exactly halal. Better yet, butter chicken poutine. Yes! That's it. Given all the Indians and Pakistanis in the U.A.E., it'd be a sure hit. Not that most of them could afford to eat in the hotels, and the owners of the labour camps sure as hell won't put up money for cheese curds, but the middle managers might find it within their means, supervisors and the like. And if butter chicken poutine, why not mixed grill? Or falafels. The Jordanians regularly put French fries in their falafel sandwiches anyway. Topped with hot sauce. Hadeel knows this is crazy, but she can't help herself. When she gets hungry, her mind goes on and on. Binge-thinks. Since, at the moment, she's not so much into binge-eating. Mexican? It might be on the menu at Cantina Laredo in the Khalidiyah Mall—french-fry base, with a sizable dollop of enchilada sauce, a mix of Monterey Jack cheese, young cheddar and a bit of asadero for meltability, topped with strips of chicken that have been rubbed with Yucatan spices before slowcooking in a pot. The picture is so vivid, Hadeel knows the Cantina must be serving Cancun-style poutine as she thinks it, and the minute she's out of Syria and back in Abu Dhabi she'll drive to the mall and order it. Two orders. And eat them right there. With a virgin mojito and a virgin margarita. *If* Hadeel can get out of Syria, by God's grace, she'll also get her sorry ass to Montreal and have that foie gras poutine and wash it down with a good vintage champagne or a well-oaked chardonnay. But first things first.

Hadeel al Rimali must get out of Syria.

In some ways, she can't believe she's in Syria to begin with, can't believe she let Ibrahim convince her this was a good assignment. She should have listened to Marc. But no. She'd let her ego call the shot. Or was it the id? This adventurous, instinctive part of herself. It wasn't only about sniffing out stories, about having one more placeline to add to her growing portfolio of clips. Up there in LinkedIn, something to tweet about. It wasn't ferreting out the fabrications, calling truth to power, following the money, afflicting the comfortable and comforting the afflicted. It was all that and more. There's a rush in the blood, to the head, in the heart, when Hadeel hears the pop and hiss of tear gas canisters launched in a protest, or when she confronts a Gulf politician or government official with a fact to disprove a statement he'd made the day before. Knock him off his dais. She gets off on the unpredictability, the what-comes-next, the uncertainty and unknowability. If Hadeel is to be honest with herself, she can't place the blame squarely on the shoulders of her editor. Ibrahim said Hadeel had done such a marvellous job on the Arab Spring protests in Bahrain that she should consider Syria next. The drought had sent thousands into the cities, and anti-Assad protests were escalating and about to get ugly. It was a risk, of course, but you should think of it as a reward for such solid work on the ground, he'd said. "And wouldn't it be a proud occasion for an Emirati to be filing from Damascus?" Never before. Not even in Abu Dhabi's Arab press.

And maybe never again. Hadeel stretches out her leg, the left one, and lifts the pant leg to get another look at it. She wishes it would heal better. Pink was a sign of new skin growth, and this was not pink. It was red, inflamed and crusted black. At first, it didn't seem too bad. A gash not even half-a-centimetre deep and about five centimetres long. Hadeel doesn't remember injuring herself. Two months before, she had made telephone contact, through someone who had proved reliable and connected, with one of the insurgent groups. They were reluctant to meet but over time were convinced by her work in the country, the source said, because they had read it online. The interview would be short. Would be at a place of their choosing. At a time of their choosing. All of it smelled like shit, but Hadeel has since stopped kicking herself over all she'd done wrong. Including not calling the paper. Even the taxi driver thought she'd slipped off her rocker and dumped her half a block away from her destination. When she saw her fixer spying her from the opposite side of the street from their agreed-upon meeting point, Hadeel knew she'd erred. She ducked into an open doorway, fled down a plywood ramp into what had been the atrium of a once-upscale apartment building. She heard shouting behind her. Desert sand and the white dust of plaster everywhere. Trees dying in their pots. Paint peeling, food rotting, rats scurrying. Pictures of Hafez Assad and his son, the president, Bashir, hanging askew in frames with broken glass. Hadeel hurtled across the space toward a back door, once glass, now open air, which she shoved through before she careered down another street in search of yet another door, or an alley, any portal into the labyrinth of Old Damascus and to safety. Smell of roasting meat in the air. Cumin and cinnamon, and vegetables left to rot in the streets. The kids would've caught her in the car anyway, but tripping and falling on stones in the rubbled street didn't help. Her capture had happened even faster: a nine-millimetre to her head, then a hood. That was all.

Marc had begged her not to go to Syria. They'd sat across from each other at one of the picnic tables set up in the courtyard in the compound *Abu Dhabi World* shared with the pan-Arab media company that owned the paper. It was as close as they could be together without raising the eyebrows of the Emirati women on staff. It was scandalizing enough that Hadeel unveiled in the office.

"Ibrahim's never been a reporter," Marc said. "He's been a desk-bound editor since he began in newspapers. And that wasn't all that long ago. He doesn't know what the weather is like out there. How life can go sour in less time than it takes to run a hundred metres."

Hadeel hears footsteps down the hallway. It may be time to eat. But she doesn't hear any doors open, like other times when food arrives. Then it's nothing. Probably one of the kids gone to the bathroom. She doesn't know how many there are. Sometimes she hears them talk in another room, but it's muffled. It's not Arabic they speak when they're together. It sounds like English, though spoken in a range of fluency. One of them couldn't order a falafel sandwich. She tried to engage one once. When he brought her food. But he'd slapped her.

"Nice backhand," she'd said. "You could go to Wimbledon with that."

"Shut the fuck up, you traitorous twat," he'd said.

"So you're British," she'd said.

Not the Canadian English that Rasha has. Or the BBC English her brother Hamsa speaks. Nor Maggie's Levantine-inflected English, or Marc's English, which is Montreal English. She misses hearing them. She misses *them*. The engagement, the banter, the gossip, the touch.

So she shut the fuck up, for a little while. But she felt bitchy and emotional and when she got that way, shutting the fuck up was the last thing she could do.

"You kidnap a woman, this is what you get," she said. "Deal with it."

This she'd said in Arabic. To test them.

The kid answered in broken Arabic. A newbie. A recruit. None of these little shits were Arab, she thought. Never mind Syrian. They didn't belong here. It wasn't their country; the Syrians weren't their people. Caliphate, my ass.

He frowned and shook his head. Didn't know what she was talking about.

"I need to take care of this leg," she said. "I need gauze, medical tape, you know. Some kind of antiseptic. If you can't find that, a bottle of vodka would do—"

Hadeel saw the kid was about to hit her. She backed away. "Oh, right. You don't drink, do you?"

Instead, he got her a half-squeezed tube of antibiotic ointment, a roll of toilet paper, which she used piece by piece to clean her leg. A day later, he took the roll back.

"I'm gonna need more," she said.

He shut the door.

"My leg's not any better!"

Hadeel sat on the wooden chair, lifted her pant leg and worked under the light of the single bulb left in the ceiling lamp. The ointment had expired nine months before, but even if the medical ingredients were inactive, it was better than nothing. Done, she kept the pant leg rolled up.

A week passed and then another. The second wasn't any less hot or airless. This week Hadeel has kept to herself. She would like to eat, but the kids have kept their distance too, kept contact to a minimum. No words. No eye contact. Were she to get out and be in a position to have to identify them—to army officials (but whose army? Assad's? the Americans?) or the police or in a dispatch or a book—she would be able to say: This one bit his nails and had a white scar right here on his hand that crisscrossed with his blue-green veins; another one smelled like matted camel fur; the third, who called her a "traitorous twat," spoke British English moulded by the Aravali mountains and the rivers that spill from Kerala into the sea.

The idea of writing again distracts her. She needs to keep her mind occupied—more than just obsessed. It's imperative she doesn't let this situation get to her head, her soul. It's enough that the leg has been so slow to heal. She thanks God she has not had her period while here.

The kids would absolutely freak, she thinks. Maybe it's the stress. Stress might also be the reason she's lost weight. Her pants are definitely loose. Hadeel must challenge herself by the day, by the hour. Keep her thoughts from turning into sludge. She sings Abba songs. If Twyla Tharp can create a full-length choreography to the songs of Billy Joel and Elton John, she should adapt *Mamma Mia* as a modern ballet. Tharp should work "Fernando" into the storyline.

The kids mustn't infect the core of her. Thoughts about food can keep them from devouring Hadeel's spirit. She's designed a memory palace of the sparse room. She tells herself stories, like the ones Grandfather Rasul used to tell. She concocts recipes to make when she gets home, meals for the next time she has friends over— not Ibrahim though, screw him—or designs menus for restaurants that don't even exist. Hadeel tries to remember her first byline and goes back to… first newspaper byline, or first, like, college-paper byline? First byline for a real newspaper would've been *The Gazette* in Montreal and would've been a freelance piece because Hadeel was still at McGill. She'd written a first-person piece about the sadness of life away from home at Ramadan and Eid. Soon afterward, the paper accepted a story on halal butchers and soon she had an internship. Her first college byline had taken longer to score. The editor was a senior with a stop-the-press ego and no time for women. He wore a blue Oxford button-down shirt, tan slacks, brown loafers and brown leather belt, even though no one wore that uniform except in movies. But wasn't Hadeel the surprised one when she got to the *World* in Abu Dhabi and found all the American editors on staff wore the same? Must save them a lot of time in the morning, she used to think. Not Marc, though. He was always handsomely turned out. White shirt tucked in khaki-green or khaki-tan pants, sometimes blue jeans. Black shoes. Relaxed.

First college byline: an interview with a finance professor who predicted a global financial crisis because of the U.S. sub-prime mortgages and what the effect would be for international students at the university. It was buried in the paper as "important but boring," though it caught the attention of the *Globe and Mail*'s Montreal bureau chief, who picked her as his McGill stringer. The college paper editor, Delancey, didn't speak to her for the rest of the semester.

Hadeel wonders where he is. If Delancey's in newspapers somewhere in Canada. If, when the *World* publishes a story about its Damascus correspondent, Hadeel al Rimali, being missing and

THE EMPTIEST QUARTER   141

the news gets picked up by the Associated Press or Reuters hack in Dubai, then by the wire's Middle East desk and broadcast around the world, whether Paddy Delancey will see the story on his computer and will think, "Wow, I knew her at McGill. She was great," knowing that, when he knew her at McGill he hadn't thought so well of her, had considered her precious, a sheikh's daughter. But because life is a continuous series of makeovers, and memory comes with a restart button, Delancey will remember Hadeel al Rimali with fondness as a "tough-as-nails reporter who always got her story" when he is quoted in *The Gazette*.

"Always got her story." What does that even say? Even a wine critic "always gets her story." Hadeel had landed *The Gazette* internship because the paper needed someone who could write with some intelligence and sensitivity about Quebec's emergent Muslim and Arab communities to, one, bring in more readership, and, two... bring in more readership. And then she'd scored the *World* job because of the country's Emiratization program and the fact she was one of the few female Emirati reporters who had a proper command of written English. Afterward, she used her family name to secure interviews—the name had *wasta*, for sure—and to "get her story." And look where it landed her.

The Pearl Roundabout in Manama, the day after Valentine's Day, the Day of Rage, 2011. Scattered, translucent streaks of cloud, mild temperatures, a funeral march of a thousand, Sunni and Shiites, to the cemetery from the Salmaniya medical centre, which also served as the morgue. They would bury two. The march was peaceful and Hadeel wrote eight hundred words for the *World*. The next day, pretty much the same as far as the weather went. But the road to the Pearl was blocked.

"Everyone is leaving their cars on the side of the road," said the Indian cab driver, who she'd found outside the hotel apartment. "This blockage is an inconvenient mess. I must drop you here, miss."

Hadeel got out and guesstimated how much the full fare to the roundabout would have been and handed it to him through the passenger window. He bobbled his head and said thanks and did a three-point U-turn to leave.

In the centre of town was a carnival atmosphere. Families had raised tarps and tents and a couple of the Shia volunteer mourners groups had organized kitchen areas from which they served biryani,

Styrofoam coffee cups of pomegranate seeds, plus black tea, sugary fruit juices and water. Two nurses and a doctor staffed a medical tent and under another large white tarp sat folding tables and chairs, plus charging stations for mobile phones and laptops. The area resembled the start of a springtime road race. But then a loudspeaker crackled into life and onto the podium jumped a polite, serious young man who demanded "an increase in the rights for Bahrain's stateless Bidoon." From another tent, set back from the Pearl, came an ill-timed cheer. A minute later, news came back up through the crowd that Arsenal had scored in the football game being watched in the tent.

It all turned sour overnight. What had begun as a quiet, joint protest of Sunnis and Shiites was painted by the Sunni-led ruling family as the nascence of a revolt of Shiites under orders from Tehran. It had to be crushed. The government instituted a six p.m. to six a.m. curfew. No one was allowed out of doors. If you were out, you were up to no good. Even guests leaving hotels were suspect. Hadeel conducted her interviews over her mobile, the company-issued BlackBerry, rather than risk arrest, then emailed her stories to the paper.

Journalists, she knew, were suspected of sympathizing with the protesters. The rulers believed the media would react to the uprising in Bahrain the way they had in Tunisia, Libya and Egypt, where Mubarak had fallen on February 11. In the second week of protests, a male colleague of Hadeel's who worked for dpa, the German agency, was blindfolded, handcuffed and beaten in a Manama jail room. A woman who reported for France's iTélé hadn't been heard from for three days before she was released, battered and bloodied.

Hadeel made connections among members of various activist groups, did her duty quoting government spokesmen, writing in a non-judgmental fashion. Regardless, she ended up in a Bahraini cell, where she was questioned for four hours about who she knew and what she was up to. Though he claimed he didn't have to—"This is not the television, you know"—Hadeel's inquisitor allowed her to make a call, which she placed to Ibrahim, who set in motion a chain of calls that led to Hadeel's release with: "We were so honoured to meet you today, Miss Al-Rimali, and please keep up the good job. We will read you in the newspapers, *insh'allah." Wasta* again.

Within a month, Hadeel had written her obituary of the Arab Spring in Bahrain, even though, like waves batting the sands at Jazair beach, the protests would come and go, as would the government's reaction to them. "As it was, so it is and so it will be," Marc wrote her.

"You're such a cynic," she wrote back.

"Yes, but an adorable one."

"You're stealing my lines."

Although Ibrahim insisted he was under no pressure from the government—"We are government-owned, not government-run. There's a difference"—Hadeel's article pleased the rulers of the U.A.E. who, along with Saudi Arabia, had sent military police at the request of Manama to intervene in the protests. Ibrahim was more than happy. "Finally, someone's told the truth," he said.

"Likely about as far as you could go," Marc texted. "To even hint at the real causes behind the failure of the protests would guarantee you a ticket home."

"I'll have to save it all for a book," she responded. "Can you get me a deal?" A couple of smiley emoticons.

To which Marc answered with a couple :) of his own. "On it." And then "Send me author pic."

Hadeel's shock was pleasant. Marc had grown bold texting. Part of the joking around, the easy banter between them, but he'd asked for her photo. It felt like the high school trade of senior-yearbook signatures.

Back in her hotel apartment in Manama, she examined herself in the bathroom mirror. She removed the hijab. Plain pastel blue, like a UN peacekeeper's helmet. Smooth skin, eyebrows plucked and shaped like smiles around her chestnut-dark eyes. Bright eyes, intelligent and confident and caring eyes. A memory of a scar on her upper lip from stitches earned while trying to ride a bicycle. A smile. My smile. What's not to love? What's not to love, Marc? She applied a touch of lip gloss. I see what I see, and so must he. Hadeel was sure he did, but there were times, when they'd talk, she could see him laying bricks and she didn't know whether to push against the wall or to come back another day and hope what he'd constructed wasn't brick but straw. Or not there at all. Something had hurt him out there and she didn't know what it was. Didn't know if she'd ever have a full grasp of it. Perhaps he didn't himself. And when he got quiet and fragile and susceptible to wounds of the heart and psyche, Hadeel felt it personally. It made her more open to him, weak and helpless. He was her mirror. His vulnerability is mine, she thought in her Manama hotel and, even now, in the confines of this puny, dusty room. He was a natural remedy to her wounds in the way she believed she was the healing balm to his.

Hadeel wants a cup of coffee. A caffè macchiato would do the trick. An almond croissant as a snack. She'd settle for water and a banana. She wonders where Marc is now. Maybe Lulu's. She sees him descend the mall escalator, eyes searching, hand on the gliding black rail. He pulls out a shopping cart and quietly enters the produce section, always aware of where he is in relation to objects and people. He stops before the avocados. Picks one up in his hands, squeezes it with gentleness like it's the small breast of a new lover.

Or he's at the office joking around with his best friend, Christopher, from the copy desk. They'd met in Abu Dhabi, but one would be forgiven thinking they had known each other all their lives. Secret sharers. Hadeel asked Marc once about their friendship. "He's just a really solid guy," Marc said. "He's there for me every day." She knew what that meant. She had such a relationship with Hamsa, her twin. Like a shared language. She wished she could fulfill that need for Marc. But the way Marc said it Hadeel knew she couldn't. Not now. Perhaps some day she could be there for him in an everyday way. If he'd open the door to her.

When Hadeel and Marc had figured out they'd both lived in Montreal and may even have overlapped in the early part of the decade, all they could do was talk about food and restaurants. His brother owned Le Matou, a top-end restaurant in St-Henri. Marc said he'd worked the line or helped prep on occasion, in the custom of family-run restaurants. She dreams about the day he might cook for her. Knows he might not ever ask.

The western journalists were scolded in their first week on the job, a "Don't pretend you're from here" speech in which the men were told not to behave as if they were at home. "Don't swear, don't give someone the finger, keep your road rage down even if you've got just cause, don't drink outside designated areas, and by all means do not strike up a conversation with a woman not related to you. If she's Emirati, you'll get deported. If she's a non-Emirati Muslim, her family might turn on her. If she's not local, you *both* might end up in jail," said the man, a British expat, who'd somehow married into a branch of the ruling family. Hadeel and Marc confined their friendship to the office.

What did it mean to identify as Emirati? Hadeel had both an Emirati passport and a Canadian passport yet the map imprinted on her heart was Syrian. When it pleased her or worked to her benefit, however, she played Emirati. This might have been what angered some of her Emirati colleagues at the paper, the ones who called her virtue into question. Her bestie in the newsroom, a reporter named Maggie Qassem, who was part-Druze and part-Irish, told her to ignore the others.

"Don't worry. I know who I am, and I know what I've done and not done," Hadeel said. "Besides, they're not the only ones to have ever called me a spinster."

"I can't believe people still use that word," Maggie said.

Hadeel shrugged. "Political correctness and feminism haven't caught on here."

"Yet."

They tipped their cups of juices—avocado-mango-guava for Hadeel, kiwi-lemon-mint for Maggie—toward the other and plastic-clinked.

"Though it kinda has, hasn't it?" Hadeel said. "More women in college than men, more women in post-grad studies. The marriage age is on the rise. And no wonder, right? I'm not about to marry a man who wouldn't allow me to study or work, who isn't as educated as I am. Screw that."

"Hear, hear, sister," said Maggie. "It's disingenuous of these women in any case. Insulting you when they're doing the same, getting their degrees, getting the jobs, holding off marriage."

"Yes, but I'm almost thirty," Hadeel said. "They're twenty-two, twenty-three. You watch. They'll get married within a couple of years and drop the careers."

The food court was busy that Friday night, the middle of the weekend—everybody back to work on Sunday—no moment should be missed. Some labourers shared a bucket of ice cream from Baskin-Robbins; Emirati dads corralled their wives and children and nannies toward seats in Pizza Hut; in front of the KFC, teen boys elbowed each other when a girl swished by in her textured rayon *abaya*. Hadeel and Maggie had bought juices from Forty Fruity before heading to the movies.

"How did you get to thirty," Maggie began, "without getting engaged?"

Hadeel was about to say she'd never been. That would have been easy to say, and then drop it. But it was Maggie, her friend, who was in her mid-thirties with a boy of ten, and who'd shared confidences about her abusive husband, the bastard she'd left to come work in Abu Dhabi.

"I was. Briefly," Hadeel said.

"Briefly? How's that?"

Hadeel's sigh was heavy with the weight of memory, a bit of a scoff, a bit you're-not-going-to-believe-this, a bit of unresolved anger. "My mother had already left my father. I mean, she lived in the same house, but on the other side of the villa, like I told you, to care for my grandfather and Zayd, I've told you about Zayd. And my father, without consulting her—I think it was almost his revenge—engaged me to this guy."

"Holy cow," Maggie said. "Without talking to her? She must have been livid."

"Not nearly as much as I was," said Hadeel. "The men are all in the *majlis* and my father comes to find me, which he never did, so I knew *something* was up, and tells me I'm to serve the men juice. Then I knew for sure. It was my *showfa*. He wanted me out there, without my veil, made up, hair down, with a tray of juice to serve the men, including, presumably, the guy I was supposed to marry. I start making myself up and he shouts there's no time getting dolled up, so, forget it, no veil, no makeup, hair still up in pins. I get the tray, get the juice and walk into the *majlis* and there's all these men looking me up and down like I was an entry in the camel beauty contest."

Maggie couldn't stifle her giggle and Hadeel joined her. "I know, right?"

"Anyway, my father made some introductions and all of a sudden, I start shaking. This is really happening. I'm supposed to be back at McGill in the fall, but I might be getting married also. Or instead! I'm shaking. The tray's shaking. The juices are moving all over the tray. And the guy—I can't tell you his name because you might recognize the family—he stands. He's about five ten, clean-shaven, not one of the meticulous beards most of the guys have these days, solid like a weightlifter, and he takes hold of the other half of the tray to steady it, looks me straight in the eyes to calm me and, together, we serve everyone. It was the sweetest. And I agreed. My father asked me and I said okay."

"Oh my God," Maggie said. "So how brief?"

This time Hadeel smiled, but the smile quickly veered upside-down. "I don't even know if it was a week. A couple of days later we were on a chaperoned trip to Marina Mall to begin shopping for our villa, which was already under construction in Khalifa A. Can you believe it? He was so obviously in the market for a wife he'd started on the house first! Anyway, it was a Friday afternoon after prayers, like today, and we had placed a few items on order here and there. I'd ordered a whole furniture set for the *majlis*! We had surprisingly similar taste. Either that or he was just going along with whatever I wanted, you know, because home furnishings are a woman's thing. Oh, one small detail. It turned out, yes, he *was* a weightlifter. Not even competitively. That's all he did. All day. He'd gone to school, which was great, you know, I could talk to him and he had opinions. But he saw no point in work."

"You're burying the lede, Hadeel," said Maggie.

"C'mon, sister, I'm building suspense," Hadeel said before she sipped her drink. "In the mall, we saw a group of special needs children with their teachers and aides. Some were in wheelchairs. They had neurological disabilities, developmental delays of some kind, CP. A couple had Down syndrome. Beautiful children. The ones with Down were pushing the wheelchairs of those who couldn't wheel themselves.

"And this guy, my supposed fiancé, says to me, 'What are they doing here? They shouldn't be out in public like this.' "

"No! He didn't say that."

"Oh, yes, he did," Hadeel said. "And I turned on him. 'What did you say?' And he was stupid enough to repeat it: 'They shouldn't be out in public.' "

"How did you… what did you say back?" Maggie asked.

"I reminded him I have a brother with CP. And he goes, 'C- what?' 'Cerebral palsy, you asshole.' And I turned to one of the chaperones, an aunt, and told her to take me home. 'The engagement's off,' I said. And that was that."

Hadeel gets up from the spent and sweat-stained mattress on the ground and bends forward. She drops her palms to the floor and stretches her hamstrings. Exercise is good. Yoga's good. Keeps her limber. Pushes away the fear, the loneliness, the longing, the uncertainty, the anger. For a time. Everything now is *for a time*. She works her way back into a jackknife position before standing straight as a mountain again. She raises her arms above her head, reaching, reaching. Looks up. Hadeel hears the scratching sound of a loudspeaker coming to life and then the familiar "*Allahu akbar*" calling the faithful to end whatever they're up to because God is greatest and there is no greater activity in life than prayer. Since they took away her BlackBerry and watch, the *adhan* is how she tells the time of day. From the faraway rooms come a scrape of chairs on the floor and the sound of water splashing in the sinks and the floor, and when the *muezzin* has stopped his call, she notes the muffled male voices of the kids praying. She imagines them on their rolled-out rugs, playing being Muslim, pretending being righteous, acting out a fantasy life of purity and prayer. From her upright position, palms together in front of her heart, she swoops her arms in an arc over her head again, bends, jackknifes, drops again with a heavy head and loose neck, then rises to begin the sun salutation again and again and again until she's focused on her breathing and has blocked the sound of these phonies, these imposters, and their pretend prayers in the room next to her. In the distance, a deep, rumbling thunder. Planes from above the clouds will rain bombs, anti-bunker, cluster, barrel. Rain, rain, rain.

When the men are done praying, she hears footsteps in the hallway and her door is opened.

"What are you doing?" asks the kid who smells like camel fur.

"Praying," she says, "like you."

He glances. "Then where is your rug?"

"You never actually gave me one, did you?"

He advances toward Hadeel.

The slap is hard enough to turn her head. Hadeel raises her arms to protect her face as the kid raises his hand again. But it's a feint. To scare her. He laughs. Hadeel reaches for her hijab, which she adjusts as she tucks her hair back under the fabric. The kid puts his hand to his side. Master Camel looks hard at Hadeel, then at her bedspread. Then at Hadeel. She backs away and lowers her gaze, her head.

Thunder.

"Why do you act this way?" he asks. "We treat you well, with food and water. With a bed. You are our guest here."

"I'm your guest?" Hadeel mocks him. "Fuck you! I'm not your guest. Fuck you." The kid looks angry enough to seriously harm her, but he turns and walks out. Slams the door behind him.

Hadeel crumples onto the mattress, her body folded over her knees, and cries. Can't believe she spoke with the Camel this way. It goes against everything she'd learned in the conflict-zone reporting course and all the advice from Marc. Do not antagonize. But dammit! Who were they to do this? This one, the kid, the youngest one. Blond hair, light brown eyes, shaggy Salafist beard. Pimply. To treat her with such disrespect. I am your equal, she wanted to shout at him. Hadeel, who had been taught at a young age that whatever her brother Hamsa did she could do. And she did. School, riding a bike, going out with friends, university abroad, travel. She doesn't know how long she cries, but the tears turn into prayer, something she hasn't done in a long time. God, let me see Zayd again, and Hamsa and Marc and Mother. Even Father, change the hearts of these men, these... these... boys, these kids, these kidnappers, to let me go, and if that isn't in the plans, then—but Hadeel can't go there, can't think of what she must do or ask for if she is not allowed her freedom.

The summer after Hamsa had been allowed to stay in Damascus with their grandparents, it was Hadeel's turn. Hamsa had protested, thrust himself onto a couch the last day and insisted he wasn't leaving.

"You had your opportunity," their mother said. "Now it's your sister's."

"But she doesn't even know how to ride a bike!"

"Neither did you when you came last year," Rasha said. "This year is Hadeel's time to learn."

Hadeel can't remember what persuaded Hamsa to get off his bum, but they got him out of the house and she had Elyas and Amena to herself.

"What shall we do today, *habibti*?" her grandmother asked when Hadeel's parents and Hamsa had gone. "Shall we start on dinner? I can show you how to make *shish barak*."

Hadeel nodded, though it wasn't what she'd hoped to do.

"Or we can go for a bike ride," Elyas said.

Hadeel squealed. "Yes, please! Teach me the way you did Hamsa."

"Of course, of course," Elyas said.

"And we can cook later, right?" Hadeel turned to ask her *jidd*.

"Yes, dear," Amena said.

Hadeel got up. "One second," she said, and she raced down the hallway to the bedroom. Five minutes later she returned with an inexpertly pinned headscarf over her hair. "*Jidd*, can you help me?" she asked.

"Whatever for, *habibti*?" Amena said. "Come here. You're too young to veil."

"But all my friends wear one in Abu Dhabi," Hadeel said.

"You're not in Abu Dhabi now. Come here."

Hadeel advanced and Amena unpinned the scarf. Hadeel's thick hair fell in jet waves to her shoulder blades. "Turn around. Give me your brush." One stroke at a time, Amena worked out knots. When she was done, Amena took her by the shoulders and turned her around. "Isn't your granddaughter beautiful?"

Elyas agreed. "My most beautiful granddaughter."

"*Jiddo*! I'm your *only* granddaughter!"

"Ah, yes, so you are." He smiled. And he kept smiling. Running alongside Hadeel as she weaved and teetered on the bike, wind blowing through her hair.

He was at her side, hand ready, when she finally balanced herself and biked steadily in the middle of the street. Fifty yards, sixty yards, then she stopped, turned. "You did it!" he said. And Hadeel was all smiles.

"Now let's turn around and go back to the house. We will show *Jidd*."

With Amena on the sidewalk, Elyas ran alongside again, but this time Hadeel looked over her shoulder. "Don't touch," she said. "Let me do it."

"You are doing it, *habibti*," he said.

But she looked one more time, tugged too hard to the left and lost her balance. Abraded shoulder, a tooth that pierced her upper lip. A small amount of bleeding. At the clinic, a few stitches.

"Did you see me, *Jidd*? Did you?"

"I saw you, Hadeel." Amena held a handkerchief to her granddaughter's lips.

"That was fun."

"Don't talk, dear. You'll only make it bleed more."

Hadeel doesn't even know who her tormentors are. Are they Daesh? Are they al-Nusra, Jund al-Aqsa or any of the hundred other rebel groups or assemblages of gun-toters with gripes against Assad? That these kids in the rooms on the other side of her door can't speak Arabic doesn't help identify them as a group. There are foreigners on both sides of the battle. From Jersey City or Calgary, teens have joined ISIS or the rebels either out of some perverse sense of jihad or glorification of Islam or the Prophet Muhammad, peace be upon him, or to defend Syria against the lunatics.

Behind the door, in their set of rooms, have they made a ransom call? *Who knows I'm here?*

Hadeel hears footsteps again and pulls herself up to standing. She straightens her hijab, wipes her fingers over her eyes and runs her hands over the front of her shirt. Another kid walks in. This one she hasn't seen before. She's about to ask where he's from, but his scowl silences her. He places a plate of rice and bread on the seat of the chair and a smudged glass of water on the ground next to the legs. Then he's out of the room.

The sound of exploding ordnance is louder. The thunder-peal nears. Not shake-the-building close, but nearby. Half a mile? In the city. She wishes she were better with direction. When the sun is low in the sky, she can tell whether it's east or west and that's pretty much it. Moving to Montreal for school hadn't helped. Everyone kept talking about Sherbrooke West and Ste-Catherine East and north side and south side of the island and none of these compass points had any basis in reality. In Montreal, the sun rose over the South Shore and set in Montreal North.

Hadeel pictures her Montreal family at the start of their day. Her grandparents have been up an hour already and have made breakfast. Some homemade *labneh* and a small dish of *fuul*, some scrambled eggs with *zataar*. Zayd would get Froot Loops. Rasha heads straight for the *dallah* on the stovetop and pours out a small cup of coffee for herself. They sit at a round table in the kitchen—or perhaps her mother has an island now, a nice, black granite-topped island, with white drawers that glide shut by themselves and a little wine fridge humming day and night to keep whites and reds at a stable fifteen degrees. Lord knows she's talked about getting an island forever. And the television is on and they watch *Daybreak* or CNN. No, they watch BBC to keep on top of world events, unaware of the events in the world of their own family. Ignorant of Hadeel's kidnapping and her wish—from the east or south—that tomorrow she'll see the sun rise.

She's met no one from CNN here. The BBC correspondent left the month before and Hadeel doesn't know when he'll be back. Journalists in Syria are an endangered species. There are one hundred and thirty-one fewer in their family of truth-seekers and chroniclers since the advent of the war. Hadeel could with no effort have been, or become, one of them. Hangings, beheadings, executions. Neither Daesh nor any of the rebel groups have a clean conscience regarding journalists though they make pretty good use of social media. Even their executions. Unfiltered.

"You're going to get shot," her father said, fat index finger pointed at her. "Or worse." His hand under his chin.

"My God, *Baba*, do you have to go there right off? I've had my safety training," Hadeel said. "They tell you how to report in conflict zones."

"Conflict zone? Is that what Syria is now?"

In a rare moment, Nadim had left his bedroom, which substituted as his office. He'd heard Hadeel and Hamsa in the living room and had come down to knock some sense into her thick head, he said.

So far, all he'd done was to antagonize and confirm in her the need to go. He'd said she didn't know anything about world affairs, or what was happening in Syria, or anything at all for that matter.

Hamsa had been quiet, the way he could get sometimes when their father criticized them. And it was only them. It was never Zayd, who was blameless. Or their mother, who had absented herself.

"At this training they teach you what exactly? How to wash after you've soiled yourself the first time you hear mortar fire?"

"You're not being helpful, Dad," Hamsa said, "and your sarcasm isn't advancing your cause. Listen, when I found out the paper was sending Hadeel, I consulted with the teachers of the hostile-environment workshop. Mercury and Mars, it's called, based in London, but the classes for reporters going to Iraq and Afghanistan and Syria were here in Abu Dhabi. Hadeel's getting the finest preparation for war outside of being a soldier herself. Risk-assessment, emergency first aid, rape prevention—"

"*La samah allah!*" Nadim said.

"Even how to encrypt stories and notes so she can communicate safely."

Hamsa stopped.

"Does that put you at ease?" asked Hadeel.

Their father snorted. "Look at the two of you. Out to save the world. One with a pen, one with a sword. You will both get yourselves killed."

Then he turned and walked back up the staircase to his bedroom. And Hadeel was left with her answers and her retorts—in short, her words—much the way she was every time she argued with her father. He had his opinion and none other mattered. His opinion was fact.

"I'm glad he cares so much," Hamsa said.

Hadeel punched her brother in the arm.

In her room, Hadeel finishes her rice with one last sweep of the plate with her bread. She chews with deliberation, draws out the repast as if it were the best meal in the best restaurant on the best date she's ever had. Then she washes it down with the water after wiping the rim of the glass with her shirttail. She pretends it's sweet and cold, as if it comes from a glacier in the north of Canada, though the water has a salty edge, is warm and has the chroma of diluted rust. She'll have diarrhea again in a couple of hours. She'll bang on the door and ask to be let out to the bathroom and the kids will argue among themselves about whose turn it is to get up and let her out of her cage to relieve herself. As if she were a dog, a female dog, and someone had to take the bitch outside for a walk.

If she ever gets out, there'll be two things she does first: kick Ibrahim Jibril-Otway in the nuts and tell Marc Dion she loves him. She should have listened to Marc. He was right. He's been around the world twenty times. He's covered Bosnia, been in Grozny and Gaza. And Aceh province, the tsunami. He knew about war and disaster and Hadeel should have put more faith in his advice. Instead, she had listened to Ibrahim, who, Marc says, was in fact Abe Otway, who'd taken on the Arab identity when he married Fairooz Jibril, a Palestinian raised in Jordan. He'd converted and learned the language—his accent is an abomination—and, as Marc said, Ibrahim had never stepped out in the field as a reporter. And by "field," Marc was generous. Ibrahim had never covered a city council meeting, never mind a coup or a war. The sole article Hadeel could find online that Ibrahim had ever written was a first-person piece about waxing ear hair. So how could he be running a newspaper?

Hadeel remembers hearing about the shouting match between Ibrahim and Marc. The whole newsroom had heard it even though the two men were in the editor's office with the door closed. Ibrahim had promoted the foreign editor to deputy editor of the paper a few months before and given Marc the desk to run until a permanent hire could be made. Marc had gone into Ibrahim's office asking for clarification: Was he in or was he out? And Ibrahim had, according to Marc, because no one had heard this part of the conversation, told him he was doing a lousy job in foreign. Marc lost his normal reserve somewhere between "are you" and "kidding me?" Everyone had heard "fucking," however. The argument escalated in volume, and descended in respect, from there, neither man willing to have his reputation questioned or besmirched. There was no doubt whose side most staffers fell on and no doubt as well who was boss.

A town hall meeting the next day put the matter to rest. "If anyone knows a good foreign editor, come speak to me," Ibrahim said. And Marc, on the phone at the time with the paper's reporter in Cairo, laid his forehead in his hands.

Hadeel called Marc from Bahrain after Maggie texted when it was over. She could tell he wanted to talk, so she let him. "You should have heard the shit he said to get me out here to work." Hadeel was this close to telling Marc to get his ass on a plane.

A week later, a former Jerusalem bureau chief for AFP was offered the job. But after talking to staffers, he rejected the offer. The environment seemed toxic, he told Marc.

"Ibrahim told him he wants someone who knows the region, someone who speaks Arabic," Marc confided to Hadeel. " 'Then why aren't you hiring Marc Dion? He's the best in the business,' the AFP guy said. To which Ibrahim answered, 'But he doesn't know the region.' "

"Listen to me," Hadeel said, when she called later. "If Ibrahim himself knew the region, he'd know any Arab editor would do exactly what you're doing. These stories Ibrahim keeps spiking are the very reason no Arab editor would work for him. Arabs are getting imprisoned for freedom of the press. Fuck that."

"Thanks for saying that, Hadeel."

"Should I say it again?"

"Sure," Marc said. "Once more with feeling."

"Fuck that," she repeated and Marc laughed.

"This will pass, *habibi*," she said. "His days are numbered."

In the end, Ibrahim hired from within, a kid from Perth who came over from the sports desk, and Marc went over to write editorials.

Hadeel asked why he didn't quit.

Marc said he couldn't. "Not now. Not in this way."

"I understand," she said.

He wasn't a vain man, but he had his pride. If he left now, he'd be conceding.

And that man, solid and proud—and handsome—is what she's looking forward to returning to. To hell if Marc's not Emirati or Muslim. Her mother, though Muslim, wasn't Emirati, yet her father had married her. Hadeel will return to Abu Dhabi and sit Marc down and tell him: "I know you love me. And you know I love you. So you stop being all bashful and worried about cultural impropriety and age differences and ask me, okay? I will marry you."

She smiles. She knows it will probably not happen that way, but wouldn't it be nice? He would look up and there'd be the hint of water in his sympathetic eyes, a soupçon of that Marc Dion gentleness, and she would move one step closer, take his face, with that scratchy midday beard, in her palms and say, "I want to share a life with you. I want to look up with you at a kind, blue sky with firm earth under our feet. I want to lie with you and wake up at dawn with you whispering in my ear. I want to bear and raise children—

we will name them Paul, Mariam and Martin—who will race into the kitchen after school each day, clambering over each other to get my attention to tell the story of their day, a piece of each one of those children reminding me of some fragment of you, Paul's black hair, Mariam's calico-brown eyes, the upturned corner of Martin's lip. Then you will come home and fill us all with some hilarious story of what happened at work." *Ta route est ma route.* "My life would be empty without you."

A scraping noise returns her to the present. But soon it turns quiet and Hadeel fills the void with daydream. Maybe there's somewhere she can dig a tunnel to. Wouldn't that be a tale? The flip side of the sad demise of Marie Colvin. It was Marc who introduced Hadeel to the American reporter's story. Though a piece of shrapnel had pierced Marie's left eye, she continued to report in war zones, wore her eye patch as a badge, like a soldier's combat medal. And now Hadeel's hero was dead. Killed by an IED, here in Syria.

Hadeel gets up with her plate and bangs on the door for someone to come and get it and allow her access to the bathroom. She has to knock several times. She hears shouts and whoops in the house and can't tell if it's from the kids or their computer. It takes a while, but someone comes and takes the plate from her.

In one of Hadeel's escape fantasies, she drops the plate, which shatters when the kid comes to the door. He slaps her with such force she falls and when she rises, she's got a shard in her hand she uses to slash the kid and take his gun from him. She shoots him and the rest of the little bastards when they barge into the room. Then she sprints down the street to a safe house. That's as far as Hadeel's imagination carries her. She doesn't know where she is in the city. If she is in the old part of the city, there are passages between the low-rises and narrow back streets to duck into, the teeming hive of the *souq* to take advantage of, where every sort of person congregates. A mosque or a church to hide in. Sanctuary. She could just as easily be on the urban fringe, however, beyond the gates, away from the city centre, in one of the massive, isolated apartment blocks that form sectarian ghettos. There aren't distinctive noises, like the sound of planes, which would indicate the airport, or sirens suggesting a nearby police station, no light to seep into her room through the cracks between the boards covering the one window. Hadeel doesn't know of any safe houses either. What can be safe when Assad targets hospitals and the Russians use bunker bombs to destroy underground clinics? If the kids were Daesh, she might be near or even in the Yarmouk Palestinian camp by Al-Orouba. But she's been inside here long enough her news might be old. Maybe Daesh no longer controls this area.

"I have to use the bathroom," Hadeel says.

"You know where it is," he says.

At the other end of the hall, she sees a laptop on the kitchen table. On the screen are a couple of men in orange jumpsuits and someone dressed in a black, ninja-style outfit with a black mask. The way he holds a large knife and thrusts the hand out and back, he is declaiming something.

The kid who'd responded to her knock rinses her plate and then sits at the table, having passed in her path of vision. He notices Hadeel and says, "What're you looking at?"

"Nothing," she says promptly.

"You're next, you know," he says and laughs.

Hadeel hurries into the bathroom. She wishes she could lock the door behind her, but there isn't a lock on this door, not even a knob. Not like the bedroom door, which is locked from the outside, like maids' and nannies' bedrooms in Gulf villas and apartments.

None of the kids has ever said that to Hadeel before: You're next. For the first time since coming to Syria to cover the war, she thinks she might not get out of this alive. She will die as Marie Colvin died. But would they kill her just like that—no negotiation with the government in Abu Dhabi, no ransom demand? Don't they parade you in front of a television camera and make you read a statement? Take a photograph of you like a kidnapped aid worker holding a newspaper so everyone can verify the date of the video? Hadeel's been here for weeks. They took her phone, took her passport. She doesn't know if they've made contact with anyone in Abu Dhabi. Worse, she still doesn't know their intentions.

Hadeel wipes herself, then tears off more toilet paper and wipes her eyes and blows her nose. A glance at the leg, healed by time. She flushes and washes her hands, her face. She feels dirty. It's been weeks since she showered. She's allowed five minutes in the bathroom with a facecloth every three days. She stinks.

"You've been in there long enough," says a voice from the other side of the door.

Where's a plate to break when you need one?

"I'm sick," Hadeel says.

"You're better," the voice says.

You're next. Such bullshit.

They're playing, trying to unhinge her. She's heard stories like this from Marc. Sometimes he's elusive on what he's seen. Talks about what he experienced, but in the third person, as if it happened to someone else. Like the guy he worked with at the *Journal* who was taken out twice in front of an execution squad, his passport taken, spat on, rubbed underfoot in dirt. Pissed his pants one time, vomited the next, and twice was allowed to live. It's a form of torture no less effective in inducing psychological stress than waterboarding, Marc said.

She opens the door and is thrust back by the kid in the hallway. He's got his hand over her mouth and has yanked off her hijab to better grasp her hair to pull her head back. He's behind her and she glances in the mirror, where she sees a man in a black uniform like the ones she saw live on the computer. He marches her out the door and out the hallway, past the kitchen and out of the house into sunlight so bright she forces her eyes shut.

Hadeel knows not to panic, but her pulse is rapid and her breathing shallow. She tries to calm herself. She takes deep breaths. The guy pricks her with what she thinks is the tip of a knife. They're headed for a car. The motor's running and the exhaust chokes with grey smoke. Another man, also in black ninja-wear, opens the rear door and her captor shoves her into the back. He throws the hijab in behind her. "You're indecent," he says. "Cover yourself, you *jahiliyyah* whore."

When the car has left and Hadeel's hijab is secure, she scans the neighbourhood, but nothing about the place is familiar. She knows this is not unusual. Nothing in Damascus or Aleppo or Homs is as it was. She forces herself to believe her family's traditional place up in the mountains might be the one place in all Syria that has withstood the devastation wreaked by Assad, the rebels, the caliphate. She has to believe this. There has to be a safe place, somewhere she can go. Somewhere she can smell jasmine. Sweet, calming, nighttime jasmine. Marc once told her that when under threat, he would imagine his brother's restaurant in Montreal.

They pass a Catholic church. The stained-glass windows are gone, concussed, the Palladian frames splintered. The driver and the other man have taken off their masks. They do not look familiar. A man outside a four-storey building shaved of its façade sits in a halved barrel full of water, trying to scrub his back. Water soaks into the dirt outside the tub.

The car stops. The driver opens the window and a man in a dust-covered black and green uniform of some type approaches. She can't tell what rebel group he might be part of—they have no insignia of any kind—but he's not a police officer or Assad government soldier. He exchanges greetings with the driver, who speaks better Arabic than the kids who've kept her captive. The uniformed guy scans inside the car, looks at Hadeel.

"What are you?" he asks.

She doesn't understand the question. Is he asking what she does or is he asking about her nationality? Hadeel looks at the driver, at the kid with the knife. How do they want her to respond? How she answers a question can mean the difference between her life and her death. Perhaps their life and death.

She decides to go with the truth. Could be he's on the right side of this conflict. If so, he can help. If she can plead with him in some way.

"I'm a journalist," she goes with. "I work for *Abu Dhabi World.* I have no quarrel with anyone here. I am an observer. I—"

"Shut up," he says. "What are you? Show me your papers."

"I have no passport," Hadeel says. "They took it." She nods toward the front seat, even though she's not sure who among the kids had taken it and in whose possession it might be.

"Emirati," the guy in the passenger seat says.

The uniform nods.

"Why are you alone with two men? Are you a prostitute?"

The question deflates her. He will be of no help.

The man looks away, distracted by a noise down the street, then his attention returns.

"I told you," says Hadeel. "I'm a reporter."

"You talk too much," he says. "Go," he says.

As the three drive away, she hears the staccato pulse of automatic weapon fire and she falls into a fetal position in the space between the front and back seats. The two in the front laugh. She squats, looks in the rear-view mirror and sees the driver grin. He lacks a canine tooth. The others near it are stained, by tea perhaps, by smoke probably, by poor care definitely. She decides she's safer crouched between the seats.

What am I? Whatever you are, Arab or foreigner, it is identity that keeps one alive. But who you are could also undo you. The Emiratis have been part of the U.S. coalition. If Hadeel's captors were fighting with the caliphate, her being Emirati could be her death warrant.

Because here and now you are as much who you are as who others believe you are.

Still, answering that she's a journalist feels right. What she does is what she is. The storyteller tells stories. And if this last story is to be told, Hadeel must stay alive. Who will tell it otherwise? The toothless driver? The black-clad kid in the passenger seat? Misguided, rudderless kids swayed by self-serving, cruel and clueless fanatics. The passenger wraps his arm around the back of the driver's seat, peeks at her between the seats. Laughing.

As they drive, Hadeel can see from her protected position there are fewer multi-storey apartment buildings. The odd shop is open on the first floor of the remaining blocks. There's a strip of stores, a tiny *souq*, a mosque, an internet café. She must empty her mind of worry. She returns in her mind to the room she's been captive in and the lists she compiled to keep herself sane and alive, during these Scheherazade days and nights of captivity.

Hadeel feels the bomb in her ribs before she hears it.

For less than a moment, the dusty city road they're driving down is bathed in intense yellow-white light. All colour disappears in the wash.

Then the light gives way to deafening noise, a thunderous force so positive it seems to push out the light, to occupy the space the light once had occupied, as if the light has become a vacuum, a hole, a negative.

Air pressure drops.

Then silence. Then black. And then smoke, acrid and choking.

Hadeel lies face down in the car. What feels like an incredible weight on her back keeps her from rising. She feels her head, her face, her shoulders, looks at her hands. They are bloody. The back of her shirt is wet. She lifts her head. A dreamlike pillow of black smoke rises in the sky. She coughs but can't hear it. There's movement in the front seat. She attempts to sit. Whatever was on her back slides off in a puddle. Hadeel shrieks. It's an arm. It's the passenger's. She flashes back to moments before the blast. The rat-a-tat of the gun and her ducking into the crevice between the seats and the two of them laughing in front. The kid relaxing in the front seat with his arm draped around the back of the driver's seat as if they're going to the drive-in.

With care, she looks up from the seat. Then back down. Up, then down again. Each time she scopes a different area. No telegraph of further danger. She tries not to sit in the man's blood, looks around her inside the car. Her head feels thick and her ears are stopped up.

Hadeel slides to the door and opens it. She gets out of the car and enters the pandemonium of the street. People running, others gathering around what had been the centre of the blast. Was it a car? Was it a barrel bomb? She hadn't heard any planes beforehand. But then she wasn't paying attention as she should have been. She pulls open the driver's door. The driver looks up. Where his jaw should be is a yawning hole. Hadeel pulls on the front of his shirt and yanks him out of the car. He's heavier than he looks and it takes several tugs to move him. Finally, he's on the ground, and she's tempted to drive the heel of her boot into what remains of his face. Instead, she steps around, says a short *dua*: "Allah, forgive him, make him among the guided ones, raise his status and be his deputy among the grieving." *You shit.*

On the other side, the kid who'd grabbed her in the bathroom and forced her into the car doesn't move either. It's his arm that was torn off and fell on her. She pulls him out too, he's even heavier and more lifeless than the driver, and when he's flat on his back in the dust of the road she notices something small and black in his waistband, a handgun. She pulls it out and tosses it in the foot well. She finds the knife he'd used on her and puts it in the car too. She thinks she can use the car to leave, but then realizes the car is still in gear. She pulls the keys out of the ignition and goes to the trunk, where she finds a backpack and bottles of water. There's a camera bag as well and a video camera in it. Had they planned to videotape her? Or was this a more elaborate way to say "you're next?"

Hadeel opens the pack, throws in the water, then returns to the front to retrieve the knife and the gun. In the pack she finds a rudimentary first-aid kit, some clothes, sunflower seeds, her passport. Looking around her, through the commotion, the confusion, Hadeel thinks she can get away with removing her bloodied shirt and changing into the one in the backpack. She slips into the back seat and wipes herself clean. She gives herself another quick scan, feels around, seems to be okay. She pours a touch of water onto her old shirt and wipes her face of tears and plaster-white dust. Then Hadeel walks out with the backpack and camera into the one thousand and one stories she hopes to tell.

She hears crying up the street. It's a baby in a navy-blue stroller. Kneeling in front of the stroller, a woman, not much older than herself, hijab slipping to her shoulders, jacket open, jeans torn at the knees. Reaching in to comfort the baby with her left hand. The right wrist bent at a wrong angle. Blood is dripping from the baby's ear.

One man's body hisses. It is wrapped in a blue gassy flame. In the man's charred hand, a newspaper turned to a thick, rolled wad of ash.

One siren after another pierces the mayhem, demanding attention for a short while. The sound stops Hadeel. When had she started to hear again?

A body, curling wisps of grey smoke emanating from beneath a quilt someone had already placed atop it.

A man on his knees vomiting by the curb in front of a building. All is covered in a thin white film.

Shouting. For help. To help. "*Allahu akbar!*" Prayers and cries.

A bullhorn, from somewhere. "Please remain calm. Please do not form large groups. Please remain calm. Emergency personnel are on their way."

Hadeel walks. A half-hour, an hour. Through one indistinct city district after another. She undoes her veil, lets her hair fall over her back and shoulders, puts the scarf back on loosely, as she does when she's in Montreal. A western look. The sun is almost overhead. In navigational terms, that must mean something. Hadeel knows, though, that if she walks and keeps walking, she'll make it to another neighbourhood, one that will stand out for being unlike all the others, where there wasn't a bombing at noon on this particular day, where there wasn't a journalist held hostage for almost six weeks by a bunch of misguided, wannabe terrorists, where a girl might get a good bowl of poutine.

III

"Would you like to talk about the birds, Marc? What was that all about? Marc?"

■ ■ ■

Marc had told them no. No interest in a Middle East comeback tour. Mentor/editor-at-large. Make your own hours. No, no and no. Abu Dhabi isn't what you think, they'd said. You don't know what I think. It's not Dubai, they'd said. Yeah, well, neither is Beirut.

He hated conference calls. Always an answer misheard, a word dropped. Sounded like talking underwater. No interest in a correspondent job either. He was through. But Ibrahim was impervious to argument. Soon as we can. We know it's what you want. We've gotta show the world what we can do here. We're gonna be the *New York*

Times of the Middle East. We want you to be a part of it. We know what you're good at, you know the region, pick of assignments blah blah blah burr burr burr. That was so Ibrahim to be using "we." Marc stopped answering his emails. He started screening his calls.

And then he got a call from Pierre in Montreal. Their mother had died and Marc did what everyone tells you not to do when someone close has died. He made a snap decision. His brother asked if moving so close to Iraq was the smartest thing, you know, considering what happened. His old editor at the *Post*, Jay, asked if moving to the Arab Gulf was the wisest thing, you know, considering what happened. His old girlfriend, Mireille, told him he was nuts. Marc said he'd been over all the pros and cons with Dr. Abramson. Pros and cons for leaving, pros and cons for staying. "Very Jesuitical, for a Jewish Montreal psychiatrist." The doctor discouraged him, but Marc thought he could handle it with the right meds, if he avoided stressful situations, kept in regular contact with Abramson, attended meetings, found a reliable sponsor.

The cottage in Nova Scotia was easy enough to unload. A couple from Boston paid handsomely for it. Said what sold them was the ocean view. Marc also found an agent who for a small sum said he'd rent and manage the apartment in Georgetown. You'd make good money if you sold, he'd admitted, but Marc wanted a place to come back to should the "*New York Times* of the Middle East" turn into an advertising supplement.

He hadn't planned to fall in love.

"I see you met my grandfather," she said.

It was about ten on a Sunday morning in November and staff were starting to pad, shuffle and roll into the newsroom. The teaboys waited by the kitchen like Bengal tigers. The translators had been in for an hour scanning the Arab news websites. Maggie Qassem was on rotation as the assignment editor and reading the competition, alternately swearing because her team had missed something or laughing at some boneheaded mistake.

The *World* had that weekend launched its U.S.-style Sunday edition: sections that included travel, auto and real estate plus a weekly style magazine and a book review, not as big or fat with ads as the *Times*, so Marc had no worry the paper would turn into a shopper. The opposite might be true though, and the "*New York Times* of the Middle East" could die of starvation. One year on, it hadn't happened yet. Someone had deep pockets. For the inaugural edition of the Sunday paper, Marc had persuaded Ibrahim to allow him to write a monthly oral history, in which he interviewed at length someone in the region who had lived through a momentous occasion, had a different perspective on a well-known time in history or had an interesting story to tell. The series was called "Nasib," a word meaning "fate" or "destiny" in languages from Arabic to Malay. Marc said he imagined an aged storyteller walking in from the desert who crouches down over a bed of coals and tells a story about Bedouins who'd passed by there a hundred years ago or points out an old building and talks about the people who'd pitched a tent on that very spot during the search for oil. Where we are today marked in the ash. As if the present had been forecast. The first Nasib segment had been an interview with Rasul bin Bashir Al Ghurair al Rimali, a ninety-some-odd-year-old Emirati whose grandfather was born in the eighteenth century. Three generations of one family, spread over four centuries. Marc hadn't thought it possible until he did the math.

"He's something else, your grandfather," Marc said and spun away from his keyboard to look at her. "Loves to talk."

"Grandfather Rasul has a story for every occasion," she said and removed the *sheyla* from over her head and face. Her hair, thick and black, she kept pinned in the back. She wore no makeup, simply a touch of gloss on her lips. She stood about four inches shorter than he, so five-five. Slender, hundred ten. And cute. Late-twenties, thirty at the outmost, he thought. Stop. Stop. She stepped forward half a foot and reached out her hand in a most un-Emirati female way. "I'm Hadeel al Rimali, by the way."

Marc hesitated for a second, then stood up and shook her hand. Firm, confident handshake. "Always nice to match a byline with a face."

Hadeel laughed, and tucked the veil in her handbag. "I'll never get used to this. It's one thing to be outside in public, but inside I can barely see my screen."

Now it was Marc's turn to chuckle. He liked her direct manner. He tried to place where she'd learned English and picked North America. He turned it professional. "That's some good work you're doing. The scoop on the corruption behind START University was stellar. Frankly, sometimes I wonder how you get away with it. Particularly a story like that. Ashok Sengupta was like Midas around here."

"The family name doesn't hurt, if that's what you mean," Hadeel said. She reached into her handbag again and brought out a bottle of water.

"No, no," Marc said, shaking his head and waving a hand. "Look, we all use whatever connections we have. I'm a bit surprised, you know, given your family name, you haven't gotten into any hot water. You've uncovered shit, excuse me—"

"It's all right," said Hadeel.

"—that the rulers believe doesn't smell."

Hadeel smiled. "We're in the honeymoon phase," she said. "The rulers wanted a western-style newspaper to show the U.A.E. has western-style freedoms—you know, to attract western investment—but they'll start to grow tired of living under the magnifying glass. I give it a year."

Marc nodded, heard the sarcasm. "And then?"

Hadeel finished a sip. Shrugged. "I don't know," she said. "You have a Plan B?"

■ ■ ■

"It wasn't the war, whatever war it was. It was the people. I needed to… well, obviously, I needed to get close to the front, to the action, to be able to get the story, but to *tell* the story—you see the difference, right? there's a difference—I needed to… it wasn't just about the fighting. It's about the men doing the fighting, the women and children *living* through the fighting. They're the story. The analysis, the politics, the big-picture stuff? I could do that from the hotel room. But the magnum opus weekend newspaper shit, the heart beating in the chest, the tears burning down cheeks, I couldn't do that if I wasn't at the front line, if I didn't put myself on the line like those people."

■ ■ ■

Marc had drifted into war journalism. Over his mother's objections, he took a gap year after university and it, he was fond of saying, "never ended." Thumbed and hashished his way around Morocco with a translation of *The Sheltering Sky* in his backpack. Wrote long letters home that his mother, a professor of Quebec culture at the Université de Montréal, edited and submitted to *La Presse*. They weren't travel pieces, they weren't news. They ended up on the opinion page. The remuneration was abysmal, but North Africa was cheap then. If you fell in with the right bunch of guys you could have a couch to crash on, or you could head out in the sands between towns and no one would bother you. And the food, well, the food was worth writing home about, so he did that too.

What pushed Marc onto the news pages was the student unrest, the "black riots," in Algiers in 1988. Marc had been in Algeria for several months before the demonstrations began in early October. He'd written home about the out-of-work kids his age he saw on the streets and how expensive produce and spices were in the *souqs*. The youths' complaints felt familiar to Marc. The political uncertainty which had followed the separatists' election in Quebec a dozen years before had undermined the provincial economy. Montreal went from economic power station of Canada to half-vacant warehouse in less than four years. It would take until the 1990s before Nortel and Bombardier became the backbone of the high-tech and aerospace industries and many years afterward before Montreal became a centre of gaming and pharmaceuticals. What Marc heard and saw on the streets of Algiers would be understood by people back home.

The letters and these first attempts at newswriting became the hallmark of Marc Dion's journalism. On the street, in the markets and public squares, on the ground floors and rooftops of the cities and villages, he'd talk with anyone who would talk to him and wrote their stories in ways that resonated with people. At first, he talked with anyone who'd talk to a sweet French-Canadian twenty-something who refused to switch to French or English so he could practise his Arabic. As his Arabic improved and his storywriting transformed into reporting, his list of sources expanded from vendors, floor-washers and soldiers to generals, executives and presidents. What Marc found in common among all of them was they all had something to say, each tale as distinct as the individual who told it, each story with its own DNA.

From Algeria he crossed the Maghreb into Egypt. The first intifada had begun in Israel, but Marc was refused entry because of the stamps from Arab countries in his passport. He skirted Israel by boat over the Mediterranean from Alexandria to Cyprus and then on to Turkey. When he thinks about then, it is without regret. He could have pushed more perhaps. Tried again with a new passport. Truth was, it also scared him. Over time that changed. And now... but there is no "now," is there? His sponsor and friend from his twelve-step program, Christopher, suggested Portugal. So here Marc is, in Lisbon. It's supposed to be his vacation. He hasn't made up his mind about whether to return to Abu Dhabi.

When Marc Dion was at the height of his game, a regular contributor to *La Presse* and *The Washington Post*, he relied on the instinct of experience and a network of friends in hotspots around the world. He wasn't so jaded as to believe there was never anything new, but just cynical enough, on a (multiple cliché warning) quiet night in a smoky bar in a bullet-pocked hotel in some hole-in-the-ground city in a war-torn country, he could always say, "What's up in Israel?"

Marc's base in Turkey wasn't far from Taksim Square. "You know, where all the protests are," he would tell people. And they'd nod, vacant looks in their eyes. To anyone who'd spent any time in Istanbul he'd say he was near the Besiktas stadium and the university, crunched between students on weekdays and football fanatics on weekends. Closer to downtown, he met correspondents not unlike himself, though more seasoned. It was a pattern he came to find in every corner of the world. Conflict, hotel, bar. Many of the writers knew each other, "served" with each other, shared sources and cabs, borrowed sat-phone time and dodged bullets. War stories got told at these bars. Grousing, griping, brotherly sniping. There was a social contract, an unspoken rule you didn't boast about where you'd been or what you'd seen, except in the most general terms. But you couldn't control what was said when you weren't there. And sometimes the novices, they'd shoot their mouths off before noticing the bar around them had grown quiet, a silence akin to reflection, though often it was an alcohol-induced avoidance of the serious shit. Voices, faces, faraway places. And the reporters all sighed and knocked back a shot.

Marc lingered in Istanbul for a few months, used it as a base for sporadic travel into Europe and the Gulf, until his editor at *La Presse* said he wouldn't take more columns about Turkey, Greece and Bulgaria—*chus tanné, câlice*—and besides, didn't he know the Soviet Union was breaking up? Why didn't he make his way to one of the republics?

In April 1989, Marc stood in the middle of Rustaveli Boulevard in Tbilisi watching a peaceful protest of Georgians—they numbered in the thousands—in front of the Supreme Soviet. It had started days before with a hunger strike by university students demanding changes to the constitution and Georgian independence from the U.S.S.R., whose teetering could be felt throughout the republics. Marc knew no Georgian and had picked up only a few handy words of Russian, but when the priest stood on the steps of the parliamentary building and began a call-and-response prayer, Marc recognized the rhythms of "Notre Père" and, despite himself, whispered along.

"You pray in French," said a woman standing at his side. She looked at his notebook. "And you write in French too."

Embarrassed, he identified himself. "Guilty. French-Canadian and Catholic… though I don't often find myself praying in the street."

"Neither do I," she said. "But," she cast an arm about, indicating the crowd, "lately…"

Her hair was black, spikey. She wore a black leather jacket, black jeans and black, low-heeled boots. She introduced herself as Tamara, then took his pen and notebook to write down her last name. "It is long and hard to pronounce." She smiled. "If you are not Georgian." She said she was a linguist at Tbilisi University down the street, but Marc didn't believe her. She looked no older than he. "And you look too young to be a foreign journalist," she said.

"Well, I'd hardly," he began, then dropped it with a smile.

Tamara interpreted for Marc for the rest of the night. But when dawn came around—after the Georgian Orthodox priest had called "Stand up! Lift your souls!" and the people had shouted "Long live Georgia!" and after the armoured personnel carriers thundered down the thinly treed *prospekt*, rolled up on the sidewalk and virgin-faced Soviet soldiers stumbled out with tear-gas canisters and automatic weapons, after twenty unarmed demonstrators were counted dead and four thousand people were injured—Marc couldn't find Tamara anywhere. They had been separated in the tumult. He searched near the gymnasium school, in front of the Kashueti Church, down toward the sulfur baths and as far up Rustaveli as the Philharmonic. He had no phone number, no address. The university was closed. Marc filed his story, one of the few western newspapers to have a reporter on the ground. The Soviet ambassador in Ottawa raised a stink, and submitted a copy of the official Kremlin report to *La Presse* to "prove" the wounds had not been inflicted by Soviet troops.

Marc hung around Tbilisi, drinking wine from the nearby Telavi vineyards and eating *khachapuri* cheese-bread and steaming bowls of deeply seasoned dark beans called *lobio*. He was proud to learn to go heavy with black pepper on his *khinkali* the way the Georgians did. He never found Tamara. Perhaps she was among the dead. The morgue had refused him entry. Then the uprising started in South Ossetia and Marc travelled north into the Caucasian foothills and then the uprising started in Abkhazia and Marc edged along the southern perimeter of the mountains west to the Black Sea coast, parked himself in Sukhumi and filed to *La Presse* and U.S. papers taking freelance copy.

The Soviet Union was falling apart. Conflict, it turned out, was exciting.

■ ■ ■

Marc lands, collects the key to the apartment rental facing the river in Lisbon and sets out to get his bearings. He's always done it this way. A nap to try to make up for lost sleep on a plane never works. New city, new placeline, new conflict, new story, new buzz. Jacked up on dopamine and coffee, out came the laptop and the notebook and he was lining up fixers or contacts and sources. Who had time to sleep? It's no different today, even when he's no longer the correspondent, the war journalist.

He leaves his luggage in the living room of the apartment on 24 de Julho avenue in the Cais do Sodré, grabs his camera and the city map Christopher gave him, and heads into the bright Lisboeta afternoon. First, a half-chicken with *piri-piri* sauce and fries and a bottle of carbonated water in the Mercado. Flights make him hungry. He refuses to pay for the food in economy and the paper was too cheap to provide him with a business seat for his annual leave. He didn't mention he has no definite plans to return. They couldn't just give him the foreign desk. And with Hadeel gone to Syria, what was the point?

Ibrahim never flies economy, he bets. Before the publication of the salary list on Wikileaks, Hadeel confided to Marc she'd heard through friends in the parent company what the editor-in-chief, Oliver Townley, made. Six hundred grand a year U.S. and that didn't include the villa, the car (with driver), the other car (no driver), private school education in Europe for his three smarty-pants brats, an entertainment budget and flights home twice a year.

"And an enormous discount on Aussie wine at African and Eastern," she added by way of punctuation.

"His booze account is separate from his entertainment budget?" Marc whistled. "Shit. I don't want to know what else the entertainment budget can include."

"I know," Hadeel said. She took a sip of juice from her cup.

"You know?"

Hadeel laughed. "No, no. I meant I understood what you mean. Alcohol is usually what people mean by entertainment around here."

"Karaoke, maybe?" Marc said. They were outside at the picnic table for lunch. Full view. No one could accuse them of impropriety.

He paused, pulled the paper wrapper down so he could take another bite of his falafel sandwich. They were three dirhams a piece when he'd started. A year later a basic one cost four dirhams, the equivalent of about a buck ten, one cheap sandwich.

"Did I ever tell you the time I bought Oliver a falafel sandwich?"

Hadeel shook her head.

"He'd never had one before."

"What?!"

"Yeah, yeah, it's true. Oliver Friggin' Townley, Mr. Fleet Street, had never had a falafel. Christopher and I went around the corner and came back with a couple. Oliver'd offered to pay and of course I said no. You offer to buy someone a coffee or a sandwich you don't accept money. He enjoyed it, I mean I never saw him eat another one, but he said he liked it. And of course, now we know how much he's making… that falafel sandwich. A little annoying. He could buy the restaurant itself with two-three months' salary."

Marc sighed. Sipped his water. "Christopher said he wished he'd choked on the hot sauce."

"You're funny," Hadeel said and stood up to leave. She fixed the *sheyla* in place. "Gotta make myself invisible again."

"You are so *not* invisible," Marc said.

Hadeel faced him with her full black veil. "I'm smiling under here," she said.

"I know," Marc said.

"You *do*?"

"Yup," he said. "I can see you."

"I'll let you in on a secret." Hadeel brushed her hand on his forearm for the tiniest fraction of a second as she was picking up her paper lunchbag. "I can see you too," she said, and then *"Ciao,"* as if they were in Montreal.

Marc watched the diaphanous black figure float away. Light moving back into the shadows.

I have to stop, he thinks. Have to stop letting her go.

So why have I put an ocean between us?

Because.

Because why?

You know the reasons why.

■ ■ ■

Marc finds himself winded. He stops on a tiny bridge on the Rua do Alécrim and looks onto the street below. Tiny cars bounce over cobbles. Tiny cafés with tiny black iron tables, tiny chairs. Tiny waitresses serve tiny cups of espresso and tiny glasses of port. Looking down the street from where he came, Marc can make out the River Tajo. A few subway stops down and he'd be at the mouth of the river and on the Atlantic. What dreamers the early explorers must have been to believe something else was out there. Or maybe they didn't believe. They took a gamble. Mireille, his ex, asked him once, "What do you expect to find out there?" Carry-on packed, ticket in hand, he'd kissed her and said he didn't know.

Marc takes a large lungful of air, looks up the steep hill and sighs. He's no longer in wartime shape. The years of desk jobs and meds have taken their toll. A tile place on the left and the familiar, Arabic feel of it catches his eye. Marc ducks in for a moment, to look. The place is chock-full of mosaics similar in style to ones he'd seen when he'd started on his never-ending gap year. The Arab influence is in part what attracted Marc to Portugal and, before, to Spain—along with Christopher's recommendation. Christopher's from Goa, a de Souza, a popular enough name in that part of India. He's worked in the Gulf for ten years, always at English newspapers, which proliferate because of the expatriates. He's a steady hand on the desk, and, like Marc, he hasn't touched a drop in many years. When they're together, Christopher doesn't pester him with war questions like others do. He's heard enough in meetings, knows it's not a subject to broach casually and Marc appreciates that. Instead, they talk cricket, the Catholic Church, and Indian politics, the kind of subjects people always tell you not to talk about. Christopher teaches Marc some Konkani phrases in exchange for French. They play chess. They cook. They're never bored. They are the last person each texts every night. Always the same thing. A list. Three things that day for which they are grateful. Christopher believes it helps him stay sober. Attitude of gratitude, he calls it. Marc thinks Christopher's list tonight will include gratitude for Marc finally listening to him about taking a holiday. He can tell Christopher envies the hell out of him now. But the desk couldn't spare him. Marc was relieved in a way. The type of thinking he needed to do was best done alone. Even if alone meant catching his breath in a musty tile shop on a hilly street in central Lisbon.

Roosters everywhere. Every souvenir shop selling postcards, key chains and coffee mugs displays a preening, puffy-chested, resplendent cock. Absently, Marc flips through tiles with pastoral scenes, shepherds and their sheep, religious scenes, blue on white, blue on blue. Broken ones, chipped ones, are under five euros, stacked in a torn cardboard box, like vinyls in a used-record store. Marc smiles at the man behind the counter, balding, glasses, slight paunch, not much older than himself. He fingers a chipped, painted tile. Six inches long by half that wide. Gold filigree and baby blue flowers. Hadeel will love it.

What is my *Plan B*? If the paper folds—ads and subscriptions are one-quarter of what was hoped for by this point—and he doesn't find work in Canada or the U.S., does he go the international route? Another risk. Maybe he plops down somewhere in the eurozone and opens a shop selling old maps and oceanographic charts. Maybe tiles.

He pays the shopkeeper. "*Bom dia*," he says and exits. He holds the door open for an older tourist couple. "Oh, honey, look at the rooster," the woman says.

An anonymous mass of people, most of them probably Portuguese, even though it's mid-afternoon on a Monday in late April. Rua Garrett begins in a wide pedestrian area that reminds Marc of Place Jacques-Cartier in Old Montreal though it could be Campo Santa Margherita or Union Square Park. He scans the square and glides in. Waiters hustle between the cafés and restaurants and their outdoor setups. People bake in the heat despite being under patio umbrellas. The *pasteis* look wonderful, the custard slightly torched, the crust flaky. A man in silver body paint dressed like the Statue of Liberty poses motionless until a girl of about three with a balloon tied around a wrist takes a euro coin from her father and drops it on the felt mat in front. The statue winks, the girl shrieks and throws her hands in front of her face and the balloon jumps up and down on its string. The scene is all on video and tonight will probably make its way around the world via social media. Marc hears "El Condor Pasa" on the panpipes. If he were to walk down the street in the direction of the sound, he would probably find the same Peruvian musicians he's heard on every public square or piazza in Montreal and Venice and New York. The absurdity and the truth of this amuse him. We're attracted to the same. We find comfort in the same. What separates us are the details.

Marc couldn't have come to these conclusions when he'd left for Abu Dhabi two years before. He's different today. Hadeel's made the difference.

A loud pop. Marc flinches. A screech pierces the air. Marc turns. It's the little girl. Her balloon has popped. She's crying and her father picks her up and takes her to the Statue of Liberty, who must be doing something funny because the girl is laughing again.

Rua Garrett T-bones with a street Marc can't find the name for on his map. He's got a choice between up or down. Uphill, he can see yet another square a hundred metres away. Downhill, he doesn't know whether he'd have to walk back up to return to the apartment. It's up, or it's down. He goes up.

In the square a short woman serves beer and wine from a green hexagonal kiosk while people sit at bistro tables and chairs. On the grass, on steps and along a stone wall, people chat and smoke and text and drink and laugh. Squirrels, dogs, cats, birds. It's all so normal. Don't they know there's a war on? As Marc makes his way through the crowd, he can't fathom what has brought all these people out on a Monday. Is the economy so bad this many people are out of work? How can they afford to be out? Across from the square rise the ruins of a Carmelite convent. He descends the steps and checks the door, but it's locked. Next door, however, a line of people waits. Ruins here are like ruins elsewhere—other than scale, the Roman columns of the old temple at Evora aren't all so different from those at Baalbek or Byblos. And sadly, not so different from the new ones ISIS has made of Palmyra. But sometimes, local history provides a bit of context, so Marc gets in line behind the others. Let's see about these Carmelites.

Except this isn't the site of the ruins at all, he discovers once in. First, there's the free admission. Don't ruins need upkeep? Second are the guards at the door, both armed. Not the typical dress of a docent. But he's now inside and decides to continue. It is free, after all; Marc will not be the first journalist in the world to pass up such a freebie. Soon it's evident he's entered the museum of the Portuguese national guard. The first placard reminds museum-goers that on April 25, 1973, the army brought about the downfall of the authoritarian Estado Novo and installed a socialist government. The coup had started out as a military one, but soon became a people's revolution. Like dictators everywhere, the rulers must have been surprised by the widespread disgust and distrust. Everyone came out then, and everyone's out today. It's a national holiday. The museum's free for the same reason. Party on, then. Marc joins the people streaming around the exhibits.

But the crowd shuffle like dutiful jurors. It might be the one museum in the world where people read every single word on the cards describing the archival photographs and various artifacts, uniform shirts and jackets, hats, ornamental swords, boots, gloves and belts, and guns which, after a while, begin to blur. The crowd breathes and sweats and moves in unison. The room is warmer. The air smells of garlic and fish and wine. Marc tugs at his collar. He seeks a chair, a bench, anything to sit on for a second, catch his breath. Maybe he shouldn't have come out so soon after landing. Maybe he should have taken a nap. He's not the man he used to be. He's not a twenty-three-year-old in Marrakech. He's forty-five now, and he's been around the world and he's seen shit no one should have to see, and now he's in a museum in Lisbon where the pop of a balloon reverberates in his head and Marc feels sweat run down his back. He's in front of a Plexiglas display and trying to breathe, but then finds himself back outside on Rua Garrett where the diners are talking over the music and over each other and all of it's bull and the Peruvians can't play worth shit and the girl, if she can't watch her fucking balloon she shouldn't have one, and Marc tells himself to breathe and to breathe again and to count and breathe to five, to ten if he can make it, and tells himself, it's okay, it's a balloon, they pop, life goes on. But it isn't working. This isn't Rua Garrett at all. It's Baghdad and the pop is the one he hears in his dreams, only ever in his dreams, only ever imagined because he'd never heard it in reality; it's the one he talks about with Dr. Abramson. "One minute everything was fine, you know, relatively, and then, we weren't, and… she… she…"

Marc jerks to cut the queue and push ahead, but he's blocked by someone in a wheelchair. So he turns and tries to exit the way he came in, but the river of people entering the room is a tide against which he's unable to swim. He's an overturned surfer rolling in a wave of people. It's futile. He can't move. An armed guard tells him to turn back and somehow, instinct kicking in, Marc knows this is the right thing to do. Listen to what the man says, turn around, forget you ever saw him and pray he does the same, what happened here didn't take place, go back to my hotel where I belong. He sees a sign for the toilet and follows it into the men's room, where he splashes his face with water, enters a stall and sits and waits and sits and waits until it's safe.

■ ■ ■

"If you don't like it," Ibrahim said, "leave."

■ ■ ■

His old editor at the *Post*, Jay, had said: "I don't have to tell you who these people are."

Marc: "Doesn't sound very PC."

Jay: "Fuck PC, Marc. They're involved in drugs, human trafficking, arms smuggling. And this isn't any camel jockey racing along the Corniche on National Day. This is the leadership. They're money-launderers, tight with the Taliban, in bed with bin Laden. Money for 9/11 was routed through the U.A.E., for fuck's sake."

Marc. "Look, Jay, I know you mean well. You've been a great editor, more important, a great friend, but what am I to do? I can't work out in the field anymore. I'm shot. And there's no room for me at the paper. No paper of any size or reputation in North America is hiring."

Jay: "The pilot of UA175, the one who flew into the South Tower? He was Emirati."

Marc: "*Câlice*, man. Give me some credit. I'll be there a couple years, save money, get out. Write a book. Write it while I'm there. Keep me busy."

Jay: "The paper's gonna be a propaganda sheet, an Arab *Pravda*."

Marc: "You think I don't know that? I don't expect a free press. Three, four years, and I'm out of there. With luck, by then the situation here will have stabilized and you'll be hiring again."

Jay: "*Insh'allah*, man."

Still no sign of a free press.

∎ ∎ ∎

"I don't even know what kind of birds they were."

"Does it worry you that you don't know?"

"Details, Doctor. Details are important. It's what separates us."

"Separates whom?"

"The professionals. If I don't get the details right, I shouldn't be doing my job."

"But you can't be expected to know the names of all the birds. You can't *know* everything."

"If I did, I wouldn't be here. Name a thing, own it."

∎ ∎ ∎

Marc couldn't remember heat like this. Afghanistan was hot, but drier, except in the mountains. India was wetter but not as hot. Definitely not in the mountains. Possibly Iraq, near Basra. But in Abu Dhabi, the humidity refused to burn off in the heat and only this amount of heat could hold that amount of moisture. Abu Dhabi was a beach towel that could not be wrung.

"You couldn't have hired me in the winter, eh?"

"Don't worry," Ibrahim said. "You'll get used to it."

No one got used to it. Editors who'd come over with their families sent their wives and kids back to wherever they came from or sent them on two-month-long holidays in northern Europe to avoid the sauna of Abu Dhabi. When Marc left the air-conditioned confines of the office at six, hot and humid, his sunglasses would fog over and remain steamed for five minutes. The only other time he'd had that happen was entering an indoor pool in Montreal in the winter.

Marc tried to describe this once to a woman he'd met, poolside, at Le Meridian. Turned out she was from a land colder than Quebec. The Meridian hotel was where the paper had placed him while he waited for the company apartment building to be ready. Construction was taking so long, its long-suffering, eventual residents had begun to call it "Insha'allah Towers." "When's your building ready?" "Next week, *insh'allah*." While at the hotel Marc had a few massages and used the pool and hung onto one of the hotel's blue-and-white striped towels, the guest-only ones handed out by short, brown cabana boys or left expertly folded on deck chairs. When at last he'd been allowed into his apartment, Marc would return to the hotel with his towel. No one ever questioned whether he was a paying guest.

It was a boiling Friday afternoon and Marc lay on his chaise-longue, watching behind dark glasses the bikini-clad mothers and their nubile late-teen daughters sunbathe and take the occasional dive into the pool, taking their time exiting, the water sluicing down their browning shoulders and downy arms and pooling for a second in the small of the back, confident they were under watch. A woman, tall and toned, blonde though not by birth, stood by the empty chair next to Marc's.

"Is this taken?" she asked.

In Russian, Marc responded it was all hers.

The woman laughed. "Good trick," she said, and flattened her towel along the chair. "How many other languages can you do that with?"

"Don't know," he said. "Never done it before."

"Nice try," she said.

"Okay, five in which we can have a full conversation. And then a few more I know what you're saying but I wouldn't want to embarrass myself."

Marc pulled the seatback straight and took off his glasses. She was pretty. An expat professional, he figured. Didn't look like one of the many trafficked eastern Europeans who come in through Dubai, who seemed hungrier, tougher, scratchier.

"Nadia," she said and reached out to offer her hand.

Marc sat up straighter and shook it. "Marc."

"Are you a guest of the hotel?"

He smiled. "Can you keep a secret?"

She had a pleasant laugh, an I-get-your-joke laugh. Maybe she worked for one of the oil engineering firms in town. The Russians had been late to the party in the Gulf, but were catching up. Here and there you'd see Venezuelans too. Their presence in the U.A.E. was nothing compared with the Americans and the British oil and gas men, most of whom were Scots.

"So you live in town and come here when the temperature rises to about thirty-five," Nadia said. She straddled the chair and pulled her blouse over her head. She wore a modest one-piece suit. It flattened her breasts, but not too much.

"Guilty," Marc said, "been living here a couple of months. You?"

"Well," she said with hesitation.

"You work here at the hotel, don't you?"

"Guilty," Nadia said. She spread sunscreen on the exposed parts of her body while she spoke. "Events coordinator. If the American Dental Association wants to hold its annual convention here, I handle the logistics. Guest rooms, meeting rooms, dining rooms, AV equipment, incidentals all the way down to water bottles and dental floss."

"They don't bring their own dental floss?"

"I don't know if they even *do* floss!"

Now it was both of their turns to laugh and Marc thought it had been a long time, such a long time, since he'd done this. Have a normal, relaxed, doesn't-mean-a-thing conversation with a woman. Or anyone, *tabernak*. The kind he used to have with Mireille before it all went south. He grew quiet for a second and thought he might cry from the relief of it. *Crisse*, was he raw. *Tune it down, bring it back under control.*

"So you won't blow my cover?"

"I don't know yet," she said. She lay back. "It depends on how dinner goes."

Marc chuckled. He could get used to this. He lay back as well. "You can always spot someone who's lived abroad for a while."

"How so?"

"They don't mess around about meeting people," Marc said. "None of us is here for all that long. You make friends quickly and deeply because you don't know when you're going to go."

"That's almost profound enough to be Russian," Nadia said.

"*Spasiba*," Marc said.

"Where did you learn it?" Nadia asked. "No, wait, don't tell me. Let me see if I can pick it out. As you did. Say something."

Marc was tempted to say "something," but that joke was as old as it was sophomoric. "I'd like to drink your bathwater" was a line out of *Esquire* magazine somewhere back in the 1980s. Instead, he said, "There's a frost this morning—three degrees, and the cherry trees are all in bloom."

"Chekhov, that's a good start." Nadia was quiet, weighing, and then said, switching back to English, "Somewhere south."

"Wow, that's good," Marc said. Tamara had been a linguist, he remembered. Spotted him praying and writing in French, a language he used with decreasing frequency, in parts of Africa should the occasion to revisit take him there, and in Lebanon. But by and large reserved for calls home to Pierre or Clémence, his goddaughter, Mireille if he was up to it. And every February to wish happy birthday to his father, if he could catch him between rounds of golf, retired in Florida six months of the year. "I was in Georgia for a while."

"Tblisi," Marc continued, pronouncing it the Russian way. *Keep it light.* "And you know… travelled around. Wine country, the north, and the coast. Can't miss the coast."

"But that's not where you learned your Russian," Nadia said.

Shit, Marc thought. *Do I have to go down this road?* He could hear Dr. Abramson saying, yes, he did. He did have to make small talk—even if he saw it as unimportant—and he would on occasion have to venture down conversational paths that might be uncomfortable, risky even, that might trigger unpleasant reactions, an outburst, or worse. But you have coping mechanisms now, don't you? Dr. Abramson asked. We've been over these. You said it yourself: name it, own it.

"I picked up some Russian there," Marc said, "but I learned it in Chechnya."

Nadia turned onto her side. "Chechnya?!" And she used a derogatory term Marc had heard many times from the lips of otherwise decent Russians to describe people from the Caucasus. "Why on earth would you go there?"

Marc shrugged. Not an answer, he knew, but sometimes deflection worked.

Nadia's natural hair colour and skin tone were as dark as those of the people she derided, and he let her comment slide. Plenty of women dyed their hair in the Gulf. Arab men seemed to like it. More streaked blondes than brunettes featured on billboards along the highways. Americans didn't have the global lock on racism. He'd seen it in every conflict he'd ever covered. It was human. It was nature. And nature was brutal. "Sometimes you go where you need to go," said Marc.

"Are you with the Red Cross?"

"No."

Marc noticed Nadia check him out. "You don't look like a mercenary." She whispered. "Are you one of those weapons smugglers? Are you one of Victor Bout's men?"

"None of the above," Marc said. He'd have sighed if he could, but what signal would that send? "I'm a journalist. I was in Georgia during the civil wars and made my way across the border into Ingushetia and then Chechnya."

Nadia's smile dimmed. "Better you are a journalist than a soldier."

"Thanks, I think so too."

"Less likely to get your head blown off."

"I wouldn't say so," Marc said. And then he did the most curious thing, he chuckled. It was laced with darkness and cynicism, but it was a laugh nonetheless and it felt good. Thinking: I can talk about this. Head bobbing up out of the waves, coming up for air. But for how long? How long before he'd be dragged down into the depths again?

Because nothing had prepared Marc for Chechnya. Not Tbilisi. He'd seen wounded students there, he'd interviewed the director of the morgue but couldn't get in to verify the number of dead. He presumed Tamara was among them. Not South Ossetia or Abkhazia, which were schoolyard skirmishes in comparison. Marc remembers being pinned by a sniper in Sarajevo. None of the guys with him could see the shooter, who had the advantage of height and distance and kept them hunkered down in a bullet-pocked Tito-era building. All the windows had been shot out and a cool wind blew through the rooms. Lying on glass, chips of wood and chunks of chalky plaster on the floor of a kitchen he assumed once belonged to a Bosnian Muslim family. Exhausted yet wired, thirsty. A box of dry spaghetti from a cupboard he and Roland from the *Telegraph*, Craig from the *Star* and Soumik, who freelanced for a number of papers in South Africa, India and Australia, passed around and crunched on. Then Roland's cellphone rang. It was his wife. She'd lost her NIH card, and what should she do? God, did they laugh when Roland, who had barely held it together on the phone, ended the call. "Look, hon, I've got to go. There's a war on." It became their catchphrase for the duration of the fight and whenever they'd meet up elsewhere. Marc would hear a phone ring in another godforsaken city under siege and someone who wasn't even in that room with the four of them in Sarajevo that day would say, "Hon, I've got to go, there's a war on." It was the war journalist's meme. But that was Bosnia. You could be covered in the white dust of war, keeping your head down so as not to get a bullet drilled into your skull by some crazy-arse sniper or about to shit your pants at an armed checkpoint, and then two hours later you could be in a bubble bath in Vienna, or ordering *cassoulet* in Toulouse or at a show in the West End. Being in Europe in a war versus being in Europe *not* in a war. It was a box of dried noodles or a croissant. Making the transition wasn't easy. Some couldn't handle it. Divorce was common. Roland, God bless him, made it okay. Moved back to Wales and raised kids and sheep.

But none of it was Chechnya. Grozny, by the time Marc made it there, had been bombed back to the Stone Age. Hollowed-out buildings resembling concrete honeycombs, denuded trees, roads stripped down to gravel fill and the bent streetcar tracks like fingers pointing to the street life of a not-so-distant past. No hotel bars for foreign correspondents. No hotels at all. In Grozny, the writer lived the broken life of the war victim. It suited Marc fine. Smoke in the air, smoke in the lungs. Streets flooded by water from broken mains. The putrid smell of sewage and human waste. Yet, life, everywhere life, incongruous and inconstant, contradictory, things that didn't belong in the same picture. Women went out in the morning with their yellow plastic bags folded in their hands and came back with them filled with boxes of this and cans of that. Straight and proud. Not a button undone. Boys rode bicycles or played king of the mountain on mounds of asphalt chunks and the rusty fangs of snaking rebar. Sharp switchblades of grass sliced through cracks in the pavement. Men prayed on worn wool rugs.

Once, a woman in her thirties, nice figure, floral pattern dress to the knees of the type popular in North America in the forties, stylish nonetheless, dark hair done up just so, coming from a market. With one hand, she pulled a two-wheeled wire grocery basket. With the other she held a wound-up rug. The basket had a large plastic bag in it. She smiled at Marc as she passed him and he said good day, and she said yes it was, and he watched her as she continued along her path, struggling with the weight of the cart, with the plastic bag, and the weight of the rug in her other arm. Marc looked at the woman again and saw the bag was leaking, the rug in her left hand was sodden. In the centre of the rug, wrapped like a bloody cut of meat, was a severed arm, blue-grey fingers limply pointing downward.

Marc took a photograph of the woman walking away, the basket on her right, the rug on her left. He sent it in, but the paper wouldn't run it. He hadn't expected them to. People had no stomach for the images of war, and unless newspapers were committed to consistent coverage, readers' outrage and curiosity withered like the unclenching fist of the dying. No matter how much Marc pushed, there were days when editors weren't interested in what he was filing. His indignation stood no chance against the indifference of readers. The war of the journalist was as unwinnable as Chechnya or Afghanistan or the morass of Bush's Iraq. The flowery pattern of the dress is what he remembers most. White with blue and pink flowers, bleached from repeated washing.

Russia was under pressure from the UN, the International Red Cross, les Médecins sans frontières and other humanitarian organizations to demonstrate it was not committing war crimes at its southern border. Select journalists were allowed to see some of the prisoners it was holding. The Chechen Muslims whom Marc saw— men and boys—numbered over a hundred and were split in two train cars. Marc interviewed a dozen. The men told him they had been roused from their homes in the middle of the night, taken from their families, made to walk miles to the station and then shoved as if bound for abattoirs into sweltering cars, which were kept on the move day and night. Sometimes it seemed they were southbound, sometimes north. Once, the train stopped and the men were forced out and handed shovels. A couple of dozen soldiers, a year at most out of secondary, ordered the Chechens to dig a trench ten feet deep and the same in width. When the work was finished, the men were ordered to stand along the edge of the trench and face it. "*Allahu akbar,*" someone shouted and fell into the ditch. "*Allahu akbar,*" others repeated.

"I felt for certain my time had come," a Chechen elder in a white skullcap told Marc. "There were the machine guns, and dirt was spraying up everywhere, and we looked around to our left and to our right, but only the one fell into the trench. We were too scared to look behind us at what was happening. The gunfire stopped and all we heard was laughing. We turned. The soldiers were bent over from laughing. A few of my neighbours were retching into the trench. Our execution was fake, torture only, to terrorize us."

Not one man Marc interviewed didn't have some kind of visible sign of abuse: filed teeth, gaps where teeth had been twisted off, broken arms that hadn't healed right, eye patches, limps.

Marc closed his eyes and sighed, looked over at Nadia. Her eyes were serious. She'd really been listening.

"Someone's turned on the oven," he said and pushed off his pool chair.

"I'll join you," she said.

He jumped, she dove, and they stayed in the deep end of the pool for at least a half-hour. By the wall, Nadia asked why he wanted to be a journalist in Chechnya. And he fed her the usual answer, the dinner party response people wanted to hear, were most comfortable with. About moral responsibility and commitment to bearing witness, keeping the world informed.

Marc pushed away from the wall and floated, Nadia trod water close by.

"My brother died in that stupid war," Nadia said. "We don't know how. We don't know where. The army never told my mother what happened. He was nineteen."

"I'm sorry, Nadia," Marc said and he righted himself in the water so he faced her.

"It killed my mother, the not knowing. All the stress, the wait, the letters, the meetings, the lies."

Neither said a word for a while. The water lapped against the sides of the pool. Beyond, the occasional call of a mother to a child, the screech of a deck chair being pulled. Another Abu Dhabi afternoon fading.

"It was an inhuman, senseless war," Marc said.

"It was a stupid war," and she repeated the word: *chernota*.

And again, the word unsettled Marc. But an hour before they had been laughing. He didn't respond. They were quiet. The pool emptied.

■ ■ ■

"Do you think you can tell me about your father? What was he like?"

It was about time Dr. Abramson got around to the question. His mother was next, Marc figured.

Marc saw himself in Florida. At his father's beachfront apartment condo. He'd come to make right with the old man, though not because the old man deserved it. He'd never asked for forgiveness, never exhibited any signs he deserved it. It was Marc's own thing, what he needed to do. Standing at the condo door, every damned insult, every abusive word the bastard ever shouted at Marc's mother, every bimbo Maxime Dion sucked and screwed and cheated with, all that hurt was present in the pressure Marc was about to exert on the doorbell. The way he left *Maman.* The way he left *us.* We were kids, the oldest ten, *câlice.* It's a wonder we all turned out as well as we did. Pierre preparing the meals the old man never cooked. Nathalie nursing wounds that will never heal. Simon, the baby, the truck driver, making more than all of us, god bless him, picking up hitchhikers on the *autoroutes* and highways of eastern Canada and New England, hoping to recognize something in someone's face. But Maxime wouldn't know. He walked. *And me, Marc, your second. Telling truth to power in places no one can find on a map.* But Marc grew unsure of what he was doing there. He could type a mile a minute on deadline, stories woven in his fingers as explosives rang in his ears. But with his finger on the doorbell, he'd forgotten his speech, words dried up for lack of use.

Marc's hand closed in a fist, his arm dropped by his side and he turned.

"No point," Marc answered Dr. Abramson. "I mean, I made my peace with him. Or rather, I made my peace with myself about him. I just try to make sure I live my life in a way that isn't his."

"And how well do you believe you've done that?"

■ ■ ■

Every thirty seconds, every ten seconds, this ruckus would rise up and a black cloud of feathers and beaks would pulverize the quiet, then land back down on the branches and chirp chirp chirp and couldn't they just shut the fuck up? And then back up in the air. No reason behind it. No dog or cat at the trunk, no crackhead squirrel, no backfiring truck cruising his D.C. neighbourhood. The stupid fucking stupidity of birds. If you don't have a reason for doing something, don't do it! Marc called the paper.

"Can't come in today, Jay. The birds, man, I might buy a gun."

"Okay. You want me to come by? You need anything?"

"No, no, not coming in. Gotta sleep."

The phone rang an hour later and it was Pierre. Why not come up and spend a few weeks at home? "*Tu nous manques*," he said.

"I miss you too," Marc said and the tap of tears opened.

He called Jay and said he wasn't going to come in.

"I know, Marc. You called earlier."

"No, I mean, I'll take a couple of weeks. Go home to Montreal."

"You take all the time you need, Marc. You deserve it."

"Jay."

"Yes, Marc."

"I mean, I've been doing this half my life and I can't do it anymore."

"It's okay, Marc. Bring me back some cheese curds."

The Amtrak train from D.C. would be slower but felt safer than a plane and Marc bought two seats for himself and slept most of the way up to Montreal. There were the odd flashes of light, loud sounds. There was the dream where Marc is sleeping on a riverbank in Baghdad and a shell explodes nearby, sending chunks of dirt and metal and stone into the air, propelling Marc in a roll down the bank into the river. Marc woke up wet, his shirt spotted at the waist with a warm, dark fluid he couldn't identify until he smelled it, tasted it and found it was chocolate sauce from a leaking backpack in an overhead bin.

Pierre picked him up at the Gare Centrale and took him, first thing, to the restaurant in St-Henri, where the family had gathered. Marc wept in his mother's arms. For no reason. Except she had grown small and her arms were tiny wings unfolding to bring him in, and there was much to drink after the restaurant closed and Mireille was there, why not, she co-owned the place, and Marc wondered to himself why he'd never married her though he knew the answer, he didn't have to ask the question, he knew he just knew, and she knew, she's the one who said even when you're here you're not here. And Pierre had dimmed the lights, lowered the metal shade and locked the door, and Marc hadn't heard his mother sing "Quand le soleil dit bonjour aux montagnes" in such a long time.

Two weeks turned into a month, during which Marc volunteered to help in the restaurant. One night, Pierre put him to work, alone because all Marc could handle was solo work, making the fancy-ass poutine for which Le Matou was famous. But the sparrow chatter of the cooks and the swallow-like movements of the busboys and servers got to him and the smell and pop of grease in the deep fryer nauseated him. A glass slipped from a serving tray and shattered on the kitchen floor. Marc shouted at the server, Pierre's older daughter, Clémence. She cried, he cried, and Mireille said what the hell, Marc, *qu'est-ce-qu'isse pas avec toé*? and he apologized, Clémence apologized, and the next morning Pierre drove his brother to the Jewish General to see Dr. Abramson.

"I'm sick, Jay," Marc said when he called Washington.

"I know, Marc," Jay said. "I'm the one who called your brother. I'm putting you on leave, short-term disability. You've gotta get well again, Marc. You're an indispensable part of this newsroom."

"What if—?"

"No 'if's,' Marc," Jay said. "You're gonna get better."

"Will I—?"

"Yes, you'll have a job when you get back."

Dr. Abramson noted his "patient shows signs of intrusion: periodic, involuntary images of distress, interrupted sleep patterns, difficulty with task-focus, and exaggerated response to extrasensory arousal. Patient has difficulty warding off distressing thoughts and tries to avoid situations that might prompt unpleasant memory."

The doctor and Marc were at it for over a year, during which time Marc didn't write a word, didn't read a newspaper, avoided the internet. Instead, he read novels, saw movies with his mother, biked with Clémence, swam with Pierre, went antiquing with Mireille. If he healed, it wasn't solely his doing. His family was his bandage, his salve.

Marc did go back, deputy foreign for Middle East and Europe. The downsizing began four years later. He accepted a buyout—three weeks per year served and a bonus of two thousand to leave within two weeks. A lot of snap decisions were made in the newsroom.

"You're in no position to retire," Jay said.

"Probably not, man," said Marc. "But I *am* tired."

With his pension, it amounted to a hundred and thirty thousand. Which was not a nest egg. When you're over forty, it's just an egg. Money got tight and though the market was hot for offloading real estate, selling meant buying again or paying sky-high rent. Meanwhile, the bank kept raising the credit card ceiling. The *Times*, the *Journal*, *The New Yorker*—no one was hiring. Marc asked around the think-tanks and foundations. Rand, Brookings. Nothing.

"You're in no position to retire," Ibrahim pointed out over the phone from Abu Dhabi.

"Don't think I don't know that," Marc said. "But the condition of employment remains: I'll edit, I'll do analysis and commentary, but I won't go out in the field."

■ ■ ■

Marc grabs a bus out of Lisbon and heads out to Sintra. Downtown is full of tourists so he takes off for a walk alone. He wants to avoid another freak-out like the one at the National Guard museum. There's a park with public art. Hadeel would like this. Mixed old and new, winding paths, stone steps. He's comfortable there, for a while. Lies on a bench. Snoozes. Wakes to the alarming sound of a splash in the brook. Breathes. Breathes again. He lunches at a table for two outside a café. Imagines Hadeel with him. Why isn't she writing back?

Other than the castle, Marc finds nothing of interest in his guidebook. Though there is the toy museum. It'll have to be spectacular to beat the carriage and coach museum in Belém. He sits up and heads off down the hill toward the toys, but when he gets to the address, the museum no longer exists. In its place is the News Museum of Portugal. Marc shakes his head at the irony of it, rolls his eyes, thinks, "What the hell," and enters.

On the ground floor stands a globe about ten feet in diameter with a touch screen that pops up facts about press freedom around the world. The U.A.E. entry is no surprise. He's been working under ever-straitening rules for eight years now. On the second floor a history of war reporting consists of talking heads for the most part. Marc is still, surprised by the flash of strobe lights. He shuts his eyes, presses his fingers to his ears, waits for the follow-up, the crash of mortar splitting space from time. Lifts his head, surveys the room. Breathes deep. There's the voice of Walter Cronkite. Marc exhales. Leaves the room.

In the middle of the spiral stairwell, a column of television screens flashes images. Each TV tuned to a different international channel broadcasting the news in real time. There's CNN, the Beeb, SkyTV, CNC World out of Beijing, iTélé. There's Al Jazeera. There's Hadeel. There's her face, her hijab. The same one she wore the day she left. The scroll in Arabic is gone by the time Marc thinks to read it. He scans the other screens. Was that her? Was it a live feed?

Marc's thumbs dance over his BlackBerry. "Saw you on TV. What's up? You look fine. Hardly think you're in a war zone." Looks at the screens again. She's not there. He blinks. He's not sure what he saw.

He is certain what he remembers though. They were seated on fake leather couches in the reception area of the media building, waiting for the company car to take her to the airport. "I can't change your mind, I know," Marc had said. Opposite them the security guards and the scanner everyone had to slide their briefcases and backpacks through. Every now and then someone ordered a muffin to go from the little coffee kiosk around the corner. "Make it hot, sir?" asked the Filipina behind the counter. Despite the bustle around them, Marc and Hadeel occupied a space all their own. As they had since they'd met.

Hadeel in black jeans, light canvas boots, a T-shirt and jacket, headscarf thrown around her head the way western women wear them when they visit the Grand Mosque. She had chosen not to wear Emirati dress. In Abu Dhabi, the *abaya* and *sheyla* freed her to move where she wanted, made her visibly a woman and therefore apart, untouchable and, paradoxically, invisible, but in Syria she'd stand out for no reason. In Syria, Hadeel was proud of saying, women no matter what they wore were given a wide berth, a measure of freedom they couldn't find in other Islamic countries. She felt protected in Syria in a way she didn't feel in the U.A.E., Egypt or Lebanon, or even in Canada, where a low-intensity anti-Islamic sentiment simmered among the less empathetic and the ignorant.

"I appreciate everything you've had to say, Marc," Hadeel said. "I do. You're the voice of reason, of experience."

"Then I wish you'd listen to that reason," Marc said.

"You don't understand."

Marc held Hadeel's eyes.

"I'm sorry," she said. "Of course, you do. You more than anyone."

Marc's eyes moistened.

"It's my home," she said. "More than this place ever was or will be." She looked out the window and gestured with her chin.

"But their war isn't your war."

"We all have one war in us," Hadeel said. "You said so. You said the guys you worked with, a lot of them felt the same. Bosnia was Vietnam to them. Well, Syria is mine. And yes, I know there's a bit of self-deception in here. That I can go in and do my job, which involves putting my life on the line, with some amount of impunity. But that's it, isn't it? If I didn't believe that—if you yourself hadn't believed it for most of your career—we wouldn't be able to do what we do. If I don't do this, I won't know who I am."

Marc, looking out the window, nodded. Without you, I won't know who I am.

Hadeel was silent long enough that Marc turned back to face her. He smiled, if that's what it could be called.

"You're right," she said. "Their war isn't my war, but it is my story."

■ ■ ■

"You told me to leave, Ibrahim, and now you want me to come back," Marc says. "I haven't been in this apartment a week yet. I have another week still. Will you make up your mind?"

"You want to know why it is you didn't get foreign, Marc?" Ibrahim says. "You want me to tell you the honest-to-god truth?"

Marc lies on the bed. He looks at the vintage maps the B&B owner had framed and hung. Sighs. Audibly.

"See? That's it right there in a nutshell," Ibrahim shouts into the BlackBerry. "You treat me with no respect! And that's why you didn't get the job."

"*Ciboire*, Ibrahim," Marc says. "Is that what you want? I thought you wanted quote unquote someone who knows the region. It's taken me this long to know what you meant by that. You wanted me to pay fealty, like you're some sheikh doling out gifts from a chest of treasures."

"Don't be an asshole, asshole," Ibrahim says. "You know what I mean by respect. We've been playing this game since before you started. You always thought you knew more and you made sure everyone knew it."

Marc is overcome by fatigue. He closes his eyes and draws in a deep breath, holds it, then lets it go, lets go all the striving, all the doing, all the arguing. "You're right, Ibrahim."

There's a pause.

"I know why you called."

"Hadeel," Ibrahim says.

Marc waits. It's been days of unrequited texts. Marc wrote Ibrahim about his suspicions the afternoon he'd gone to the News Museum, but Ibrahim didn't write back. Marc called, but he wouldn't pick up.

"We think she's missing," says Ibrahim.

"You *think*?"

Ibrahim would never admit it was a mistake to send Hadeel to Syria—and in many ways it hadn't been: she'd done stellar reporting and her photography was stunning, prize material, no one else on the

ground got as close to tell such personal stories in a visual way. It felt, to
Marc, like the photographic version of what he used to do with words.
She could do it all.

"I'm coming back."

"Not why I called," Ibrahim says.

"I'm coming back, Abe. We've got to bring Hadeel back."

Marc's not sure how much Ibrahim knows about his relationship
with Hadeel. Workplace romances blossomed in the Abu Dhabi desert,
but this one would be unusual—for the differences of age and faiths—
and Ibrahim would be one to frown on that. Yet sometimes his editor
could be so obtuse.

"Look, Marc, I've made some calls, sent out feelers," Ibrahim says.
"This is being handled at the highest levels. Highest. Talking with
Syria. We don't know who's got her or even if she's being held. If it is
the case, we don't know if it's Assad, ISIS, al-Nusra. It could be anyone.
No one's claimed responsibility. There's been zero contact."

"You're saying the government's on it and you don't need me."

"You're doing it again, Marc."

Marc feels he's about to say something he will regret for a long
time. He counts to himself, breathes.

"It's my sources you need. On the ground."

"Fine, Marc. I'll say it," Ibrahim whines into the phone. "It's your
sources. It's you. You know the region."

Marc pushes the cancel button, then connects to the WiFi and
changes his return ticket for the next morning flight. Then he drops to
the bed with his phone at his side. Maybe tonight, go out to hear some
fado. Drown his sorrows in someone's maritime melancholy. Until
then, rest.

She comes to him unbidden, the way she always does, the way she
did when Marc first laid his eyes on her. He feels her palms on each side
of his face to calm him, reassure him, comfort and give him courage.
He searches for sleep. Instead, he remembers Iraq.

Bound by a desire to remain independent in the most absolute
terms, Marc had refused to be embedded with the military, but through
years of honest, reliable reporting had earned a modicum of respect
from the military and entry into the actions and thinking of troops.
In 2003, months after the U.S. invasion had begun, he was allowed to
follow a platoon along the Euphrates. They had been assigned to clear
the banks of obstructions, any object someone could hide behind or
leave a bomb near. Marc kept to the middle of the group of soldiers.

It was hot and the pace was slow and the men's eyes were keen. It was summer and Haifa Street had become ground zero of Sunnis pissed off over the emasculation of the Baathists. The area had slid quickly into bread-, water-, and gas-starved antipathy and desperation. This was the start of the insurgency many anti-war activists and commentators, journalists among them, had predicted. It was here. It was Najaf and Fallujah and Tikrit. Marc worked his contacts to establish a relationship with the former Baathists, who, it was suspected, wished to stockpile weapons in an attempt to rearm a militia or rearm the army. In the meantime, small groups of U.S. soldiers patrolled the streets and, like that day, on the riverbanks, trying to make the city safe again.

The patrol had bored Marc. His thoughts drifted downstream, away, far and away. Lying in bed with Mireille. She's driven down, a furious nine hours, to Washington to meet him at the airport, but the flight is late and he's exhausted, yet the hunger is there and she throws him on his back and tells him not to move, not to touch her, not to blink and he does as he is told, and she climbs on top, and slaps his hands away, and kisses him on the eyelids, the cheekbones, the lips, the neck, she kisses him and licks him and still he won't harden, nothing works, no amount of skin, contact, pulling, rubbing, lubricant leads him to an erection. Finally, Mireille flops on the bed and says, "What am I doing wrong?" And Marc says, "*C'est moi.* It's not you. I'm just, I'm just tired." "But this has never happened before," she says. "You're always coming in late and exhausted and…" Marc rolls over and kisses her with all the love he can muster, but it isn't enough to reassure her.

"We *can* talk about it," she said. "I'm always here." "There's nothing to talk about," Marc said. "I'm fine." "But you seem quiet. *T'sais.* And, you know, what happened before." "Nothing happened before." "I know! That's what I'm saying." "Mireille, how many different ways do I have to say it? I'm *fine.* Drop it, okay?" So she did. A few minutes later, she was crying. Marc could have rolled back to face her, but he didn't. What was the point?

"Ugh, ugh, ugh." They all heard it. And all knew what they heard. The sound, out of place, was unmistakable. When the patrol and Marc came upon the couple, she was on her hands and knees and a man was pounding away at her from behind. The skinny-assed guy jerked upright and yanked his pants up by the drawstrings and ran up the embankment. The woman yanked up her underwear and pulled down her chador in the fluid motion of someone who'd done this before, but in her attempt to escape, she slipped on palm leaves and fell to the ground. Marc broke from the ranks and rushed to her side. He caught himself before reaching out to touch her and help her up.

"Are you all right?" he asked in Arabic.

She looked at him startled. "Yes," she answered. "No."

"May I help you?" he asked. "How may I help?"

She shook her head and tried to stand, but she'd twisted her ankle.

The soldiers had gathered around, back to the action, eyeing the perimeter, guns hiked to their chests. "Who the hell is she and what the hell is she doing here?" the lieutenant, Royson, asked.

"Are you asking me to interpret here, Lieutenant?" Marc said. "Because I'm not—"

"I know what your job is here, Mr. Dion, but you see anyone else who speaks towel-head around here?"

As she answered, the woman kept tugging at her hijab, shoving her hair in, looking away from the men, up the hill, toward the river, at Marc, back to the soldiers.

"Her name is Umm Lailah and her husband's dead and she doesn't have any way to make money to buy food or gas for the stove," Marc said.

"So she's a whore," Royson said.

"You don't have to be that way," Marc said.

"Get her out of here," Royson said.

"*Yallas*," Marc told the woman and pointed up the embankment. "I will help you. Let's go."

It wasn't a long walk, a hundred yards back up to the road above the Euphrates, but it took ten minutes, a long time to walk a hundred yards in Marc's estimation, but not long enough to extract a story from her. Umm Lailah's ankle may have been more than twisted. She leaned on him, reluctant to ask for the help, but reliant nonetheless.

"I'm a reporter," Marc said. He asked if they could meet again. "I will bring food if you want," he said. "For the children." Any trick to get her to talk. She said nothing. In her eyes, he knew, it would not be permissible. Though he understood her reluctance, the barriers standing in their way then, he longed for some western liberalism, openness. And, considering the way he'd discovered her here at the riverside, her unwillingness was curious.

They emerged from the canopy of palm trees. He looked across the street, then scanned left to right. Quiet, empty. Apartment buildings across the street. No windows, no doors. No signs of life. It didn't feel right.

"Okay," he said. "We can cross here."

He turned to Umm Lailah to help her up. He'd put out his hand and she'd reached out with hers and then she regarded him with an expression of such fear and surprise he thought he might be looking in a mirror. He screamed. He threw himself over her, as one would over someone who'd caught fire, and rolled them back down the riverbank. He'd never heard the gunshot. The linnets squawked and yakked and whined, they rushed and flustered out of the branches and, then having forgotten the fuss, resettled elsewhere in the same trees. When Marc and Umm Lailah had stopped rolling, he rose on his elbows, then knees. They were covered in mud and dead leaves. Pebbles stuck to where their clothes were wet. He looked down at his shirt. Looked down at her. "*Crisse!*" A red flower of Umm Lailah's blood blooming. He shouted, a cry wrenched from his lungs and stomach, as if something had reached in with its hands and twisted and pulled, an emptying, painful and complete. But Marc couldn't hear it. Didn't hear the screaming. Didn't hear the firefight happening around him. He just saw the bloodied body of Umm Lailah, no way to stanch the flow, no way to blunt the hurt.

■ ■ ■

The Lisbon apartment is, as advertised, full of maps. The owner, Roberto, is an artist. Large canvas stuff. Multi-genre, collages, photographs, some archival, some more recent, or charts and nineteenth-century maps. Roberto works nine months of the year in Macau, has corporate clients in China. "The Chinese," he said when he and Marc chatted about his art for a while, "love maps. They love knowing their place in the world."

Examining the maps, considering the countries he's visited, at war or at peace, Marc thinks every nationality loves knowing its place in the world. Britons, the Québécois, Turks, Armenians, Greeks, Russians… *merde*. Americans design maps so the U.S. is always in the middle.

A framed, old map of the Gulf hangs on the wall of the bedroom. The world calls it the "Persian Gulf." At the *World*, and at the *Gulf Times* and all the other papers in the region, the body of water is called the "Arab Gulf." As if the change of name changes history. As if history means anything. Persians, Arabs, Shiites, Sunnis, they fished and pearled and traded in these waters forever. Did a kid diving ten metres into the muck to pluck an oyster from a sand bed and barely able to catch his breath before going back down, give an *Allahu akbar* what the Gulf was called?

But there is the map and Marc sits up in bed to study it, the way he considers all cartography, out of curiosity, interest, and finds himself staring at the Trucial States, where Abu Dhabi is rendered Abu Zabi, where Trucial Oman still exists, past and present marrying, at least on paper. Sometimes they are together in the ground forever as well. Marc had visited Muscat for the first time after three months of work in Abu Dhabi because his work visa was about to expire and his permanent residence ID had not yet cleared. He found the country was a fair rendering of what Abu Dhabi might have been like forty years before. Simple, friendly, dusty. Emiratis were always on about their cultural identity and heritage, yet Abu Dhabi had destroyed its *souq*. Historical Abu Dhabi was Heritage Village, a puny collection of palm-frond *arysh* houses and a scrawny camel even the tourists found pathetic. In Muscat, if you looked hard enough, you might find signs of the Portuguese colonization four hundred years ago, just as in Lisbon and Evora and Oporto and Coimbra, you could find signs of Arab colonization of eleven hundred years ago.

We're all stuck in that past, aren't we? Marc thinks. Shackled and bound, in fact. History doesn't repeat itself. It's a leghold trap. Only the fox who chews off his own leg survives it. Oman and the Portuguese, the U.A.E. and the Brits. Chechnya and Russia. Syria and the French and the British and the Ottomans. Who's the fox?

The BlackBerry buzzes again. Marc picks it up and reads the caller ID. It's not Hadeel. He didn't think it would be. It's Ibrahim. Marc texts his boss, then puts the phone down and begins packing.

■ ■ ■

At the airport, Christopher takes one look at Marc at the baggage carousel and takes his carry-on from him. "Dammit, let me take it," he says when Marc protests.

In the car on the way back to Marc's apartment in the Insha'allah Towers, Christopher says, "Marc, uh—"

"I know, Christopher," Marc interrupts.

"Are you okay?"

"*Boro asa,*" says Marc.

Christopher laughs. "I have taught you well."

They speed along a silent mile or so of Airport Road. It's featureless out here. Trees line the road, a feeble attempt to mask the anorexic desert scrub that goes on for miles. The carnival-like illumination of an Adnoc gas station brightens the desert night. Then he spots the lights of one of the Khalifa cities. A or B. Marc always mixed them up.

"Do they know what happened?" Marc finally asks.

Christopher shakes his head, shrugs at the same time. "You know better than anyone what it's like out there."

Marc nods.

"I left a packet of clips in your office mailbox," Christopher says. "But there is not much there. She was found some days ago."

"Did they say where?"

"Outside Aleppo."

"Aleppo? She wasn't… she was supposed to be in Damascus."

Christopher says yes, she was. He puts his turn signal on, checks the rear-view mirror and looks over his shoulder before entering the passing lane. He's learned how to drive like a North American, checking his mirrors, looking into his blind spot, since living in the Gulf. "Ibrahim says—"

"Fuck Ibrahim," Marc says.

"He is not, as you say, 'my type' either," Christopher says.

Marc sits quietly. It's funny, but not funny in this moment and he knows Christopher regrets making the feeble attempt.

"But she's okay?"

Christopher nods. "Yes, Marc, she's okay."

"And the paper's heard from her brother Hamsa?" Marc asks.

Christopher nods again. "He's with her."

Marc rests his head on the window and closes his eyes. When he opens them minutes later, they are driving by the Sheikh Zayed Mosque, Abu Dhabi's Grand Mosque. The third largest *masjid* in the world, it's said. At night, programmed lights tint the eighty-two domes and reflect the phases of the moon. It's a pale, mottled mauve tonight. The pattern resembles a map, with dark landmasses and light oceans, and, if Marc were to look closely, he might see himself. He might know his place in the world.

AUTHOR'S NOTE

The dialogue attributed to "you" in the novella "Oil" includes modified quotations of Sheikh Zayed bin Sultan al Nahyan, the father of the modern-day United Arab Emirates. Although some historical details might lead one to believe Zayed is the character Rose addresses in her story, "you," like the other characters in this collection, is a work of the imagination.

The words attributed to Freya Stark and Wilfrid Blunt in "Oil" come from *Passionate Nomad: The Life of Freya Stark* (1999) by Jane Fletcher Geniesse. There are many versions of the relationship of the Prophet Mohammed with his young wife Ayesha. The one retold in "Oil" is a reworking of one written by Karen Armstrong in *Muhammad* (2006).

For insight into post-traumatic stress disorder among war correspondents, I read *Journalists Under Fire: The Psychological Hazards of Covering War* (2006) by Anthony Feinstein. Stephen Starr's *Revolt in Syria* (2102) and Toby Matthiesen's *Sectarian Gulf* (2013) helped jog my memory about the very early days in the Arab Spring in Syria and Bahrain, which were heady times to be working on a newspaper in the Arab Gulf. I learned about the early days of pearl diving in the Arab Gulf from Emma Plouffe's scholarly paper from 2012: "Pearling in the Gulf Explored: The Life of a Pearl Diver."

The Emptiest Quarter is a fiction about a relatively young country in a very old part of the world. Yet for all those years, the books written about the U.A.E. are few, and what books exist are dated, or focused on a specific time in an ever-shifting place. When I arrived in Abu Dhabi in January 2008, a French-Canadian engineer I met took me up to a part of the Abu Dhabi Mall overlooking the Gulf islands of

Al Maryah and Al Reem. "If you were to leave and come back in five years, you wouldn't recognize the place," he said. When I left in late 2011, construction of the Paris-Sorbonne and residential towers had begun there. By the time of publication of this book, they've been developed. The island beyond, Saadiyat, is home to NYU's Abu Dhabi campus and the Louvre Abu Dhabi, both of which were shrouded in labour controversy, as many projects of such magnitude are.

For those interested in knowing more about the country, I would recommend Christopher Davidson's trilogy, *Dubai* (2008), *Abu Dhabi* (2010) and *After the Sheikhs* (2013); Mohammed al-Fahim's *From Rags to Riches* (2008); Jo Tatchell's *A Diamond in the Desert* (2010) and *Mother Without a Mask* (2004) by Patricia Holton, which are all non-fiction; as well as Deepak Unnikrishnan's *Temporary People* (2017) and Denise Roig's short-story collection *Brilliant* (2014).

I would like to thank Karen Haughian for structural edits that breathed new life into *The Emptiest Quarter*, Cate Myddleton-Evans for an early edit of *The Emptiest Quarter* and Andrew Foster for his kind words of support and advice. As always, the greatest thanks are reserved for Denise, who's always been up for an adventure, none greater than love.

ABOUT THE AUTHOR

Raymond Beauchemin was born in Western Massachusetts and has lived in Boston, Montreal and Abu Dhabi. He currently lives in Hamilton, Ontario. He has worked as an editor for the *Boston Herald*, Montreal *Gazette*, *The National* and the *Toronto Star*. He is also the author of *Everything I Own*, a novel.

Eco-Audit
Printing this book using Rolland Enviro100 Book
instead of virgin fibres paper saved the following resources:

Trees	Water	Air Emissions
3	1,000 L	180 kg